CONTEMPT

MICHAEL CORDELL

TCK PUBLISHING.COM

ISBN: 978-1-63161-080-6

Sign up for Michael Cordell's newsletter at
www.michaeljcordell.com/newsletters

Published by TCK Publishing
www.TCKpublishing.com

Get discounts and special deals on books at
www.TCKpublishing.com/bookdeals

Check out additional discounts for bulk orders at
www.TCKpublishing.com/bulk-book-orders

To Kate,
My love, my life, my light.

I can't see my reflection in the water
I can't speak the sounds that show no pain
I can't hear the echo of my footsteps
Or remember the sounds of my own name

Bob Dylan

CHAPTER ONE

FIVE YEARS HAD PASSED SINCE the two lawyers last faced each other in a court of law. Five years—or a lifetime, depending on which lawyer you asked.

Thane Banning was struck by how cavernous the L.A. courtroom felt with only four people present. At the original trial, a crush of spectators had overwhelmed the space; each morning when the building opened, the mob would scramble forward, fighting their way inside as if it were a lifeboat on the side of a sinking ship.

But today, Thane's voice echoed off the marble walls.

Five years ago, the press had laid siege not only to the courtroom and the adjacent hallway, but also to the front steps of the courthouse and down each sidewalk. TV news vans parked bumper-to-bumper for five blocks. It had been dubbed the trial of the year, the decade, and even the century, depending on which cable news pundit was talking. But today there were no members of the press, no microphones, no cameras, no news vans puttering outside. Judge Bennett Williams was conducting today's hearing as surreptitiously as possible.

Judge Williams, who had served on the bench for thirty-eight years, hadn't presided over the original trial, but it was his unfortunate lot to draw today's arguments. The uniformed guard posted next to the locked door was also absent last time, but his presence today wasn't just for show. Today his leather holster was unsnapped, providing easy access to his service revolver.

Of the four men in the courtroom, only the two lawyers were back in their original places. Bradford Stone once again assumed charge of the prosecution, although this time he did so as the District Attorney for Los Angeles. At forty-seven, Stone's features, like his designer suits, were a collection of sharp angles. Thane figured the courtroom artists would have to fish for their finest-tipped pencils to draw his face. His dark eyes were those of a hawk on a wire, surveying the landscape, scanning for prey.

Thane once again stood at the defense table across the aisle from Stone. The DA hadn't changed over the years, but Thane knew the same couldn't be said for himself. Instead of an Armani suit, today's thread-worn jacket was three sizes too small, too tight to fasten the buttons. His black hair was as thick as ever, but he had seen tendrils of white worming their way to the surface over the past few months— not a distinguished gray like the judge's, but white, the kind of shock-white most men would dye away.

He was only thirty-six years old.

But it was on the inside that Thane had changed the most. There had been a time when he might have felt overwhelmed by what was happening to him, but today he felt nothing at all. Nothing but contempt.

"Your Honor," Thane said, "I contend that Defense was denied an opportunity to pursue a reasonable line of cross-examination. The fact that the witness and detective knew each other prior to the incident was not disclosed by the prosecution." He spit out the last two words as if he'd bitten into something sour.

Bradford Stone sprang from his chair before Thane even finished his sentence. "Detective Gruber encountered hundreds of people in his work. For him not to remember one witness is understandable."

Thane turned from the judge and faced Stone directly. "But it has come to light that you learned of this during the trial and said nothing."

"Because it was irrelevant."

"Not to me," Thane shot back.

Judge Williams banged his gavel. "Gentlemen," the judge said, "if you could at least pretend to address your arguments to me, I would appreciate it."

"I apologize, Your Honor," Stone said, "but I vehemently disagree with what the Defense believes is important. A thirty-three-year-old woman was knocked unconscious by ether and dragged down a dark alley where the killer stabbed her seventeen times as she regained consciousness. Those are the facts. That's what's important."

Thane turned once again toward Stone, not to respond, but to fully absorb the prosecutor's words. He held his tongue, though it took tremendous effort.

"I understand the gravity of the crime, Mr. Stone," Judge Williams said.

Thane wondered if Williams was working solely off the transcripts, or if he had also examined the photos from the original trial. It was one thing to read that a young woman's life had been ripped away in such a heinous manner; it was quite another to see the horror printed on her face as she lay sprawled on her back, her right cheek pressed against the pavement at an impossible angle. Yet despite all the blood, what had stunned Thane most was the close-up of her eyes: vacant, glassy, and wide open, as if frantically searching for God.

"In addition," Stone continued, "Ms. McCoy was not only a public servant, but an important member of the District Attorney's office. I had the honor of working with her on many cases prior to becoming DA, and her memory deserves better than to see her killer set free. Requesting that the court throw out the witness's testimony would be tantamount to dismissing the case altogether. It's been five years, Your Honor, and the key witness passed away three years ago."

"What about the arresting officer?"

"He didn't see the defendant attack the victim. The witness in question provided the foundation of our case. Without him . . ." Stone stopped, a note of frustration starting to push his tone off-key.

Thane took this opportunity to jump in. "Your Honor, I have provided numerous precedents. *'Sheffield versus Michigan Court of Appeals', 'Spearman versus the State of Colorado', 'Goldman versus—'*"

"Yes, Counselor, I have reviewed them," the judge said. "I understand your arguments."

"Your Honor," Stone said, "overturning this verdict and releasing a depraved murderer would be an outrage. A complete and moral outrage."

"I agree, Mr. Stone," the judge said after a moment's consideration. "It would, indeed, be an outrage." A look of relief flashed across Stone's face. "But I'm afraid that just might be what the law demands."

Stone blanched and Thane stood motionless as they each absorbed the weight of the judge's words. Not wanting to leave anything to chance, Thane said, "Your Honor, I'd also like to reference three other court decisions—"

Judge Williams raised one finger, stopping Thane in mid-sentence. "If I were you, Mr. Banning, I would quit while I was ahead."

When Thane hesitated, the judge leaned forward, the rusty squeak of his leather chair prefacing his final words. "And you are ahead."

He rose and strode from the courtroom.

Stone remained seated for a moment, lips pursed. Slowly he rose, bullied a stack of papers into his leather briefcase, and thrust his way toward the door. The guard stuck his key in the lock, turned it, and stepped aside, allowing the DA to march out of the room. The guard then shut and relocked the door, keeping his attention on Thane.

Thane remained standing at his table, staring at the papers scattered in front of him, miles away in his mind. Years away. Finally, he collected the documents, sliding them into a brown paper bag and placing them under his arm.

"Leave the bag on the table," the guard intoned. "I'll gather everything for you."

Thane obeyed. Then, upon hearing the familiar jangle of the handcuffs, he shuffled to the narrow end of the table, turned his back to the guard and leaned forward slightly, placing his hands behind him. The inch-thick metal shackles around each ankle, and the six-inch chain between them, made walking even a short distance a humiliating ordeal. Or at least it had the first few times. He was long past feeling humiliated these days.

The past five years had broken him of that.

CHAPTER
TWO

HANNAH BANNING SWAM UPSTREAM AGAINST the lunchtime crowd that filled the sidewalk on Grant Avenue. The restaurant was two blocks away, and she was already half an hour late. Bad enough asking Paul to meet her so they could talk about the break-up in person: making him wait felt like an insult.

When she'd gotten out of bed that morning, it was simply Wednesday. Two hours later, though, it had become the last full day that Thane would spend in prison. Everyone around her was going about their business as if nothing extraordinary had taken place, but she knew the world had shifted. The projects she had been working on, the ever-growing tasks on her to-do list, the upcoming appointments on her calendar—none of it mattered now.

She finally reached the restaurant and entered. As she maneuvered her way toward the table, Paul stared, his face missing the usual half-smile and raised eyebrow, the one he lifted like a tiny boomerang to welcome her into a room. The best Hannah could offer was a meek wave and the nervous smile of a fourteen-year-old, but Paul's frown never wavered.

"I'm sorry. I hope you haven't been here long," she said as she sat down, unable to think of anything else to say.

Paul looked at her incredulously. "That's pretty much the least of my concerns right now, wouldn't you say?"

His six-foot-five frame, most of it muscle from working construction, was rigid and pitched forward. His usually friendly smile, like a German Shepherd wagging its tail, was gone. Today he looked as though he could bite. His work attire—torn flannel shirt and dirty blue jeans—stood in contrast to the dark. clean suits huddled around the nearby tables.

Hannah reached up to pull at her hair, a nervous habit she thought she'd broken years ago, but her fingers brushed against her shoulder instead. Her face suddenly felt as red as her shortened locks as she realized one more thing Paul might seize on: she had just come from cutting six inches off her hair.

"Is that how you wore it back then?" Paul muttered. "Trying to make it look like old times?" Even before he finished his sentence he had turned his fiery eyes away from her, directing them toward the table.

A waiter heading toward them abruptly stopped in his tracks and beat a hasty retreat, acting as though he had forgotten something.

"Thanks for meeting me," Hannah replied, ignoring the question. "I just didn't feel this was a discussion we should finish over the phone."

"Doesn't a discussion imply two people working through something? I was under the impression you'd made up your mind—and to hell with what I want."

Hannah felt like she'd swallowed a mouthful of ashes. Figuring it might be a while before the waiter ventured a return, she reached for Paul's glass of water, leaving him with the gin and tonic already in front of him. But when she began speaking, she wished she'd taken the cocktail instead.

"I'm sorry," she repeated. "For everything. I know this is hard for you, but you know what? It's even harder for me."

"I don't see how," Paul said. "I'm the one who's going to be alone."

She looked at him, her eyes welling up with the tears she thought she could hold in check. It had been two years since she'd allowed herself to cry. Tears never changed a damn thing, and anyway, she figured there were no tears left inside of her. Wrong again. She grabbed her napkin and unfolded it, methodically placing it on her lap; there was no food on the table, but it gave her something to do and provided an excuse, however feeble, to look away from Paul.

As she stroked the linen, Paul's tone softened. "Baby, look," he said, "I didn't mean that. Well, yeah, I did, but I know this isn't easy for you. But damn it, you think I'm just going to step aside quietly?

You may not know everything about me, but you oughta know I'm not someone who just gives up. I fight for what's important."

"I'm not looking for you to fight. And it's not a matter of giving up. I'm doing what I have to do."

"Bullshit. You don't have to—"

"Paul, I do. He's my husband. And yes, maybe you're right that I don't have to do it, but I'm choosing to do it." She threw her napkin on the table, no longer needing its comfort. "Don't you realize this is a shock for me? Do you have any idea how scared I am?"

"Well, I'm scared for you. That son of a bitch liberal judge, what the hell was he thinking? I've read about your husband. I know what he did, and I can't—"

"No." Hannah narrowed her eyes and aimed her index finger at him. "Don't you dare go there. I'm not scared for my safety. Thane did not murder that woman. I don't give a damn what you've read. I'm scared because . . ."

She paused, catching her breath. She understood what Paul felt, but if she was honest, her relationship with Thane was none of his business. Not anymore. "I'm sorry," she finally said. "I really am. I wish I could tell you what's going to happen, but I honestly don't know. I haven't even spoken to Thane in over three years. For all I know, I'll be on your front step tomorrow, begging you to let me in."

Paul shook his head. "You won't have to beg. Ever."

He pulled out his wallet, threw a twenty on the table, and downed the rest of his drink with one swig. Then he rose and walked away without saying goodbye—although by then, goodbye was the only thing left to say.

Hannah opened the door to her bookstore, hoping to slip in unnoticed, even though she knew the bell would announce her arrival. It was a compact space, smaller than the fiction section of an average Barnes & Noble. She instinctively checked for any customers. None. Her only employee was a twenty-one-year-old college student named Caitlin, whose round face and round wire-rimmed glasses made her look like one of those cartoon owls holding a book. She sat reading in one of the side chairs near the register.

"If you worked at one of those big chain bookstores, you'd never have time to read," Hannah said.

"You're telling me," Caitlin responded without looking up. "I worked at a Books-a-Million for a month. It almost killed me."

"Spoken like a woman who doesn't have to pay rent." Hannah walked to the counter and picked up a smattering of mail, glancing through the pieces but not seeing anything worth opening.

Caitlin set the book on her lap and looked up at Hannah, eyes wide. "How'd it go?"

"It was great. We laughed and laughed, then left with a big ol' hug."

"Was he pissed?" Caitlin asked, not even trying to hide her eagerness.

"Let's just say he started off pissed. It went downhill from there."

Caitlin bounced on the chair cushion in an effort to sit up straight. "I just want you to know I think all of this is so cool. I've never met anyone who has had anything this romantic happen to them."

"Kiddo, you and I obviously have different notions of romance."

"You know what I mean. But tell me the important stuff. What are you going to wear tomorrow?"

Hannah thought for a moment. "I don't know. What does a woman wear for something like this?"

Caitlin leapt from her chair like a cat who heard food rattling into its dish. "I saw this movie once. I think it was from the sixties or something because the color was all faded, you know? And there was this girl, and she was going through what you're going through. Kind of? Well, maybe not exactly, but you know. Anyway, she wore this real pretty sundress. It was all bright and cheery and the dress just swayed around when she moved, and her boyfriend threw his arms around her and wouldn't let go."

"I'll put that on my list."

Hannah stepped forward and gave Caitlin a hug. Caitlin hugged her back and started to step away, but Hannah wasn't ready to let go just yet. "I'm heading home," she said, letting her go at last. "I just wanted to make sure you were okay. And thanks again for manning the store tomorrow."

She grabbed her purse and turned to go, but when she reached the door, Caitlin called out to her.

"Hey, Hannah? You look real beautiful."

Hannah stopped for a moment, then glanced back over her shoulder, more grateful than the young woman could ever imagine. "Thanks. I don't believe you, but thanks."

"And I think your hair looks fantastic!" Caitlin shouted. "He'll feel like nothing's changed."

Hannah tried to respond, but the words got stuck in her throat, so she settled for a nod. Quickly closing the door, she walked toward her car, slowly at first, then faster and faster, determined to reach it before the next wave of tears kicked in. She knew she wouldn't make it.

CHAPTER THREE

Forsman Penitentiary's ability to castrate a man's spirit was legendary. Built in the thirties to incarcerate felons too savage for other prisons to handle, its thirty-foot concrete walls had turned a jaundiced yellow. A dirt courtyard in the center of the prison had been pounded rock-hard by the thousands of men who had been herded across it over the past eighty-six years.

On the far side of the courtyard, Thane sat alone on the bottom row of a rotting wooden bleacher. He was out of his ill-fitting sports coat and back in the dirt-brown uniform he had been wearing for the last five years. He stared straight ahead at the other inmates who either migrated toward the weights or the basketball court, strutting as though they owned the place. A smaller group of men stood along the far wall, keeping to themselves, as if waiting for a bus to pick them up and take them away.

While his eyes faced the courtyard, Thane's radar stayed locked onto Baby, a steroid-soaked inmate the size of a refrigerator but half as bright, lumbering towards him from his immediate left. Baby's head, larger than a bowling ball, boasted a scalp shaved so close that it reflected the sun. Thane had steered clear of the man after watching him snap another inmate's shoulder blade with one hand while holding a biscuit in the other. Apparently, the biscuit had somehow caused the altercation.

Thane leaned down and pretended to tie his shoe. Moving his hands over the shoestring like a third-rate mime, he discreetly grabbed a handful of dirt and sat back up, resuming his study of the weightlifters. He used to think if he knew a trick, then surely every prisoner in Forsman knew it, but he'd now been there long enough that he could outwit many of them. He hoped his sleight of hand went unnoticed in case it turned out he was prey.

As the behemoth approached, Gideon Spence appeared on Thane's right, casually lowering his bulk next to him. Thane didn't acknowledge him, although his clenched fist relaxed a degree or two. Gideon, a stout African American man in his early fifties, glared directly at the approaching convict, almost daring him to come nearer.

After a couple more steps toward Thane, Baby veered off-course and plodded toward the basketball court. Thane dropped the handful of dirt as though it was just another day in the yard. Such was life in Forsman. "You got beef with Baby?" Gideon asked.

Thane shrugged. "Does that ever matter?"

"Maybe he just wanted to show everyone the legend of Forsman Prison ain't such hot shit," Gideon said, a small grin crossing his face.

"Don't start."

"Hell, you not only kick yourself off death row, you suddenly get to strut your ass out the door. That's big shit."

Thane nodded, pretending to consider this for the first time. "Yeah, it is, at that."

Gideon leaned back, resting his arms on the wooden plank behind him, the cheap fabric of his prison-issued uniform straining against his barrel chest. He nodded toward the small pile of dirt at Thane's feet. "You've learned a lot since you first showed up." He nudged Thane and cackled. "We'll make a proper convict outta you yet."

Thane knew Forsman had changed him, though he didn't like to think about it. For one thing, he was stronger now, more physically powerful than he had ever been before. And he had grown cunning as well, constantly calculating—and always looking over his shoulder for brutes like Baby. "Maybe your parole will come through next time," he said simply. "Maybe you'll get out of here, too."

"Nah. I appreciate your help and all, but I never do too good at those hearings. Bunch of self-righteous, tie-wearing dickheads thinking they can judge me. Who the fuck they think they are?"

"They think they're the parole board, and like it or not, they *do* get to judge you. So try sticking to the script we practiced, okay? And quit spitting every time you think a question is stupid."

Gideon looked up, then muttered under his breath, "Speaking of things that make me want to spit."

Chuck Yoder, a prison guard with a permanent scowl, strode over and stood directly in front of Thane, his chest puffed out like he was asking for a fight. His hair was the color of a sparrow, a dirty brown that managed to look greasy even on a quarter-inch crew cut, and his two front teeth were gray. His uniform, however, was always pristine.

Thane hadn't been in Forsman long before getting on Yoder's bad side. It happened when Thane had first arrived, before he understood that reporting a guard for misconduct was a quick way to make enemies. He also hadn't realized that Yoder kicking a prisoner simply because he could wasn't a surprise to anyone. As far as prison officials were concerned, that was just a regular Tuesday. Yoder wasn't reprimanded as a result of the complaint, but he was pissed off.

As he got closer, Thane avoided eye contact, but Yoder brought out his metal baton and rapped it against his open palm. The baton had a grim collection of dings and dents on it, most of them caused by contact with human bone.

"Got something you want to say, Banning?" Yoder said.

Thane continued staring at the ground and shook his head. "No."

Yoder brought his baton down hard, smashing it into the bench an inch from Thane's hand, but Thane didn't flinch. The sharp crack of the wood caused two distant guards to whip their rifle scopes toward the source of the sound, but they resumed their positions when they saw that it was just Yoder.

"Stand up."

Thane stood slowly and raised his eyes to meet Yoder's.

"You speak to me, it damn well better have a 'sir' on the end of it," Yoder said. "You understand?"

Thane nodded. He continued looking directly at Yoder, holding eye contact far longer than was wise.

Yoder's face tightened. "Fucking piece of shit lawyer. It don't do nobody no good when death row scum like you gets sprung. This whole place is gonna be a damn monkey cage for the next few weeks cause of you, and I'm the guy who's gotta clean it up."

"You're releasing an innocent man," Thane said. "If that makes it any less painful for you. *Sir*."

Yoder's lip curled, as if he'd just heard a good dirty joke. "You think I'm just being a hard-ass? You still don't give me no credit for trying to keep things orderly around here. Maybe you should report me to the warden." Yoder slowly raised his metal baton like a hammer over Thane's head. "Although I guess I'd need to give you something to report."

Gideon stood and Yoder pivoted quickly, pointing the baton at the large man's forehead. "You don't want to be standing up, boy. I'll drop you like a big ol' black bear."

Gideon continued giving Yoder the dead eye. The commotion started to draw a crowd, including several other guards. Yoder turned back toward Thane as he lowered the baton.

"You always act like you're better than everyone else. Smarter than everyone else. But you're not. Which one of us gets to walk out of here at night, huh?" Yoder said.

"I'll be walking out of here tomorrow."

Yoder glared at Thane. "Maybe. Maybe not. A hell of a lot of shit can happen between now and tomorrow. Real ugly shit. Either way, you need to remember that as long as you're behind these walls, I'm in charge."

Thane nodded to Gideon, then turned and walked away from the guard. He heard Yoder mutter something, but it was just background noise, like traffic outside the prison walls. Yoder was something from his past now, one more thing to forget, like everything else in Forsman.

As long as he survived to see tomorrow.

Thane lay on his cot, staring up at a quarter inch-wide crack that zigzagged across the cement ceiling while he thought about what was to come in the morning.

Soon he would be sleeping in a real bed with sheets and blankets that didn't feel like they were made of asbestos. And in that new bed, would Hannah be lying next to him? The prison social worker had only sent word of transportation being arranged, but he had no idea if it would be Hannah. A small part of him hoped it wasn't. The rest of him prayed it was.

He had written to her three years ago, telling her to move on with her life and not visit anymore, a letter that took him a week and most of his sanity to write. And he'd refused to go to the visitation room the four times she came after receiving the letter, even though it tore him up to know that she was there waiting, maybe a hundred feet from his cell. But he knew that if he'd tried to say goodbye in person, he never could have let her go.

Tomorrow would be the first time in three years he'd see her face. If she came at all.

His release meant Stone had decided against trying to keep him locked up, which didn't surprise him. But being freed on a technicality didn't mean anyone believed his innocence. He would not be welcomed back to society like a hero or a martyr, the way the scenario always played out in his imagination. Instead, he would still be seen as a killer. A lucky killer.

The sharp click of dress shoes echoed down the corridor as the night guard made his rounds through the cellblock. That meant it was 3:30 a.m. There was a precision to life here in Forsman, things that could be counted on, some good, but most not so good. What would it be like to once again have control over his own time? To have ownership of his own life?

He knew one thing for certain: people would say what they wanted about him and the circumstances of his release. They would say he got away with murder, and some would make it their life's mission to ensure he continued to suffer for his sins. There was nothing he could do to change any of this; but it was all a small price to pay for never again having to tell the time by the sound of another man's step.

CHAPTER FOUR

ISTRICT ATTORNEY BRADFORD STONE HATED what he was about to do.

He sat ramrod straight at his desk as if he were wearing a brace, even though there was only one subordinate in his office with him. But even alone, his rigid posture always conveyed the look of a man testifying in front of a Senate Subcommittee.

"So where do we go from here?" his senior deputy assistant asked.

Stone paused before answering, calculations running through his head. "We deal with it as quickly as possible, then we move on. That's all we can do."

Wallace Winston nodded. A rotund man in his early sixties, he always looked as if he should have a dab of mustard on his wrinkled shirt collar. His flabby jowls were accented by a drooping, bushy brown mustache, and eyebrows that looked as though they were combed with an eggbeater.

"You still don't think we can retry him? Because I really do believe we would . . ." Winston started.

"We're not retrying him and I'm not going to keep having this conversation. We're done with this case. I just don't want to have to go through the theatrics of this press conference. The whole thing is bullshit. The public is going to say we couldn't keep them safe. They have no idea what that actually means."

Down the hall, a pack of reporters were tuning up, trying to sharpen their questions enough to draw blood. He could handle them, but no matter what he said, his office was going to look unprofessional—or worse, incompetent.

"You've done more to make this city safe than the three previous DAs combined," Winston piped up.

Winston had kept his job through four District Attorneys because of two important qualities: he was unquestionably loyal to his boss, and he had absolutely no interest in advancing his own career. His lack of ambition posed no threat to anyone, and that, coupled with the vast reservoir of historical knowledge he'd accumulated over the years, made him invaluable.

"I remember how bad things got around here when we lost Lauren," he continued. "Now Banning's going to go free and the whole grieving process will start all over again."

Stone shoved his chair back and stood. "None of this ever should have happened in the first place."

He exited his office, his pace confident as he strode toward the conference room full of reporters. Stone paused for a moment before opening the door and taking his place behind the podium.

Camera lights cranked to full intensity made the room a good fifteen degrees hotter than Stone's office. He surveyed the gathered horde, refusing at first to make eye contact with them, viewing them instead as one great faceless mass.

"The murder conviction of Thane Banning," he began, "was overturned yesterday afternoon by the Second District Court of Appeals of Los Angeles. He is to be released at three o'clock this afternoon. It is an understatement to say this office is disappointed with Judge Williams's ruling. However, as Officers of the court, we have no choice but to respect his decision."

Stone paused and looked at the podium, shaking his head almost imperceptibly. Almost. If there was anything to be gained from this circus, he wanted the reporters to know that he did *not* in fact respect the judge's decision.

"Mr. Banning may still be retried for his crime. He was not found innocent; he was only released as a result of the judge calling a mistrial on the original hearing. However, the passing years have made a second trial exceptionally difficult, in large part due to the death of our primary witness. But we have not ruled out this option. A decision will be made within the next six weeks, at which time you will be informed of any future actions this office may pursue. I will now take questions."

Reporters' voices clamored from around the room. Stone raised his hand to try to silence the group, then pointed toward Dan Larson, an older reporter in the front row. The man stood, notepad in hand, and offered up the predictable question.

Let the blame game begin.

"As District Attorney, do you take responsibility for Banning's release?"

Stone answered without hesitation. "I take responsibility for all actions in my office. But let me be clear: There was no dereliction of duty on the part of anyone working in this office. None whatsoever."

Stone pointed to a young woman sitting in the middle of the pack.

"How is it that a real estate lawyer was able to overturn a capital murder conviction? He's never practiced criminal law a day in his life."

"I'm not going to talk about the specifics of the case at this time. Next." He pointed at a reporter who looked young enough to be working for a high school paper.

"You were elected in large part based on your conviction of Thane Banning. Do you think his release will result in your being removed from office next election?"

Stone unclenched his jaw. "First of all, I disagree with your initial assumption. But be that as it may, I serve, and always will serve, at the pleasure of the citizens of Los Angeles. They should consider how safe they felt before I took office, look at the progress we've made over the past four and a half years, and then decide. But they should also remember that releasing Thane Banning was not my decision."

"Then you still believe he's guilty?" said an unmistakable baritone voice echoing from the back of the room like a bullhorn.

For the first time during his years of press conferences, Stone was thrown off-guard. Russell McCoy had somehow managed to slip in through the rear entrance. Allowing the father of the slain girl into the press conference was the journalistic equivalent of tossing chum into a shark tank. The cameras swirled toward the man, causing McCoy to squint his eyes and take half a step back, as if the heat of the lights carried enough punch to move him.

McCoy, who stood a head taller than most everyone in the room, looked over the reporters and addressed Stone eye-to-eye. "Well?" McCoy continued. "Do you?"

Stone focused his attention solely on McCoy. "It doesn't matter what I believe or don't believe, Mr. McCoy. That's not the way the system works."

McCoy shrugged his massive shoulders and turned to leave the room. "Yeah. The way the system works," he said as he walked out the door.

The reporters looked as if they were struggling to decide whether to follow McCoy or see the press conference through. Stone struggled with the same dilemma, but didn't want to give McCoy's words any weight.

"Next question."

CHAPTER FIVE

THE MAIN GATE TO FORSMAN opened at three o'clock, and the first thing Thane noticed was the sky stretching endlessly toward the horizon, not broken by concrete walls and razor wire.

A mob of press awaited him; he would have to take in this new landscape later. He had figured there might be a couple of low-level media hacks awaiting his appearance, but more than forty eager reporters stood yelling for his attention. He walked behind the three guards who were stationed like linebackers along a rope to hold the press at bay.

A stadium-sized parking lot stretched out in front of the prison: city traffic was a good half-mile away, but the sight of free people driving wherever they damn well chose stirred desire in him. He scanned the area past the reporters' camera flashes and waving hands, ignoring the barrage of questions designed to provoke him. He only looked forward, and for only one face.

His breath caught when he spotted Hannah next to her car about thirty yards away. He stopped abruptly, as if he'd run into an invisible barrier. She was an apparition, an image of hope, as her white dress and auburn hair were bright in the sun. She looked like everything Forsman wasn't. She was leaning against her car but stood straight when their eyes met, at first clasping her hands in front of her, then letting them hang by her side, and finally holding them pressed together in front of her mouth as if saying a prayer.

Her '82 Honda Civic was a hodgepodge of clashing colors: the right rear door was midnight blue, the hood black, and the rest of the body a faded yellow, except for a belt of rust along the chassis. It was a car that would have been equally at home in a prison lot or a demolition derby. When he'd been shipped off to Forsman five years ago, she had been driving a brand-new pearl-colored Saab.

Thane regained his momentum and walked toward her. When he finally got close enough for her to hear him, he nodded his head back toward the reporters and all of their cameras.

"I don't want to do this in front of them."

She glanced toward the reporters, then nodded and went around the car, sliding her slim frame behind the steering wheel. Thane pulled on the locked passenger door; Hannah fumbled as she tried unlocking the door, accidentally lowering one of the back windows first, then finally managing to let him into the car.

She put her hand on the key, but instead of turning it, she simply stared straight ahead.

"I was afraid I'd never see you again," she said, her voice cracking.

"I'm sorry I stopped seeing you," he finally said. "But when I thought there was no chance of ever getting out, I just wanted you to—"

She turned quickly to face him. "Don't apologize. You never have to apologize to me for anything. You did nothing wrong." She wiped the back of her sleeve across her eyes. "You did nothing wrong." She caught her breath, holding it tight.

"I know all of this is very sudden," he finally said. "And I'll understand if you want to take things slow. I can find another place to stay for now if you'd like."

She shook her head, although her silence made him wonder if she had considered this option as well.

"Are you sure? I don't even know where you are in your life," he continued. "I just don't want to make this difficult for you." He looked away, gazing out the passenger window, his ghostlike reflection in the glass staring back at him, trying to figure out who he was.

"It shouldn't be difficult," she said.

"It shouldn't. But it's been a long time."

"Would you rather be alone?" she asked.

"I've been alone for five years."

"Then let's go home."

He nodded, feeling as though he was already halfway there.

She turned the key and the tired engine coughed its way to life. The reporters raced toward their news vans, breaking down tripods and equipment as they scurried across the parking lot to follow. Hannah's car approached the final barricade leading off the prison grounds and the guard raised the bar, allowing her to depart without slowing down. The bar then lowered, and the reporters found themselves in a traffic jam as the uniformed guard conducted a methodical review of the first vehicle. Apparently, the prison preferred the press not talk to their inmates, which was just fine by Thane.

Driving south on the 110, Hannah merged into an exit lane five miles from their turnoff, toward an unfamiliar and rather menacing section of town. Thane's mouth tightened. She'd had to move.

Hannah glanced over at him. "It's fine."

She drove through a part of the city that wasn't yet lost to violent crime, but Thane could tell it was nearing the tipping point. Every fifth or sixth house looked either abandoned or condemned, and there were more pawn shops than convenience stores.

They pulled up to an eight-story brick apartment building, an indistinct square with windows, a front door, and an exterior that could have been designed by a five-year-old.

"Don't be disappointed when you see it," Hannah said. "It's a little small, and old, but it has a lot of character."

Thane hesitated, then got out of the car, following her through the building's front entrance. After Forsman, living under a bridge would have been an upgrade for him, but it cut him to the core to see where Hannah had landed.

After Hannah pushed the button for the elevator, the door only opened part way, forcing them to slip into the car sideways. The ride to the sixth floor was slow, the rancorous hum of the motor and the grinding gears making conversation difficult even if Thane had been able to think of something to say. He had been conditioned by years of self-imposed silence, and now he felt as though his command of language had abandoned him.

They stepped onto Hannah's floor and entered her apartment. Thane couldn't help frowning.

He looked at the tiny kitchen, where every flat surface was covered with robin's egg linoleum. He walked over and glanced out the kitchen window that led to a rusted fire escape platform, trash dumpsters in the alley directly below.

Her living room was dark, partly because the shades were still drawn, perhaps an effort to repel the squalor outside. But her place would have appeared dingy even with open windows on the sunniest of days. The once-emerald blue sofa had obviously seen other living rooms in its day—possibly even the dump. A pale red reading chair, peppered with beer stains and cigarette burns from years and families gone by, sat angled next to the sofa.

But surveying the living room more closely, he noticed familiar touches: a teacup on the floor next to the reading chair, a bowl of green apples on the lopsided coffee table, a Cherokee throw pillow on the sofa. Plywood shelves stained a dark green and stacked on cinder blocks resided unevenly in the corner of the room. One thing that hadn't changed: a wide array of Hannah's favorite books stood on the top shelf, arranged alphabetically as they had been in the old house.

But the most noticeably absent items were photographs. The mantel over the sealed-up fireplace and the scarred coffee table each displayed a few personal items—a round rock, a ceramic tile from Paris, a tiny metal bird—but no pictures. This was Hannah's world where no one else was allowed inside, even in celluloid.

Yet here Thane stood.

"It looks like you," he said.

"Old and worse for wear?"

"No. Warm and inviting. Safe."

She smiled slightly but looked as though she could cry. "I picked up some things for you at the drugstore," she said. "Toothbrush, stuff like that. I also got you a couple pairs of pants and shirts. I wasn't sure if you were the same size, since I hadn't—anyway, I didn't get you much. I'm sorry, but when I moved here, I gave away your clothes. It wasn't that I had given up. I just . . ."

She halted for a moment. "Are you hungry? I could fix you something."

"What I want most right now is to wash Forsman prison off me. But after that, something to eat would be good."

"The bathroom is down the hall on the left."

As he walked past, he lightly touched her shoulder, uncertain of his right to make closer contact yet. When he got halfway down the hall, she called out.

"Thane? Welcome home."

He turned toward her and tried to speak, but he could only offer a half-nod. He had imagined hearing those words hundreds of times while lying on his prison cot, playing them over in his mind like a favorite record. She couldn't have said anything more beautiful. He wanted to respond, but instead he turned and went into the bathroom.

He switched on the light and shut the door, studying the doorknob's lock as if it were an alien artifact. Slowly pushing the button until it clicked, he continued staring at the door. A room that he himself could secure. The concept was still strange in his mind.

How long would it be before he no longer noticed things like this?

A bath towel and washcloth were on the seat of the toilet for him, another reminder of the civility of the world he had re-entered. He picked up the towel and held it to his face, breathing in deeply. The softness of the cotton and the allure of its lemon scent reminded him of his wife and a gentler existence.

He turned on the shower, removed his clothes, and stepped into water that was actually hot. It took him a moment to realize he could shut his eyes without fear, although he still didn't totally close the shower curtain, leaving a two-inch gap so he could glance out into the room if need be. He stood motionless, content to hide within the water's warmth and security for as long as he could.

Hannah prepared pasta and a salad, and Thane limited himself to one glass of wine, although he poured a generous glass. They talked some during dinner, often lapsing into a silence that would have seemed unusual in their earlier life. They frequently looked at each other and sometimes smiled, strain and comfort mixing together.

As the evening grew dark, the atmosphere turned uneasy as neither one appeared comfortable suggesting it was time to go to bed. They sat at the table long after the food and drink was gone. Thane assumed Hannah was struggling like he was, trying to think of the right thing to say.

Eventually they both rose, Thane following her cue, and took their plates to the sink, where they gazed at each other intermittently, carrying on a broken but intimate conversation with their eyes. Hannah then stepped forward and put her arms around Thane's waist, softly resting her head against his shoulder. He wrapped his arms around her, and neither one could let go.

All of the awkwardness and hesitancy of their reunion dissipated in this embrace. It was as though they had each been trying to find words to bring them together, but there was no language that could convey their feelings for each other. It was only through touch and the warmth of flesh that he could find a starting point upon which to begin building. After holding each other for several intense minutes, they finally stepped back, turned off the lights, and headed to the bedroom.

Hannah changed into an elegant silk nightgown that embraced her curves, wrapping her like an exquisite gift. They spent their first night together holding each other, offering an endless series of tender kisses, each one opening up Thane's heart a little more. Hannah spoke in whispers, words of love and loss, fear and gratitude. Her words came easily now in the dark, and as she spoke, Thane stroked her gently. His last five years had been spent in a world of metal and concrete and rock; embracing something so soft and warm seemed utterly foreign to him.

She eventually fell asleep, but Thane found it difficult to surrender to the night, even without blazing fluorescent lights and clanging prison sounds. He simply wasn't ready to let go of his first night of freedom. It had taken him too long to get here to simply roll over and close his eyes.

There would be plenty of time for them to pull their lives back together. Plenty of time to get to know each other again. But that thought stoked fear: he wasn't the same man she'd met fifteen years ago. Once she saw who he was now, would she turn away from him?

His insides tightened. He knew one thing for certain: he would do everything in his power to get them back to where they were before his conviction. But he didn't want to think about it now. All he wanted, in this quiet, content moment, was to lie in that room, listening to the sound of his wife's tranquil breathing.

CHAPTER
SIX

THANE AND HANNAH MEANDERED ALONG the beach, close
enough to the Santa Monica Pier to hear a Michael Buble song
playing from a restaurant while the ocean waves tried their best
to hush him. Walking arm-in-arm, they tightroped along the
water's edge, navigating by moonlight in the night's gloom.

They hadn't gone out much in the month since his release,
although recently they were venturing out a bit more, realizing
they couldn't stay secluded in their apartment forever, tempting
though that was. Without acknowledging it, they gravitated toward
places shrouded in darkness, such as the beach at night. After one
uncomfortable experience in a movie theater, when an entire row of
people got up and moved once Thane walked in, they started slipping
in after the previews began.

They ambled along the beach, animatedly debating the merits of
the movie they had just seen.

"You are so wrong!" Hannah said.

"Oh come on—that part was totally unbelievable," Thane said.

"It was a children's fantasy, not a documentary." She shook her
head and laughed.

"Still, give me a break. When that monkey ran over and grabbed
the key to the lock—"

"It was a movie! When you watched *Harry Potter*, did you grumble when the kids rode flying brooms?" She lowered her voice, impersonating a muttering Thane. "I know I never had a broom that could do that."

As Thane laughed, Hannah stopped walking and gazed at him warmly.

"What?" he said.

"That's the first time you've laughed in a month."

He smiled. "I've been waiting for you to say something funny."

She punched his arm. "Uh-huh. Nevertheless, it's nice to hear."

They leaned against each other as they faced the ocean, looking up at the night sky. Gazing out over the dark water, Thane could make out the stars that were usually blanketed by smog. A light coastal breeze whispered across their faces, and the steady stroking of the waves made conversation softer.

"Beautiful night," Hannah sighed.

"You have no idea," Thane said.

He paused for a moment, gazing upward. "One of the things I missed most in prison was seeing the stars. We weren't allowed outside at night. Some people say the night sky makes them feel insignificant, but try never seeing it. Then you'll know what insignificance feels like."

Hannah turned towards him. "That must have been hard," she said.

"Everything was hard."

He stared up at the stars a moment longer. "Sorry. I'm really not standing here just feeling sorry for myself."

"I wouldn't blame you if you were. Maybe it would help if you talked about it more often."

"Maybe," he said, as he put his arm around her, turning them back toward the pier, "but not tonight. It's too perfect of an evening. Come on, let's get something to eat."

They strolled to a small diner a couple of blocks off the beach, the old-fashioned kind with a neon sign, a Formica counter, and one row of booths covered with cherry red Naugahyde running alongside the window. A booth at the far end was just opening up, so they made their way past the customers sitting at the counter and slid in.

In the next booth over, a big man in a tight leather vest narrowed his eyes at Thane as they took their seats. He looked like a human Humvee, with a broad red face and lamppost arms that stretched the sleeves of his Harley-Davidson T-shirt. A nightclub bouncer, Thane thought, or a drug dealer.

Or maybe an ex-con, like him.

A middle-aged, heavyset waitress with flame-red hair walked over to Thane and Hannah's booth. "What can I get you two? Afraid it's too late for the special."

The big man next to them leaned out of his booth and called to the waitress. "Yo, Miss."

The waitress glanced at him. He had enough food to feed a family of four in front of him, along with a full bottle of beer. "Just a sec, hon," she said, turning her attention back to Thane and Hannah. "But everything on the menu's special anyway, that's what I always say."

The man's voice bellowed this time: "I want my check now. I ain't sitting next to a murderer."

The diner fell silent except for the sound of dishes clanking in the back, although it was only a moment before that, too, went quiet. Hannah turned around and looked over the top of the booth at the man behind her. "Hey screw you, you ignorant—"

Thane reached over and touched her arm, turning her back around toward him. "Let it go," he said as he slid from the booth. "Come on. To be honest, I don't really want to eat next to him either."

Hannah looked at Thane, then slid out of the booth as well, continuing to glare. "You're lucky I didn't want to get my hands dirty," the man said as they passed. "Otherwise I'd break you in half." Hannah and Thane kept moving.

The man once again leaned out of his booth. "That's right—take your bitch and run away."

Thane stopped cold, his pulse suddenly pounding in his temples. Before he knew it, he was striding back towards the big man, who was now standing, holding his beer bottle by the neck, primed for a fight. As Thane approached, the man raised the bottle to swing, but Thane struck first, driving his right fist into the man's trachea faster than a striking snake.

The man staggered back against the booth and fell onto the seat, gasping for air as he lay on his back. The bottle of beer tipped over onto his chest, its contents spilling out all over his T-shirt. Thane reached into the booth and yanked the muscleman up by his ponytail until he was sitting upright.

"I didn't kill anybody, you dumb son of a bitch—but don't think I don't know how," Thane growled. He grabbed the steak knife off the table and pressed the point of it against the other man's throat as he gasped for air.

Hannah grabbed Thane's arm and tried pulling him away, but she wasn't strong enough to budge him. Thane leaned closer to the trembling man. "I don't give a damn what you think of me," Thane said, "but you speak to my wife like that again, and I swear to God I'll gut you."

Thane paused, then threw the knife onto the table. When he released the ponytail, the wide-eyed man collapsed back onto the seat, still gasping.

Thane and Hannah walked out of the diner and down the sidewalk. Hannah remained quiet for a while, and Thane just stared ahead, walking so quickly that his wife almost had to jog to keep pace.

"He was just a jerk," she finally said.

When Thane didn't respond, she tried again. "Are you okay? What happened to 'let it go'?"

Thane slowed his step, finally leaning his forehead against a streetlight. He clenched his fist, placed it against the metal pole, then relaxed it without taking a swing.

"I'm sorry," he said. "I'm sure you've had to deal with that before. I guess I was trying to make up for not being around the last time."

"I understand," she replied. She opened her mouth to speak again, but closed it instead, putting her arm in his and pulling him close.

"Come on," she said, "let's go home."

They turned and continued down the sidewalk in silence, stepping away from the glow of the streetlight, back into the shadows.

CHAPTER
SEVEN

THANE'S FIRST SOCIAL EVENT SINCE being released felt even more awkward than expected. On the few occasions that he glanced around, several sets of watchful faces quickly turned away, so he mostly occupied himself with surveying the food display or staring at his shoes. He knew the time down to the minute, since checking his watch offered him something to do besides standing there like a statue.

Joseph Crowell, his former boss, insisted that he and Hannah attend a gathering in honor of Thane's vindication, but the sparse turnout confirmed that few people viewed his release as a cause for celebration. It had been five weeks, but the press still trumpeted his freedom as the exploitation of a technicality—or, worse, a total miscarriage of justice.

Hannah walked up to Thane as he was studying the endless spread of hors d'oeuvres. "You've been eyeing these for the last ten minutes," she said, pointing to the canapes. "Think you'll actually choose one?"

"If you must know, I'm avoiding conversation. Trust me, I'm doing everybody a favor." As he once again looked out into the living room, a former colleague immediately looked away. "You know, we really should get out more. This is a lot of fun."

Hannah smiled and nudged him. "It was a nice gesture on

Joseph's part. And at least a few people showed up."

"These are all Joseph's people," Thane replied. "I'm sure they didn't have much of a choice."

He grabbed a couple of fancy crab puffs that were sprouting some sort of green sprig, just as the kitchen door sprung open and Joseph burst into the dining room, inconspicuous as a bottle rocket. "Eat, everybody! Eat!" Joseph shouted. "There's enough food in the kitchen to feed an opera."

At fifty-eight, Joseph Crowell had the world on a leash. He ran Crowell Architects, the boutique law firm where Thane had worked before his arrest. The firm exclusively courted high-roller developers of high-rise office buildings, helping them to navigate the whitewater rapids of city government bureaucracy.

Thane watched as Joseph instructed a waiter to refill the wine glasses of two guests, who just a minute ago had been wistfully glancing at their watches. Once they no longer had an excuse to bail, Joseph strode over to Thane and Hannah.

"My dear," Joseph said to Hannah, "I need a few minutes with the prodigal son, but whether I give him back in one piece is going to be entirely up to him." Joseph put his arm around Thane's shoulder and steered him out of the room, leaving Hannah alone with an entire tray of crab puffs.

Joseph led Thane through the kitchen and outside onto a massive patio that was built with more stones than a lighthouse and overlooked an Olympic-sized swimming pool. The deep green spotlights shining from the bottom cast the entire backyard in an ethereal beauty.

"I appreciate you doing this for us tonight," Thane said, "but maybe it was too soon."

"Bullshit," Joseph said. "Those bastards took five years from you. I won't let them take one minute more. Not one." He removed a Cuban cigar from his jacket and lit it, inhaling deeply and holding the smoke in his lungs before finally expelling it into the night air in a thick gray cloud. "Besides, I had ulterior motives for getting you here."

He shot a mischievous grin at Thane. "I want you back and working with me. It's non-negotiable."

Thane shook his head. "That's very generous, but you don't have to do that."

"In all the years you've known me, have you ever seen me do a goddamn thing I didn't want to do? I know I don't have to do it. I *want* to do it. And it's for selfish reasons: you're the best real estate lawyer I've ever worked with, and I don't settle for anything less than the best."

"Imagine how clients will react if you bring me back."

"They'll react how I tell them to react—or they can find another law firm, and trust me, that's not something they want to do. Listen, you're the best. Sure, maybe I won't have you do the presentations for the clients, but you know as well as I do there's a hell of a lot of work behind the scenes that doesn't involve dealing directly with the great unwashed. Christ, that should make the job more appealing to you."

Thane took a step back, eyeing Joseph warily. His smile never wavered; instead, he gave a single, confident nod—the one he gave when he considered negotiations closed—and extended a hand. Thane looked at the hand for a moment, then slowly reached out to shake it. Joseph snatched it, making sure Thane didn't have time to change his mind.

"Excellent," Joseph said. "As a lawyer, you know this is legal and binding. Or were we supposed to spit in our palms first? I can never remember."

After extended goodbyes and thank-yous to Joseph, Thane and Hannah drove down the interstate and back toward the seedier part of the city. Neither one spoke, despite the fact that Hannah was leaning against the passenger door to face Thane, an obvious effort to stare him down. But he couldn't restrain a smile as he watched her try and fail to outwait him. Finally, when he reached to turn on the radio, she broke, playfully slapping his hand away from the dial.

"Oh no, you don't! When you and Joseph came back inside, you looked totally different. What's up?"

Thane's smile dissolved. "Joseph wants me to come back to work."

She gasped. "Are you serious? That's great! I mean—I'm assuming it's great." She waited one brief moment for confirmation. "Isn't it great?"

"It's very generous," he said. "And also very crazy on his part. But you know Joseph. I'd be lying if I didn't say the whole thing kind of scares me, but being able to go back to work for someone who knows me and believes in me, that's about as good as it gets. Just the same . . ."

He fell silent, drifting inside his thoughts.

Hannah leaned over and threaded her arm through his. "It feels as though things are finally starting to fall our way. When does he want you to start?"

"Monday." He stared hard at the road.

"That's quick."

"Yes, it is."

Thane drew a breath. Deep down, this was something he had hoped for, but he'd never expressed it aloud. The more he'd thought about it, though, the more it confirmed his take on his former boss.

When they reached their apartment building, Thane shut off the car and sat for a moment as Hannah opened her car door.

"Go on up," he said. "I'm going to take a quick walk around the block, just to clear my head."

Hannah paused. "It's not the safest neighborhood at night, sweetheart."

"I'll be fine. Really. I won't be long. I'll be up in probably ten minutes. I just want to sort through all that happened this evening."

She looked at him, concerned, then kissed him gently and walked inside. Thane stood next to the car for a moment, then turned and crossed the street toward a figure leaning against a mailbox. Although the man had placed himself in the shadows, Thane had spotted him immediately when they pulled up outside the apartment building, recognizing him purely by his silhouette.

He'd figured at some point he'd have to deal with Russell McCoy, though it bothered him to find the father of the dead girl outside Hannah's apartment. Thane didn't slow down as he approached. He knew better than to show fear, something he'd learned early on at Forsman.

But maybe that was only true in prison. Maybe the rule didn't apply to grieving fathers.

Thane kept a sharp eye on McCoy's hands. If the big man was packing, he would most likely touch the weapon, feeling for it in the dark—or at least that's how it played out in the prison courtyard. But McCoy's hands remained motionless. Thane stopped within three feet of him, waiting for him to speak—or throw a punch. McCoy stared back with an expressionless face that could have been carved out of ice.

"I want you to know that as far as I'm concerned," he said in a lifeless voice, "there's a big difference between the justice system and true justice."

"I've felt the same way for five years," Thane replied.

"Just 'cause you found a way to get loose doesn't mean you didn't kill her."

"You're right. But I didn't. I don't expect you to believe me, but I'm saying it anyway."

McCoy studied him carefully. Although the two men had never spoken, they saw enough of each other during the trial. Whenever Thane had glanced McCoy's way, no matter what was going on in the courtroom, McCoy had never seemed to take his eyes off him.

"I spoke with Stone's office," McCoy said. "They won't confirm one way or the other, but what I'm hearing is they're not retrying you. My daughter's killer deserves to die, and if they're not going to make it happen, I will. Make no mistake about that."

"Is that why you're here?"

"Not tonight. I'm giving the DA a chance to do the right thing and send you back where you belong. But if he doesn't . . ."

McCoy pulled back one side of his jacket to reveal a pearl-handled Colt 45 tucked into a shoulder holster. "Killing a man might be a crime against the Lord, but I'll be comfortable arguing my case after I die."

"However this plays out," Thane said, "keep away from my wife's apartment. She has nothing to do with this. This is between you and me."

McCoy coughed out a laugh. "That's really something. Are you thinking it'd be difficult if someone you loved—some *innocent person* you loved—got hurt? You thinking that would be a terrible thing to happen? I suppose you're right."

McCoy turned to leave, then paused and faced Thane again. "It don't matter what you do. You can move away, change your name, get a gun, it don't matter. When I decide it's time—and it isn't gonna be long, either—then I'm going to kill you. I just want you to know that. Don't matter what you do."

"I didn't murder Lauren."

"Then you better tell me who did. You tell me what I should do with all this hatred. Because right now, buddy . . . you're it."

CHAPTER EIGHT

THANE WALKED DOWN SANTA MONICA Boulevard wearing a blue Hugo Boss suit, a lavender linen shirt, and a silk tie that had maxed out Hannah's lone credit card. The tie alone cost more than he had earned in six months working in the prison laundry— twenty cents an hour didn't go that far. As least the ever-mounting credit card bill with its parasitic interest rate would disappear soon, now that he was working again, at his old salary, adjusted for inflation.

Hannah had insisted he buy a suit that made a statement. He would have preferred something to help him blend in, but Hannah wouldn't take no for an answer. He kept his eyes downward, walking along the crowded sidewalk, feeling exposed in the daylight. Fortunately, nobody seemed to recognize him, the clothes apparently having turned him into just another faceless executive hoofing it to work.

The office building that housed Joseph's law firm loomed arrogantly above the other structures in the area. Thane walked into the expansive lobby and headed toward the elevator. A young security guard leaned against the reception desk and swung his keys around his finger as he hit on the obviously uninterested woman answering the phone. Thane's muscles tensed instinctively; even a rent-a-cop's uniform reminded him of prison.

The young man glanced at Thane, refocused his attention on his prey, then twisted around, checking out this guy in the new suit, trying to place the face. Thane had already seen that reaction scores of times. People who had seen his mug shot on the news dozens of times but couldn't quite make the connection.

Luckily, in L.A., it wasn't that uncommon to encounter people from TV.

Thane nodded at the guard and walked past the desk to the elevator, while the uniformed man continued to study him. He pushed the button for the elevator and glanced back. The receptionist had spun her chair in his direction, too, and she clearly had no trouble placing his face. She spoke rapidly to the guard, whose eyebrows shot up. Even across the lobby, Thane could make out a few words: "prison," and then, predictably, "murder." The young man puffed out his chest and patted the gun on his belt, most likely in an effort to reassure the young woman. As he strutted toward the elevator, the door opened, and Thane lurched toward it.

"Excuse me!" the guard called out. "Sir, hold up a minute."

As the guard raised his hand, Thane stepped inside the elevator. He pushed the button to close the doors, hearing the quickening clicks of the guard's dress shoes on the marble floor as the doors slid shut. He sighed and felt a wave of relief wash over him. He would suggest to Joseph that the security company be notified of his hiring.

He stepped off the elevator and into the firm's lobby, the name *Joseph Crowell and Associates* greeting visitors in conspicuous gold letters. Gold in more than just color: Joseph spared no expense for décor, especially when it came to his own name.

The receptionist looked like she could have been a model: blonde, blue-eyed, and with teeth a shade of white found only in a toothpaste commercial. She spotted Thane and offered a confident smile.

She stood and extended her hand. "Mr. Banning, my name is Brianna. I look forward to working with you, sir. Mr. Crowell is in a meeting across town for most of the morning, but he asked me to show you to your office and make sure you get settled in."

"Thank you, Brianna."

She led him through the door that separated the lobby from the rest of the firm and escorted him down a long office corridor, conversations in some of the side offices abruptly cutting off as he passed. A few of the secretarial staff across the room even took turns peeking over the top of their cubicles like a game of Whack-A-Mole.

Brianna led him to his office—a large, beautifully decorated space. Photographs of buildings, presumably made possible by the labor of Joseph's firm, were elegantly framed and mounted along one wall. "Here we are," she said, stepping to the side. Thane walked over to his desk, surprised to see his reflection in the polished desktop.

"I could use this thing as a mirror," he murmured, and Brianna giggled.

He then walked over to the sleek, ergonomically designed office chair and eased his weight down into it. "Bet you a dollar this cost more than my wife's car," he said. "Then again, I could probably say the same thing about the pen." A sterling silver Waterman pen and pencil stood upright in their holsters, locked and loaded.

A stack of folders on the gleaming desk awaited his review, the first of what was sure to be an endless torrent of documents he'd need to catch up on after five years of missed business. He swept his gaze around the room, again taking in the expensive furnishings, so far removed from his old world of concrete and violence.

During the first several months of his incarceration, Thane felt confident he would be released. He *had* to be released: he hadn't killed anyone. But after a year inside, he stopped dreaming of a moment just like this one. He felt like an imposter, an actor wearing a fancy suit while playing the part of a high-priced lawyer. This used to be his life, but now it felt like it all belonged to somebody else. Like it would all disappear if he closed his eyes.

"Is there anything you need right now, Mr. Banning?"

"No, thank you, Brianna. I'm good."

Thane stood and stretched after reviewing legal documents for several hours, the minutiae of real estate contracts returning to him like old friends. It helped that he had spent most of the last five years familiarizing himself with the nuances of criminal law which, while obviously different from real estate, still required extraordinary attention to detail.

He walked over and studied some of the enlarged photographs hanging on his wall, losing himself in one particular picture when Joseph appeared in the doorway.

"He has returned!" Joseph crowed. "All is right with the company again. So tell me—how's it feel?"

"Familiar. And . . . not familiar at the same time."

Thane turned back to the photograph of a stunning brick and glass structure with front entrance pillars extending twenty stories high. "My last project," Thane said. "I never did see how it turned out." He stared a moment longer. "Very impressive, Joseph."

"I'm sorry. I didn't know this was hanging in here. These were put up long ago. I'll have someone switch it out. In fact, I'll burn that fucking picture myself."

"That's not necessary."

"Do you remember it? We were so excited to get that job, something of that magnitude. Now I'm sure we both wish we'd never seen it."

Thane turned away and leaned on the side of his desk. His stomach churned, and for a moment he hesitated to speak. "Say, Joseph, you used to keep a security company on retainer, didn't you?"

"There was an outfit that used to do investigative work for me from time to time, although it's been a while. Don't remember their name off the top of my head. Why do you ask?"

Thane paused, then pushed forward. "Russell McCoy confronted me last night outside Hannah's apartment."

"Are you serious? Did he come at you?"

"No, but he pretty much said he was going to. Look, I can take care of myself, but I wouldn't want him doing something here after hours. I hate bringing this stuff to the workplace, especially on my first day. If there was any other way—"

Joseph raised his hand to silence him. "Listen, we knew there would be speed bumps. No need to apologize. I'll look through some old invoices and get you the name of the security outfit."

"I can do that. It's not like I have a lot on my plate right now."

"No, I got it. You just get up to speed on all the projects we've got in queue. So what did McCoy say?"

"He thinks I killed his daughter. What can I say besides 'I didn't do it'? That's not exactly a persuasive argument."

"And you can bet the police sure as hell aren't out there looking. They figure you just got loose on a technicality. Did you think of anything while you were away that might help figure it out? I'd be willing to help pay for a P.I. to chase down any leads you might have."

"No," Thane said. He looked out the window at the palm trees below. "You remember what Lauren McCoy told me when I talked with her? About her suspicions?"

"You mean about it being an internal issue? Do you think it was somebody from her department? That seems like a stretch."

"I know. I'm just grasping."

"You better hope it was some low-life. A loser like that would be a hell of a lot more likely to screw up than somebody in the DA's office, unless maybe it was a clerk or something. But let's start by getting you some protection from the father first."

"I appreciate it," Thane said. "Hopefully this will all fade away soon." But he knew in his heart that none of his problems would be going anywhere for a while.

CHAPTER
NINE

A BLACK AND WHITE SECURITY CAR prowled Ashcroft Drive at 9:30 p.m. Friday evening, looking like Andy Griffith patrolling Mayberry. The company responsible for protecting Park Heights claimed their cars added a hometown feeling to the neighborhood, where everyone should feel as safe as they did in the fifties.

It was Tony's night to drive, so the car stayed well within the posted speed limit. "You take the test again?" Tony asked the man in the passenger's seat.

"Yeah, but they don't tell you nothin' for over a month," Wes replied. "Don't know what takes so damn long to grade a stupid test. What's a test gonna tell them about whether I've got the guts to be a good cop? I ain't giving up, but this is my third try."

"Well, they give you six tries, so it's not like they're looking for just a few good men." Tony grinned at the thought of Wes taking a test six times to write traffic tickets.

Wes leaned forward, sucking on his lower lip as he studied a white two-story Victorian with a long front porch and shrubs running along both sides of the house. "Slow down a sec."

Tony peered in the same direction, but didn't see anything unusual about the unlit house.

"Shine the spot over there," Wes said, pointing through the window.

Tony turned on the car's side spotlight and snaked the beam across the yard and up the sidewalk until it reached a half-open front door.

"That ain't good," Wes muttered. "And the porch light is off. We oughta check it out."

Tony killed the light and was reaching for the radio when Wes grabbed his arm so tight Tony almost yelped.

"Turn it on again!" Wes shouted.

The spotlight kicked back on, illuminating a hunched man skulking out the front door, wearing a black ski mask and dark clothes and carrying a military green duffle bag. He turned and froze under the bright light, then hobbled down the front steps, running as best he could toward the back of the house. A pronounced limp kept him from making good time, but he was giving it all he had.

"Hit it!" Wes hollered.

Tony stomped the accelerator, his pulse racing. Wes exploded out of the car before it reached full stop, his gun sliding easily from its holster as Tony knew he'd practiced hundreds of times in front of a mirror. He barreled toward the back yard, hollering back at Tony.

"Check inside. I'll catch the bastard."

Tony grabbed his flashlight with one hand and pulled out a walkie-talkie with the other. "Unit four to base, we have an intruder at 1387 Ashcroft Drive. In pursuit. Seriously. Send help."

Tony had taken this job because he needed the money and he had been assured that encountering anything dangerous was unlikely. He crept toward the house, then stopped and checked the gun's safety. He crept up the steps of the house, his pace more deliberate than his partner's, who was probably off living out his *Lethal Weapon* fantasy.

"Security?" he said uncertainly before stepping inside the house. "I've got a gun, but I'm not looking to hurt anybody, so just let me know if anyone's here and we'll work this out."

The house stayed silent. Tony clicked on the hall light and took a few steps inside. He peeked around the corner into the living room, then slowly inched his way toward a small room at the end of the hall where an overhead light was on. Reaching the end of the hall, he glanced inside the room just long enough to see the body of a man sprawled on the floor, blood flowing from a quarter-sized hole in the back of his head.

Tony stumbled backwards a couple of steps and threw up against a wall, then turned and power-walked his way back outside. He leaned against one of the porch columns, then slid down to the top porch step, his flashlight shining toward the street at nothing in particular.

Wes appeared from the back yard. "The son of a bitch got away," he said. "There's bushes all around the back yard, but there was a hole dug underneath one of them that took me a while to find."

Tony maintained his dazed stare at the light, which was illuminating a patch of weeds in the front yard.

"You okay?" Wes asked.

"We lost a customer."

Wes glanced toward the front door and redrew his gun. He rested his hand on Tony's shoulder, then passed by him on his way inside the house.

Tony didn't join him.

The law firm's executive break room, with its dark oak walls and leather wingback chairs, looked like a back room in an exclusive country club. Thane walked in, finding it empty except for Joseph, who was making his daily ten o'clock cup of tea. He stood at the counter, meticulously slicing a cucumber with the concentration of a surgeon, placing the millimeter-thick pieces on a special type of cracker baked in Peru. This was one of the few mundane tasks he was willing to do himself: he claimed the whole process was refreshingly Zen. Thane wasn't sure exactly what that meant, but it seemed to make his boss happy.

"Morning," Joseph said, as Thane entered the otherwise empty room. "Ready to defend all that is holy?"

"Yeah—although I totally forgot to pack my shining armor this morning."

"Ah, don't worry about that, my lad: all that matters is pureness of heart."

Thane stood at one end of the counter and glanced at the front page of the L.A. Times. He opened his mouth to reply, but quickly returned his attention back to the paper, lifting it closer.

"What's up?" Joseph asked.

Thane continued reading the paper for a moment, then walked over next to Joseph. "I know this guy."

The headline read "Retired L.A. Cop Slain in Home." The accompanying picture was of a man wearing a J.C. Penney-caliber sports coat, the kind of artificially posed photo real estate agents and life insurance salesmen take at shopping malls. A stocky man in his fifties sporting a bargain basement rust-colored hairpiece, his left eye hung just a bit lower than his right. The camera had captured a failed attempt to convey authority; instead, the man simply appeared constipated.

"I heard about that on the radio," Joseph said. "How did you know him?"

"He's the detective who arrested me."

"Are you serious?" Joseph took the paper for a closer look. "Damn. Not that you'd wish anything like that on anybody, but if it had to happen—I mean, look who's still standing, you know?"

Thane shook his head. "I never blamed him. Trust me, if you had seen what he saw, you'd have arrested me too. He seemed like an okay guy, just doing his job."

Joseph looked at the article. "What was his name again? Grover?"

"Gruber. Ted Gruber." Thane ran his hand through his hair.

Joseph looked at the article again, scanning it for details. "You going to be all right?" Thane started toward the door. "I'm fine. It just caught me off guard. I better get back to work. I'll catch up with you later."

Thane walked down the corridor toward his office. He noticed Brianna heading his way, glancing back over her shoulder toward the lobby. She seemed concerned that she was being followed.

"Mr. Banning, there's a . . . gentleman here to see you," she said. "He didn't tell me his name, but I get the feeling he might be somebody you know. He's waiting in the lobby. Would you mind coming to get him? To be honest, he kind of makes me nervous. He keeps looking at me and making sounds."

"What kind of sounds?"

Brianna blushed, then looked away from Thane. "Kind of like 'mmmm, mmmm, mmmm'."

Thane followed Brianna and looked through the one-way glass out into the lobby. He had never seen Gideon wearing anything other than a dirty brown jumpsuit, but his scowl was indelibly etched in Thane's memory.

Thane loosened his tie and unfastened the top button of his dress shirt, wishing he could go so far as to untuck it. As he stepped into the lobby, Gideon shifted his gaze up from the floor to Thane. He rose slowly, apparently not wanting to scare Brianna, who was back at her desk, phone in hand, looking at Thane as if waiting for a sign to call security. She put the phone down once she saw Thane striding forward, his hand outstretched.

"Man, oh man, look who they set loose on society," Thane said as the two men clasped hands like arm wrestlers. "Come on, let's go back to my office."

Thane escorted Gideon down the hallway as several of the staff working in cubicles suddenly stood and stretched at the same time. The firm's clients almost always dressed better than the lawyers themselves, in dark suits and black pantsuits. Gideon's clothes—torn jeans, stained white T-shirt, sneakers with different color shoelaces—drew eyes like he'd set himself on fire.

Thane shut the door to his office and perched himself on the edge of his desk as Gideon wandered around the room checking out the ornately framed diplomas, whistling a long, impressed note.

"Goddamn," he said. "You didn't tell me you were the kind of lawyer with degrees and shit."

"Most lawyers have those."

"You never met the public defenders who represented me." Gideon grinned again, then strode over to shake Thane's hand one more time. "Look at you. Ain't you the hot shit."

"Don't start. I heard you got paroled a month ago and was wondering if I was going to hear from you. I told you to call me soon as you hit the street."

"Ah, I figured that was just one of those things people said, like 'how ya doin'.'"

Gideon walked over and lowered himself into an overstuffed chair, bouncing up and down on the cushion a couple of times before settling in. "Damn, this thing's more comfortable than my bed. But then, so's your desk, probably." His look turned to one of curiosity, studying Thane like a science project. "So how you doing?" Gideon asked. "How's all this been for somebody like you?"

"What do you mean, somebody like me?"

Gideon put up his hands in mock self-defense. "Now, don't be taking a swing at me," he said laughing. "Didn't mean nothing by it. It's just when we ex-cons get out, we usually screw around for a while, then end up back in the cage. That's just how it goes. But I've been wondering how all this was for someone like you. What's the adjustment like for someone innocent?"

"Long," Thane said.

"I hear that," Gideon nodded solemnly.

"So how about you?" Thane said. "Guess you suckered the parole board."

"I think it was the not spitting that did it." He laughed, then the smile slowly dissolved from his face. "Things are okay, I guess. Wouldn't mind a job where I don't have to wear a little fucking paper hat, but I'll do the fast food gig for a while. Then lose my money at the track, then probably end up back at Forsman."

"It doesn't have to go like that."

Gideon shrugged. "Always has before. I just don't seem to understand the rules out here."

"I used to think I did," Thane said. Neither man spoke for a long moment.

Finally Thane glanced at his watch, shaking his head apologetically. "I'm really sorry, but I have to go to a meeting. Trust me, if it was something I could get out of, I would."

Gideon immediately rose, nodding. "Nah, I understand. The life of an important man. Besides, you're not the only one who's got to get back to work. Lots of people lookin' for burgers, and if I'm not there to feed 'em, well, I don't even want to think about that."

"Give your number to Brianna, since otherwise who knows when I'll hear from you again. Just don't scare her."

Gideon shook his head and smiled at Thane. "That's okay. Don't feel like you got to go through the motions. Besides, all I got is a work number."

"Then leave that. I'm serious."

Thane extended his hand, taking his friend's big paw in both of his and shaking it for several seconds. Thane knew Gideon well enough to know this was more affection than he was used to receiving—even a longer than usual handshake was viewed with suspicion in prison—but he didn't care if it made the tough guy feel awkward.

"Let me teach you how the game's played on this side of the bars," Thane said. "We're on my turf now. There's no reason to end up back at Forsman."

Gideon took back his hand and shoved it in his front pocket. "I appreciate it, but things are different for cons like me. I don't get a job with a big paycheck and fancy chairs and shit. Don't worry about me. To be honest, I was kinda surprised you wanted to see me at all."

"You taught me to survive inside," Thane said. "I never would have made it there without you."

"Don't be so hard on yourself," Gideon grinned. "You might have lasted couple of weeks. Look, I got to get going."

"I'll keep my eye open for something. I owe you."

Gideon nodded skeptically, then held up his hand in a half-wave and turned to leave.

"Even more important than owing you," Thane added, "you're my friend."

Gideon stopped and turned towards him, at first looking like he figured he was being scammed. At last he simply nodded. "I appreciate that. I really do. You're a good man. But you probably oughta keep with respectable folk. I'll just bring you trouble."

Gideon opened the door to Thane's office and shoved his hands in his pockets as he walked back toward the lobby. Thane started after him, but his telephone buzzed. He leaned over and hit the intercom button; Brianna's voice came across the speaker.

"I'm sorry to bother you, Mr. Banning, but the caller said it's urgent. It might be a crank call, though."

"Why do you say that?"

"I'm pretty sure he said his name was Mr. Skunk."

Thane smiled slightly, albeit with a hint of melancholy. "It's just Skunk. Go ahead and transfer it on back."

"Yes, sir," Brianna said. "You sure do have interesting friends, Mr. Banning."

CHAPTER
TEN

Returning to Forsman hit Thane hard, even as a visitor. He remained in his car across the street from the prison for over an hour, taking deep breaths, his face drenched with sweat. There was still a piece of Forsman inside him, he realized. After finally escaping its cold grasp, he'd vowed never to return again.

Yet here he was.

He signed in, emptying his pockets and submitting to the usual pat-down: now he understood what a humiliating process it must have been for Hannah all those times. For some reason, he always envisioned her simply walking through the front entrance and into the visitation room.

Walking down the hallway, he saw Yoder leaning against the wall, grinning maliciously as he tapped the end of his baton against his open palm. The fluorescent lights only highlighted the guard's pallor. While it was possible he just happened to be stationed there that day, Thane guessed he'd come to meet him personally.

"I've been thinking about you a lot, Banning," the guard said with a smirk, "and damn, I don't know which I hate the most: Banning the murderer or Banning the lawyer."

Thane didn't break stride. "That's interesting—I haven't thought about you at all."

Yoder's face snapped back to its more natural scowl as he slapped his baton harder. "Maybe I oughta remind you."

Thane wheeled around. "I wish you would, Yoder. Then you'd be giving me your paycheck for the rest of your life, assuming they're actually stupid enough around here to pay you."

Yoder puffed up, but Thane knew it was too public of an area for him to do anything. Finally, the guard coughed up a chuckle.

"Oh, you don't want me to try. You're lying. Which makes sense, since you're a lawyer." Yoder turned and started back down the hall.

"And you're nothing but a thug."

Yoder froze, then finally turned and glared at Thane, who showed no inclination in backing down. The guard escorting Thane quickly turned him back toward their destination and nudged him forward.

Thane continued toward the visitation room. He entered an area no larger than a one-car garage: four card tables were spaced evenly against each wall of the room, and the air was stale and smelled of sweat, even though the temperature was cool. He walked over to the one open table and sat down on a plastic chair, the sort of patio furniture sold for five bucks at a hardware store, but it was light and couldn't do much damage, an important consideration when furnishing such a room.

Across the room, an inmate with satanic tattoos up and down both arms sobbed as he held his baby's hand between two of his fingers and looked into her eyes. On death row, Thane hadn't even been allowed that degree of intimacy. A couple of tables away, an inmate in his late forties whispered to a giggling young woman who looked to be in her early twenties. Whether she was the man's daughter or girlfriend, Thane couldn't tell. She could have been a pen pal: one of an endless stream of luckless women convinced of 'their man's' innocence—even if they'd never met outside of Forsman. Women who probably lived lives as solitary as their men.

Then he spotted Scotty "Skunk" Burns, a fifty-year-old African American man being led from a holding cell, arms and legs shackled. Even if the chains had been removed and he'd been given a baseball bat, Skunk probably could have been taken down by a teenage boy. At five-foot-six and 130 pounds, Skunk's posture was that of a kicked dog. He always said he was a lover, not a fighter, but it was doubtful he was either. His hair was dark, but with a single stripe of pale gray splashed along one side of his head—the origin of his strange nickname.

Skunk limped toward Thane's table, his gait the result of jumping from the roof of a three-story home during a thwarted break-in fifteen years ago. His treatment came at the hands of a prison doctor, the limp a memento of the man's inexperience and shaky hands. Putting shackles around Skunk's ankles was almost redundant.

Skunk tried a smile when he saw Thane, but the expression never looked quite natural on his face, even when it was genuine. Thane knew him during his time at Forsman, speaking with him every now and then in the prison library. It was more than a year before Thane realized the man was illiterate, having noticed one day that he wasn't turning the pages of his book. Apparently, Skunk just liked to sit with a thick book in front of him. Maybe he liked the way it made him look.

Skunk sat on the edge of his chair across the table from Thane, fidgeting as his eyes darted around like a pinball. "You a life-saver, Banning," he chittered. "You shoulda known you'd be my go-to guy, but I wasn't sure you'd take this."

"I still haven't said I would. Skunk, a murder charge is serious stuff. You need a lawyer with experience."

Skunk glanced behind him, then leaned forward. "What P.D. would believe me? But you—you know I couldn't kill nobody. I'm a thief, not a criminal. I need a lawyer who's gonna fight because he *believes* me, not just cause he's paid a couple bucks from the state to take me on."

"I don't think I'd be doing you any favors. I do real estate law, Skunk. You understand what that means?"

"You got yourself sprung, didn't you?" Skunk said. He looked broken, leaning back in his chair, dropping his head and staring at the chains clamped around his ankles. "I know I ain't nothing special. I know that. Hell, even whatever family I got don't want to admit I'm kin. But damn, Banning, that don't mean they can juice me for something I didn't do. I didn't kill that cop. I swear to God. Don't let them kill me, man."

"I don't doubt you're innocent, Skunk, but you're not listening to me: you need a criminal lawyer."

Skunk looked back up at Banning, the rims of his eyes turning red like he was burning up on the inside. "Then give me the name of a lawyer who knows better than you what it's like to get busted on a bum murder rap. You give me the name of a lawyer who'll give two shits about what happens to me."

He paused a moment as his eyes watered over. "I know I belong in Forsman. I know that, okay? But not on death row. Come on, Banning. You'd fight like a dog for me, man. I know it. Like a fucking angry dog."

Thane sat back and looked at Skunk for a long moment. Finally, he heaved a deep sigh and folded his hands on the table.

"How about you start by telling me what happened."

Things were finally turning Bradford Stone's way. The DA's office had been crucified on L.A. talk radio following Banning's release. It helped that most of the know-nothing media blowhards set their sights primarily on Judge Williams, but there was enough vitriol to go around. With city elections eight months away, the body blow Stone had taken over Banning's release hurt worse than he'd expected.

But, as usual, eventually public indignation shifted elsewhere: now the hot talk on the street was the murder of a former police detective, a murder that was going to put Stone back on offense. He even nodded and said good morning to the office receptionist when he arrived, an unusually upbeat act for him. An arrest had been made—a two-bit burglar named Scotty Burns—and Stone had already announced he was overseeing the prosecution. This would show the media he still knew how to get a killer off the streets.

He strode into his office where his top two Assistant DAs were waiting for him. Wallace Winston's significant girth rippled with laughter as his colleague Simon Keaton did a less-than-flattering impersonation of a local news anchor who had been giving the DA's office a hard time.

Keaton, who had won a national debate championship while in college, was one of Stone's best promotions, vaulting up the ranks at age thirty-six, leapfrogging prosecutors with twice his seniority. He'd been in the DA's office for six years, but hadn't advanced too far until Stone took over the department. There were rumors that Keaton and Lauren McCoy had been a bit of an item, but Stone hadn't given a damn about office romances: the young man worked insane hours and was a bulldog in court, two qualities Stone prized in an Assistant DA. And the fact that he was African American to boot was just good optics. Whereas Winston was a plodder who wanted to retire in four years, Keaton would likely, and rightfully, be offended not to be in charge of a division within that same time frame.

Even Stone's face gave up the hint of a smile when he saw the two men laughing. Ever since Banning's release, the office had felt too much like a cancer ward for Stone's liking—in some ways, literally. Winston's wife had recently been diagnosed with non-Hodgkin's lymphoma. With proper medical treatment, there was a good chance of survival, but the whole ordeal had clearly thrown Wallace off his game—so it was good to hear his coworkers laughing, especially at an anchor's expense.

"Time for you two schoolgirls to stop giggling. We've got work to do." Stone slid into his desk chair like a fighter pilot ready for battle.

"And yet, not a *lot* of work," Keaton said, as Winston chuckled in agreement. "There's no way we won't win this one."

Stone leaned forward, his eyes narrowing. "Oh, I'm not looking for a 'win'. 'Wins' are for off-election years. I want to annihilate this son of a bitch."

"We figured you'd want the death penalty," Winston said.

"Not enough."

Winston and Keaton glanced at each other.

"After they charbroil his ass," Stone said, "I want to string him up by a rope and hang him by his balls in the city square. I want to kill him twice. And if there's a way to get a temporary reprieve of the amendment against cruel and unusual punishment, then I'll torture his ass as well." Stone brought his fist down upon his desk. "Law and order is the phrase that pays this election year, gentlemen, and this scumbag is going to be our poster boy."

"Say amen, someone," Keaton said with a grin. "I have a sense you'll be able to get anything you want during this trial."

Stone looked at his assistants and their broad smiles. "Okay, I'll bite. What do you drones know that the king bee doesn't?"

Keaton smiled, looked over at Winston, then lowered his voice slightly, more for effect than any need for secrecy. "I got a call from a buddy of mine over at Forsman prison. He doesn't know the name of the guy, but the grapevine has it that the guy representing Burns doesn't even have any training in criminal law. From what I was told, he's never argued in front of a jury before."

Stone smiled. "I'm looking forward to meeting this new best friend of mine."

"No wonder convicts always end back in jail," Winston said. "His lawyer's got to be doing this just for the publicity."

"No, no, it gets better," Keaton said. "This isn't some ambulance chaser looking for his fifteen minutes of fame. It's someone the asshole knew in prison. An ex-con, for God's sake." Keaton burst out laughing, no longer able to contain himself.

Stone's smile disappeared like an eclipse. Winston noticed the grim reaction and stopped laughing.

"We'll be able to finish the trial the first day and still catch an early dinner," Keaton crowed. He smiled broadly and looked at his boss, but his smile froze on his face when he saw his boss's blooming frown.

Stone held out one moment, then two, then finally erupted. "Son of a bitch!" He sat motionless for a moment, trying to compose himself.

"What's wrong, Brad?" Winston asked. "The guy sounds like a joke."

Stone placed his hands on top of his desk and leaned forward like he did when cross-examining a hostile witness. "Burns was paroled from Forsman five weeks ago. Who do you think any convict from that hellhole is going to call, especially on a murder charge?"

"Oh, Jesus," Winston muttered, his face turning pale.

"Once again the only thing the press is going to talk about is Banning's release—and how we screwed it up. Not to mention the fact that when we win, they'll say any fool could have won it."

Stone swept a pile of documents off his desk with the back of his hand, the pages shooting out across the room like a covey of quail. He then dropped back into his chair. *This couldn't be happening*, he thought. Not now. Not to him.

There was silence until Keaton finally spoke. "I know you want to make this go away," he said, "but if we can't, then it's one way to beat Banning again." He paused until Stone looked at him, waiting for more. "The press is going to crucify Banning so bad it will look like he was retried and convicted. We just need to make sure reporters understand the real story: that Banning is putting a man's life at risk just to take a shot at you. Worse yet, if I remember correctly, Banning will be trying to free the man who killed the cop who arrested him for killing Lauren.

While this won't put him back in jail, it will be your chance to crush him in court. Your chance to finish off the cocksucker."

Stone thought about this. He wanted nothing more than to have Banning out of his life forever, but if they were destined to cross paths again, he would make damn sure it was for the last time. "I just want him to go away," Stone said, almost quietly. He reached for the phone. "But if he wants to join this dance, then I'll show him how rough the big boys play."

He called his secretary over the intercom. "Joanne, get me Jag Colter at KXLA TV right now. Tell him it's important." He hung up before she could respond and turned back to his colleagues.

"Since the press is going to eat this up," he said, "I'm sure as hell going to be the one setting the table."

CHAPTER
ELEVEN

THANE WALKED INTO HIS OFFICE after returning from the prison; within a minute, Joseph appeared at his door. He had obviously asked to be notified when Thane returned. "Sorry to have to be the one to tell you, buddy," Joseph said, "but Brad Stone is here. He wants to speak with you."

Thane suppressed a groan. He knew he'd have to deal with Stone eventually, but that didn't stop his stomach from clenching when he heard his name.

"He's in my office," Joseph said. "I told him it was up to you if you wanted to talk to him, but that as long as you worked for me, I was sitting in."

"You shouldn't butt heads with the DA on my behalf. That's not good politics."

"And that's why I'll never run for office," Joseph said with a smile.

"I'm fine seeing him," Thane lied. "It was going to happen sooner or later."

Joseph called his secretary from Thane's phone, telling her to send the DA on down the hall. Thane smiled inwardly: not escorting Stone there personally was a deliberate slight on Joseph's part.

Stone entered the office as if it were just another business meeting. Thane hadn't expected any display of contrition, but he was nevertheless irritated by the phony 'let-bygones-be-bygones' air Stone seemed to be trying to sell. The man who had sent him to prison walked over and started extending his hand, but Thane moved back a step.

"What do you want?" Thane said.

Stone lowered his hand, looking glad to be able to shove protocol aside. "Word on the street is Scotty Burns asked you to represent him. I want you to know I've decided to try this case myself."

"A high-profile murder of a cop, eight months before elections?" Thane said. "And you're prosecuting the case yourself? Knock me over."

Joseph stepped away and leaned against the wall, positioning himself on the far side of the room to watch the fireworks.

"I'm going to win this case," Stone said. "God Almighty Himself could call and offer to testify for me and I'd tell Him 'no thanks, I don't need you.' I have so much evidence, anything less than a plea bargain would be malpractice on the part of Mr. Burns's lawyer."

"If you're so confident, why do you care who represents him?" Thane asked.

"You're a real estate lawyer—and from what I understand, a damn good one."

"The best," Joseph said from the side of the room.

"But you're not a criminal lawyer, despite what you might think you've learned these past few years. I'm concerned taking this case for the wrong reason could cause irreparable harm to your career."

The caustic laugh that bolted from Thane's mouth surprised even him. "So you're concerned about me. And my career. I appreciate that. I really do. But you know what really had an impact on my career? Being sent to Forsman for a murder I didn't commit."

Thane stepped forward, in that instant wanting only to lean across the desk and grab Stone by the throat. "Yeah, all things considered, I'd have to say that's what had an impact on my career."

Stone kept his voice steady. "I can't change what happened in the past. I can only try to help you see that what you're doing now isn't a good decision for anyone. Not for you, not your client. And not this firm."

"You may not be able to change the past, but you can admit your complicity in it."

Stone shook his head. "You're a real estate lawyer. You're thinking of representing a man accused of murder, and you're doing it for the wrong reasons. That's the only thing I'm talking about today."

"I know the man you charged with murder and there's no way he did it, but I also know you don't give a damn about his guilt or his innocence. You just care about how it plays out in the press because you've got an election coming up. I'll pit my intentions against yours any day of the week."

Stone's chest puffed up, but before he could say anything else, Joseph advanced from his place on the sidelines and walked over to Stone, putting his hand on his shoulder and directing him toward the door. "You've said what you wanted to say. Thane and I will talk about this and get back to you by the end of the day. Forgive me for not seeing you out."

Stone looked at Joseph for a moment, then glanced back over at Thane. He shook his head and walked out of the office, shutting the door behind him.

Joseph turned back toward Thane. "I know you could take on anything you set your mind to."

"But?"

"But our law firm can't take on this case. We do real estate law. We help developers build office complexes. High-rises. Shopping malls. We don't defend cop killers."

"Maybe he—"

"You're right, you're right. *Alleged* cop killer," Joseph said. "But it's not a matter of publicity, it's a question of liability. Stone is right: you're not a criminal lawyer, which opens us up to all sorts of issues of legal malpractice. You would be putting the firm at financial risk here."

"That's fair," Thane said.

Joseph fixed him with a hard look. "Thane, you know I don't give a frog's fuck what our esteemed District Attorney wants. Far as I'm concerned, I'm offended that he even thought of stepping foot in your office. I also hope you know I'd do anything to help you. You're not just a good lawyer, you're a great friend, but think about what you're doing—for the firm's sake."

"I'll be honest, I never even considered that," Thane said slowly. "But you're right: I would be putting the firm at risk. I was so caught up in my own idea of what was right, I didn't think about you or anybody else here."

Thane thought for a moment as he slowly surveyed the accoutrements of his office, taking in all of the symbols of his reentry into his old world. He finally looked over at Joseph.

"You've been a wonderful friend to me, giving me this job and this office. Probably nobody in their right mind would have given me the chance."

"Well, you know I've never claimed to be in my right mind."

Thane also smiled for the first time during this meeting and nodded his head in good-hearted agreement. "And now I'm going to try to be a good friend in return."

Thane extended his hand to Joseph, who happily accepted it.

"I quit."

Thane walked toward Hannah's bookstore, having just cleaned out his office despite Joseph's protestations. It was the first time he had ventured to see Hannah during business hours since his release. He had spent numerous evenings there after hours, stocking books and installing new shelves against an empty wall, but so far he had avoided visiting when customers might be there.

Though she never spoke of it, he assumed her business suffered with the press rehashing their story, especially after she took him back. He figured the bookstore survived his initial arrest because people felt sorry for her, the poor woman who had no idea her husband was evil incarnate; but welcoming him back probably scared off more customers than she could afford. He didn't want to compound this hardship by making guest appearances during daylight hours, but today he had no choice.

Nearing the store, he noticed a man in his late thirties slouched in a pick-up truck just across and down the street. A broad-shouldered man, he sat staring at the store's front window as if it were a big screen TV. When the man saw Thane, he revved his truck engine and took off, glaring at Thane as he drove by. Thane was used to harsh stares, but this one seemed different—like the animosity was personal.

Thane had waited until after lunch, hoping most customers would be back at work. Entering, he saw two women grazing their way leisurely down the aisles. He also saw Caitlin stationed behind the cash register, her smile quickly shifting from one of welcome to a frown of disdain. He hadn't met her yet, but Hannah spoke warmly of her. Caitlin obviously didn't feel the same about him.

Thane walked to the counter, extending his hand. "Hi, I'm Thane. Hannah's husband."

She considered his hand as though he had just blown his nose on it, then gave it a limp shake before quickly letting go, her frown deepening.

"Is she around?" he asked.

Caitlin huffed, then cocked her head toward the closed door in the rear of the store. "Back there."

Thane considered trying a smile, but instead he simply nodded and headed toward the back office.

As he neared the door, Caitlin called out to him. "You know, it hasn't been easy for her, keeping this store open."

One of the women standing next to the table of half-price books glanced up, suddenly having an interesting story to share at dinner. Thane took a few steps back toward Caitlin, not wanting to have this conversation across the room.

"You think I don't know that?"

"I would have thought you did, but after today—"

Thane cut her off. "I don't usually waste my breath saying this, but I was innocent."

Caitlin shrugged. "I believe you. Or, rather, I believe Hannah. I think what happened to you really sucks. But what I think doesn't matter to our customers."

Thane noticed the second customer inching her way toward the cash register, maneuvering toward a better view of the main event. Not wanting to cause a scene—and not feeling the need to defend himself any more than he had already—Thane broke eye contact with Caitlin and went into the back office, shutting the door behind him.

Hannah sat hunched over her desk, marking an invoice with a yellow highlighter. The office was small, barely able to accommodate her desk, a tall file cabinet, and an extra chair positioned across from the desk. She spoke without looking up.

"Did you really order ten copies of *Wuthering Heights*? It's not exactly a big seller."

"Nope. Wasn't me."

She jerked her head up, looked at him for a moment, then shifted her attention back to the invoice without saying a word, leaving him to jumpstart the conversation.

"Based on the reception I got out there, not to mention the cold shoulder in here, I'm guessing I've already made the news."

She continued staring past the invoice for a moment, then finally put down the marker and looked up slowly, her eyes half-closed, as if she barely had the energy to lift her head.

"Just tell me it's not true."

Thane didn't answer, although he knew what she meant.

"A *Times* reporter called to ask how I felt about you taking on a capital murder case just to get back at Bradford Stone. Imagine my surprise. I'm back here now because I got tired of everyone staring at me like I was in a zoo. So please, tell me it's not true."

As much as he wanted to, he couldn't look away. All he could offer was a slight nod.

"Thane, you can't do this."

He turned the wooden chair in front of her desk around and straddled it, leaning forward against the back of the chair, using it as a shield. "I'm not sure," he said.

"I am. It's been five months, and things are just now starting to feel like they used to. The last thing you need is to get involved with Stone again. Or with a murderer."

"People still call *me* a murderer, but that doesn't mean I am one."

"Maybe he's innocent. All the more reason why he needs a criminal lawyer. Don't you see? This case will drag you backwards. You need to move as far away from the past as you can."

"It's not that easy."

"Then don't make it harder."

She lifted herself from her chair and walked around the desk, leaning on the edge of it in front of him. She started to speak, but her voice broke. She wouldn't look him in the eye.

"There's no reason for you to deal with Stone again. None. No reason to put yourself back in the spotlight."

"I knew this guy in prison. There's no way he could have killed anybody. I can't let Stone put him through what I went through."

"If he's innocent, then someone else can prove it. And you know what, to be honest, right now I don't give a damn if he's innocent." With visible effort, she looked him in the eye. "Please, Thane, I haven't asked anything from you since you've gotten back. Nothing. But I'm begging you, please don't do this."

She leaned over, taking his hands in hers and squeezing them, tears starting to make their move. Thane stood and put his arms around her waist: her halting breath betrayed how close she was to sobbing. He stroked her hair, not wanting to let go. She deserved better than this. For a fleeting moment he wanted to tell her why he had to do it, but she would never understand.

"I can't even imagine Joseph letting you do this," she said.

He continued holding her, unable to answer. Hannah lifted her face toward his, then pushed away from him hard when he didn't speak. He finally shook his head and averted his eyes. "I quit this morning."

She stared at him as if he were suddenly speaking in tongues, the words coming from his lips some sort of nonsensical gibberish. "You quit," she said, matter-of-factly.

"It wouldn't have been fair to Joseph or the firm."

"To Joseph," she whispered to herself. "It wouldn't have been fair to Joseph." She dropped back onto the edge of the desk like her legs couldn't hold her. "But you felt it would be fair to me? Fair to us?"

"It's not fair at all," Thane said. "And I wish I could say something that would help you understand, but I have to do this, Hannah. If I can keep an innocent man from going to prison on a false murder charge, then how can I say no? How can I, of all people, turn away?"

Thane stepped closer, putting his hands on her shoulders. "You stood by me during the trial, when everybody said I was a monster," he said. "You trusted me, and at no time did I ever feel you waver. I know it's asking a lot. I do. But I'm asking that you trust me again. Please have faith that I would not be doing this to us if I didn't absolutely believe I had to. Please, trust me."

She looked at him and didn't speak for a long moment. Then she rose and turned away from him.

"It was easier for me to trust you back then," she said. "I knew who you were."

CHAPTER

TWELVE

FIVE YEARS AGO, THANE TACKLED the biggest undertaking of his career. A prime piece of real estate in South Central L.A. came on the market when its octogenarian owner died. For years he had refused to sell his twenty-six undeveloped acres, despite multiple multi-million-dollar offers, and left the land to heirs who couldn't wait to sell it off. The expansive property, located just a few blocks from the USC campus, would easily accommodate the type of construction not feasible in the city. In newspapers, interested parties had lobbied for a new performing arts center, a shopping mall, or a development that would combine office buildings with shops and condos. Given the potential scope of the project, the city of Los Angeles inserted itself into the process, instating complex bidding guidelines to determine who would get the rights to develop the land. One significant requirement was that the development firm had to be local in order to help bring more revenue into the city coffers.

Although scores of development companies expressed vociferous interest, the reality was that only two local firms—Hexagon Partners and Wilson-Scott Development—had the resources and clout to actually build something that would match the scope of the property. Thane had previously done work for Carlin Wilson, one of Wilson-Scott's founding partners, and was asked to serve as legal counsel on the proposal, which represented the potential for tens of millions of dollars for the firm if Wilson-Scott nabbed the contract. Joseph started referring to Thane as 'Typhoon Banning', saying the term 'rainmaker' simply didn't do his powers justice.

Maneuvering all of the nuances of such a project—the political palms that needed greasing, the special interest groups jockeying for influence, the environmental groups analyzing every inch of the blueprints, and the crazies who came out of the woodwork from every direction—pushed Thane to his limits, but he kept the project on track through sheer force of personality. Near the conclusion of a brutal string of fifteen-hour workdays, some unknown bureaucrat leaked word that Thane's client was going to win the rights to develop the property.

Two weeks before the official decision was handed down, however, Thane heard through the unreliable grapevine that the competing firm, Hexagon, was planning to charge Thane's client with rigging the bidding process, a crime that would not only disqualify Wilson-Scott from the process, but also represent serious long-term legal risks to the development firm if proven to be true.

It was because of that rumor that Thane first made contact with the woman whose death would destroy his world.

Lauren McCoy was the thirty-three-year-old Assistant District Attorney assigned to oversee cases dealing with alleged corruption in projects involving the city. Thane reached out to her and asked if there was anything he needed to know regarding his client and the project as a whole. He felt he must have caught her at the end of an exhausting day because she was unusually forthcoming, as if simply too tired to play games.

"I don't think there's anything you need to worry about," she said. "I've been looking into some accusations of wrongdoing and my impression is that everything has been done by the book. But it's my job to be thorough, so I need to look a little further—because there are a couple of things that just aren't adding up, but I don't think there will be any charges brought against your client."

"Do you feel the accusations are simply a face-saving effort by Hexagon because they expect to lose their bid?" Thane asked.

"I'm not sure yet. It's just that I've come across a small irregularity that I need to understand better. I want to feel confident there wasn't any internal malfeasance."

"Do you mean internal to Hexagon, or perhaps another sub-contractor associated with that developer?"

Lauren began backpedaling, as if suddenly realizing she was saying too much. She stammered that she shouldn't have said what she did and had overstepped her bounds, so Thane stopped pressing. Lauren asked him to promise not to mention to anyone what she had just said, and Thane gave his word, since it didn't appear to jeopardize his client's chances of being awarded the project.

He was somewhat surprised to receive a voicemail message two days later from Lauren's assistant, asking if Thane could meet Lauren at a neighborhood restaurant near the proposed development site at 9:00 p.m. that evening. The message gave no other details.

As he drove to the meeting site, he received a text from Lauren saying she might be running a couple of minutes late and to wait for her if he got there before she did. She also said she had some disturbing news for him and begged him not to be too angry with her. His pulse quickened at the thought of a potential problem with the deal.

Thane arrived at the proposed meeting place—a local, family-owned Italian restaurant—a few minutes before nine o'clock, but it was closed. The entrance was just off a dimly lit dead-end alley and across the street from a liquor store. He glanced down the alley and saw what appeared to be a vagrant sleeping on the ground, not too far from a couple of trash dumpsters. A bus stop bench was in front of the alley, so Thane sat there and waited for Lauren.

When she still hadn't arrived by 9:30, Thane used the number from Lauren's text and called her. He heard the sound of a cell phone ringing in the alley. He rose and once again looked down the alley toward the direction of the noise, now studying the shadowy form on the ground with heightened interest.

Thane hung up the phone, and when the ringing from the darkness also stopped, he jogged down the alley and came upon the body of Lauren McCoy, sprawled in the middle of the alley. He slipped on the pool of blood already forming its own outline of her body and fell to the ground. He cautiously crawled a couple of feet over to her, but even without the blood he knew she wasn't just unconscious. The angle of her head, her eyes—everything told him she was dead.

She was dressed in the standard black pantsuit commonly worn by female lawyers in the DA's office. A large knife was next to her body, the kind one might use to carve a turkey, except it had been used on her. He was struck by the amount of blood: he wouldn't have thought so much could come out of one person's body.

He looked around, his heartbeat racing, ashamed at suddenly being so afraid for his own safety, but his self-preservation instincts were firing. He reached for his cell phone to call the police when he heard a sound from behind one of the nearby dumpsters. It sounded too loud to be any sort of small animal. He froze for a moment, unwilling, or unable, to even take a breath. His darting eyes were the only part of him that moved. He heard the noise again and picked up the knife, ready for anybody who might come charging his way. He hoped the person hiding didn't have a gun.

He maintained his part of the stalemate, refusing to even turn his head away from the dumpsters, when Detective Ted Gruber, who had just wrapped up his shift a couple of hours earlier, walked past the entrance of the alleyway, glancing down the dark corridor as law enforcement instinctively does even when off-duty, practicing a constant vigilance for potential trouble. The detective walked another couple of steps before stopping, as though his mind had just finished processing the bloody image.

Detective Gruber whipped out a gun from his ankle holster and strode down the alleyway toward Thane. "Drop the knife and lie flat on the ground!"

Thane started crawling away from the body so as not to lie down in the pool of blood, but another command from Gruber had him prone immediately.

"I said lie on the ground! *Now!*"

Even though Gruber had his gun pointed at him, Thane had never been so happy to see a cop before in his life. He told Gruber there was somebody else in the alley: Gruber kept the barrel of the gun aimed at Thane's head.

"I didn't kill her. I found her like this."

All the cop could see, however, was some blood-soaked guy kneeling over this dead body in a dark alley, holding a knife the size of a hatchet.

Thane slowly raised one hand and pointed toward the dumpster.

"I just found her, but I think someone is hiding behind the dumpster. Please, you need to check behind the dumpster." Thane then laid on his stomach, his hands outstretched and legs spread as far as he could to show he wasn't going to make any fast move. "Look, I'm not moving. Please, check the dumpster. I swear I heard a sound."

Gruber didn't take his focus off Thane. When he shined his flashlight on the body, the cop looked like he wanted to shoot Thane. But then a young couple on a date passed by the alley and saw what was going on. Even though they were fifty feet away, the woman saw enough that first she screamed, then she brought out her cellphone and started filming. Gruber yelled at them to get out of the way, which seemed to refocus his adrenaline. Thane knew this was a hell of a lot more than either of them had bargained for that night.

"I'll check it out, but I swear to God if you so much as twitch, I'll put a bullet in you."

Gruber approached the dumpster, keeping the pistol's attention mostly on Thane. He quickly checked behind it, and even inside of it, but returned his attention to Thane, informing him that there was nothing there. From then on, Thane remained the gun barrel's sole focus of attention. But Thane wasn't worried about that, because he knew it'd get straightened out: he just wanted to get the hell out of there.

But he continued to be the prime suspect, in part because of Lauren's text message telling him she hoped he wasn't going to be angry at her, and in part because of Detective Gruber's testimony. And the knife only had Thane's fingerprints on it, which didn't help him any, although of course his lawyer reasonably argued the real murderer could have worn gloves. Despite how it may have looked, Thane was confident he would be cleared. And then Lenny entered the picture.

Lenny Schultz was a forty-year-old low-life who looked as if he had hit rock bottom twenty years ago and just settled there. A two-bit drug dealer with an oily ponytail, his job was catching quarters thrown his way by any passers-by who happened to have spare change and a twinge of guilt for how good they had it, especially after looking at Lenny in his rusted out wheelchair. Even though he had the character of a weasel, the wheelchair wasn't a prop. He'd been paralyzed from the waist down for the past ten years, his drug distributor having taken umbrage when Lenny decided he wasn't going to pay for product he thought was bad. He saved himself fifty bucks and spent the rest of his life on two wheels.

After a couple of hot showers, Lenny looked almost respectable for the trial. The wheelchair didn't hurt either. He testified that he had stationed himself to panhandle at the liquor store across the street from where Thane had waited, and he called 911 the night of the murder. The recorded call was played at the trial, where Thane and the jurors heard Lenny telling the dispatcher that there was a couple arguing and the man appeared to be forcing the woman into the alley. When asked for more details, Lenny's description of the man matched Thane, not just physically, but also the clothes he wore that evening.

Lenny's taped voice grew emotional as he cried out to the 911 dispatcher that the man was stabbing the woman, and that Lenny was getting the hell out of there, at which point he yelled to send the cops and then hung up. During his testimony in the courtroom, Lenny identified Thane as the man he saw, leaving no doubt in the eyes of the jury that he was the murderer. Thane didn't know if Lenny thought testifying would give him a chip later on if he got in trouble with the police, or if the actual murderer resembled Thane, or if maybe Lenny was stoned out of his head and thought Thane was the guy he saw. Whatever the motivation, Lenny's testimony was all the jury needed to convict him.

CHAPTER THIRTEEN

THANE PLACED AN ARMFUL OF legal reference books on a rotting bookshelf, the wood creaking in outrage. The few furnishings that were present in his recently rented office were one step away from the dump, and several pieces should have already made the trip. His desktop was a labyrinth of deep scratches and missing chunks, as though somebody had taught shop class behind it. A rat-gray couch was shoved against one end of the room, and two chairs were positioned across from the desk, mismatched in every way except their identical musty smells.

He'd landed in this office after looking into several safer neighborhoods, but these were the safest digs he could afford with what was left of his last paycheck. The small room off the main hallway would be a reception area. It was smaller than Joseph's private bathroom, but he wouldn't be hiring a receptionist, and he wasn't expecting a line of people waiting to meet with him, although apparently he already had his first unexpected visitor. He heard the door off the hallway open and a familiar voice muttered:

"*Jesus Christ.*"

Thane stepped away from the books, waiting until Stone charged through the front room and into the office, slamming the door behind him. This time there was no pretense of professionalism in the DA's voice. "So you want a piece of me? Is that it?" Stone said. "Screw what's best for your client—you're just trying to even the score."

"You seriously think this case could come close to evening the score?"

"Step away from this. You'll only lose again."

"Yeah, too bad I was innocent the first time."

Stone waved Thane off as he would a homeless man begging for money. "You were innocent, huh? In all my years of prosecuting, I've never heard *that* one before."

Thane moved away from the bookshelf, taking a couple of steps closer to Stone. It was the first time the two men had been alone in the same room, and Thane wondered if he would be able to restrain himself from violence, since he knew that would only benefit Stone. "I was innocent and you knew it."

Stone just stared.

Thane came within two feet of Stone, but the DA didn't flinch.

"You figured something out near the end of my trial," Thane said. "You learned something. I don't know what, but suddenly you couldn't look me in the eye anymore. Even during your closing argument. Before, you couldn't stop looking at me, glaring at me, like you were putting on a show for the jury. What happened? What did you learn?"

Stone broke eye contact. "That's ridiculous."

"No, you learned something, but by then it was too late. There'd been too much press, too much publicity for you to suddenly admit you were wrong. Not during an election year. You got to be DA thanks to me: what say we go for governor this time?"

A board creaked outside Thane's office, perhaps someone walking down the hall, stopping to see if the new tenant was going to be trouble.

"Don't take this case," Stone said. "Get on with your life."

"The life you tried taking from me?"

"Just move on. Please. You won't find the justice you're looking for here."

"You seem to be taking all this personally," Thane said.

"I take every murder personally. My job is to keep the community safe from killers. Whenever someone gets hurt or killed, yes, I take it personally."

"I spent five years in prison. I took that personally, too."

Stone stared at Thane for a moment longer, then turned his back on him and strode toward the door.

"You take this case, I'll make you wish you were back in Forsman. I'll eat your fucking lunch."

He yanked open the office door and a young woman carrying two cups of coffee fell into the room, apparently having been eavesdropping. She lurched into Stone, splashing coffee on his white shirt.

"Goddamn it!" Stone jumped back and glared at the young woman, dressed professionally in a navy blue shirt and jacket, and looking as out of place in that office as he did. "Who the hell are you?"

The young woman didn't appear the least bit flustered, and she didn't apologize. "I'm Mr. Banning's associate, and if you hadn't done your Incredible Hulk impersonation on the door, this wouldn't have happened."

Stone pushed his way past the woman. "Fuck you," he muttered as he left the room, his footsteps echoing as he marched down the hallway. The young woman watched him leave, then turned toward Thane.

"He seems nice," she said. "Think he's single?" She walked over and held out the two cups. "One's black, one has cream. I didn't know how you liked yours."

Thane looked quizzically at the two cups of coffee, then at the woman. "And you are again?" Thane asked.

"Kristin. Kristin Peterson. Your associate." She held the cups of coffee up a little higher. "Pick one before they get cold."

He hesitantly took one of the cups, watching her warily. With one hand now free, she brushed back her blonde hair, which had fallen over her eyes when she'd catapulted into the room.

"I didn't realize I had an associate," he said.

"That's why I stopped by. To let you know. I'm in my senior year at USC Law and I'll be graduating in seven months. I'm currently twelfth in my class. I should be ranked higher, but I refused to sleep with my Torts Prof last semester. I'm thinking of suing his ass. I'm Editor of *Law Review*, and am looking to specialize in—"

"Ms. Peterson—"

"Kristin."

"I don't need an associate."

A tinkling laugh sprang out of her. "You're kidding, right? You're taking on the murder case of the year, going up against a District

Attorney who says he's going to eat your lunch, and you're working out of an office that looks like it used to be a crack house before it went downhill . . . and you're saying you don't need an associate?"

"All right," Thane said. "Maybe I do, but as you so diplomatically noted in your assessment of my office, I can't afford one. Especially a twelfth from USC. I'm likely not going to have income for a while, even after the case starts, seeing as how my client isn't exactly solvent."

Kristin walked past Thane and took a seat across from his desk, occupying the chair as if it were her office. She leaned back, ignoring the wobble from the chair's uneven legs, and took a long sip of coffee. "Mr. Banning, do you know what the market's like for new graduates?"

He glanced around his third-world office. "It has to be better than working in an all-but-condemned building in a high-crime neighborhood."

"There are thousands of us out there, all applying to the same practices, all with the same resumes and the same training, all trying to get the same crappy jobs."

"So you figured why not go to a barely solvent single practice. You sure you're ranked twelfth?"

Kristin looked at him and smiled like they were old friends. "Don't get me wrong," she said. "I'm confident I'll get my share of job offers at some pretty good firms, but let's be honest here: an entry level shit job is a shit job, no matter how much marble lines the lobby. I'm not exactly a corporate ladder sort of gal."

"I have to tell you, I'm still having trouble linking the pieces here."

"Here's the deal: I'll work part time for you for free once the case starts. We can think of it as an internship. Trust me, you're not going to get a better deal than that. And you're going to need help."

"And what do you get out of this?"

"Exposure. If we win, I can go to any law firm in the city after I graduate and move directly into the corner office."

"It's far more likely I'm going to lose," Thane said.

"Then I still win, because this case is a media magnet. I'll be famous just from working on it. You'd be amazed at how much cachet that sort of thing carries in some firms. None of my other classmates will have anything quite that interesting on their resume."

A two-column photo of Thane was once again front-page material for the *Times* that morning, accompanied by an editorial expressing outrage that he was risking a man's life solely to piss off the District

Attorney. Talk radio hosts didn't have to worry about finding fodder for their four-hour shifts: callers were already overloading phone lines to offer their two cents on the issue.

"People don't remember if you win or lose," Kristin continued, "they just remember they saw you on TV. Any stigma that comes from working for you will be nothing compared to the options I'll have once this case is over. No offense."

"None taken. I guess it's not an option to say I'll get back to you on this?"

Kristin smiled. "Why go through the motions? After all, what have you got to lose?"

"Aren't you worried about working for someone who got away with murder?"

"Please. I put myself through college working as a Hooters waitress. I can take care of myself. Besides, I'm on your side. If you were going to off anyone, I'm guessing it would be that little ray of sunshine who just left."

She stood and set her cup of coffee on the desk, having looked first at the rough state of its surface. "I'm assuming I don't need a coaster." She extended her hand. Thane wasn't surprised at the strength of her grip.

"All right then, Twelfth, we'll see how it goes, assuming you don't find an even gaudier legal media circus to attach yourself to."

"You know, I just don't see that happening," Kristin said with a grin.

Bernie's Burgers was packed with the after-school crowd when Thane walked in. Music blasting from the speakers shook the stack of plastic cups with each beat of the bass, but somehow the high school kids at the front counter were even louder. It was a brightly lit space, even by fast-food standards. Maybe Bernie thought kids would gravitate toward it like moths to a streetlight.

Thane saw Gideon behind the front counter, leaning on a mop next to the deep fry machine. He wore a stained white apron and a paper white hat that looked like it was five sizes too small for him. Thane caught his attention as he walked toward the counter.

"Got a minute?" Thane said.

"Sure, but one crack about this stupid hat and I'm going to hurt you."

"I have to check something out, and it's something you might be able to help me with. What time do you get off?"

"Eight."

"I'm afraid I have to go this afternoon. Never mind. Not a problem."

"Hold on a second," Gideon said. "I can take a break."

"I don't want to get you in trouble."

"Nah. Wait here." Gideon took his mop and walked over to a jittery, spike-haired teenager standing next to the milkshake machine. He was sporting a stained, short-sleeved white shirt, a plaid clip-on tie, and a dirty name tag with 'Shift Manager: Reggie' written on it.

"I got an emergency I gotta take care of," Gideon said. "I'll be back soon as I can."

"You can't just leave, man. That's not how it works. You haven't even mopped the floor once today."

Gideon gave Reggie a doomy glare and stood as straight as he could, casting his long shadow over the boy-manager. He clenched his jaw, lifted the mop parallel to the ground, and snapped the handle in half as if it were a Bernie's crispy cinnamon breadstick. The crack of the wood echoed through the restaurant, and every head turned to stare.

"Can't. Mop's broke." Reggie's body stiffened as rigid as his spiked hair. Even his breathing halted for a long moment.

"Oh. Okay, then," he finally squeaked. "I guess if it's an emergency and all . . ."

"Thanks, dude. You're all right." Gideon turned and walked back toward Thane, his adolescent coworkers gingerly stepping aside to let him pass. He grabbed a large bag of fries and a couple of pieces of Bernie's Bodacious Berry Pie before joining Thane.

As they walked toward the door, Gideon snatched the white paper hat from his head, crumpling it into a ball and tossing it over his shoulder where it landed in a booth packed with gawking teenagers.

"You employee of the month yet?" Thane asked.

CHAPTER
FOURTEEN

THANE PULLED UP IN FRONT of Detective Gruber's house. Yellow police tape still stretched across the driveway, four days after the murder. A baby-faced policeman leaned against one of the columns on the front porch, standing guard against reporters and crime scene fanatics. Thane opened his car door and started to get out, but Gideon stayed where he was, eyeing the young cop.

"You coming?" Thane asked.

Gideon grunted in displeasure, but finally opened his door, hesitantly. "You didn't tell me there was going to be cops here. I don't exactly get on real good with them."

"Today's the day we start fresh—the both of us. Come on."

The policeman standing watch straightened when he spotted them approaching. He was new enough to the force that he hadn't yet perfected that classic cop glare: he squinted at the two men, but it only made it look like the sun hurt his eyes.

"I'm Thane Banning," Thane announced himself. "Defense counsel."

"Like I don't already know that?" The young cop turned and spit off the porch. He then looked over Gideon with a skeptical eye. "And this is . . . ?"

"I'm his daddy," Gideon said.

"He's my associate. Stone said he'd leave word I was coming."

The cop studied Gideon a bit more, but didn't spit again. Finally he stepped to the side and resumed leaning against the porch column. They walked past him and up to the front door.

"We gotta work on your delivery," Thane asked Gideon, who only shrugged in response.

Thane started walking into the house, but Gideon grabbed hold of his arm and directed him to the left side of the front door, pointing out a small metal security box that had been pried open.

"Look here." Somebody had twined a couple of twist-ties around one of the alarm circuits. Gideon pointed at one of the thin wires. "Skunk always used these thingamajigs to bypass the main alarm. Kept it from going off when the door was forced open."

"How do you know?"

"Ah, he was always yapping about how easy it was to bypass security systems. Said a trip to a grocery store and you pretty much had everything you needed—even for the fancy alarm systems."

Thane leaned over and took a closer look. He was amused that all of the elaborate circuitry and wiring that filled the box could be circumvented by something from the produce section.

"That must be part of Skunk's MO that Stone says implicates him." Thane turned to go inside, but stopped when Gideon didn't follow, still staring at the alarm box.

"What do you see?"

"Skunk said he strips *all* the plastic off the wire, not just the ends. But these only have the ends stripped, just enough to hook them to the circuit."

"That make a difference?"

Gideon shrugged. "Probably not, but as much of a mess as ol' Skunk is, I always got the impression he was damn precise when it came to thievin'. I'd bet a Bernie's paycheck he'd call this sloppy work."

They entered the house and encountered another officer sitting in a chair, an old issue of *Guns and Ammo* in his hands. He glanced up at the two men and wrinkled his nose, then turned his eyes back to the magazine.

"The DA said you guys wasn't to touch nothing. If I catch you doing otherwise, I'll haul you in."

Thane looked around the living room. Ugly didn't begin to describe the furnishings. There was a sofa and two side chairs, each covered with a dirty cream-colored fabric displaying hunters and Springer Spaniels holding limp ducks in their mouths. The heavy smell of cigar smoke wafted up from the filthy gray carpet and any furnishing not made of metal. Dust covered all of the side tables except for a couple of circles that looked to be the circumference of a beer can. A pile of magazines sat on a small coffee table positioned between the two chairs. Atop the pile was a copy of *Hustler*, turned in a different direction from the rest of the magazines. There weren't any pictures on the wall or much in the way of decoration, apart from a couple of shiny knickknacks on the mantel and a battery-operated singing fish mounted on the wall. The only item in the room that looked as though it couldn't be dated back to the early eighties was a seventy-two inch wall-mounted TV.

The décor of an aging bachelor: Gruber must have furnished the place himself.

He walked over to the hallway that led to the back of the house, then turned around to check out the living room from a different angle, trying to visualize the scenario the night of the murder. "The police report says the intruder—"

"Skunk Burns," the officer interrupted, still not looking up from the magazine.

"*The intruder,*" Thane continued, "came through the front entrance. Gruber had been working part-time for a security firm and they figure when he came home from his shift he saw the hot-wired system and tried to catch the prowler himself instead of calling it in."

"Fool," Gideon said, causing the officer to finally shoot a look toward the men.

"Hey, show some respect for the dead," the policeman said. "He was a brother officer."

Gideon looked at him. "Sorry. I meant *Officer* Fool."

The policeman's face twisted up, but he didn't press the matter. Thane pointed down the hall.

"Gruber goes back to his office and takes one in the back of the head. They figure that's when the intruder ran out."

Gideon walked over and stood next to Thane, lowering his voice so the cop couldn't hear him. "Without that?" Gideon pointed to a small decorative pyramid on the fireplace mantel that reflected what little light made it into the dim room.

"What is it?" Thane asked.

"That's real crystal, with gold inlay. Real pricey piece. I'm surprised a guy like Gruber had the taste to have something like this, let alone be willing to cough up the cash for it. Betcha it was a gift or something."

"You sure it's worth something?"

"Yeah, I'm sure—and if I'm sure, you know damn well Skunk'd be sure. He wouldn't have left without that little beauty. Don't care how scared he mighta been. Besides, he come in that front door, that'd be one of the first things he noticed. He wouldn't have just walked past it to go on down no hallway."

Thane made another note on his pad. "That might be something I can use."

"Oh yeah," Gideon said. "Defense almost ready to rest now."

Gideon followed Thane down the hall and into the office, a small room cluttered with furniture and equipment which had a total resale value of probably twenty-five bucks. The particleboard desk, which looked more appropriate for a junior high student, was falling apart at the joints, its plastic writing surface curling up from the rest of the desk, and atop this squatted an ancient computer with a dusty screen.

The one spot of color was the blood.

There was a large, fading stain in the center of the mud-colored carpet, as though a bowl of punch had overturned during a party. Thane felt the blood drain out of his face, which surprised him. He figured his time at Forsman would have deadened him to this kind of shock—but here he was, getting wobble-kneed at the sight of this blood stain.

"Gruber, meet Skunk," Gideon said. "Skunk, meet Gruber."

"You really think Skunk could have killed somebody?"

"Sure." The big man shrugged. "Under the right circumstances."

Thane finally looked away from the stain and glanced around the room. "Doesn't make sense. Why would Skunk even be in this room? One glance says there's nothing here worth stealing. And if he heard Gruber coming, he wouldn't try hiding in here: he would have run for the back door."

Gideon chuckled and sized Thane up. "Whoo-ee. Baby, would you lookit you. Thinking more and more like a criminal every day."

Thane frowned—but it was true, even if he didn't like to think about it. It had begun in Forsman, and now that sort of thinking came to him effortlessly, almost by instinct. He walked over to the desk and looked at an open racing form, red circles identifying each race's horse of choice. "Do you think your time in Forsman changed you?" Thane asked.

"I never was what you'd call a good egg, if that's what you mean." Gideon smiled, but Thane didn't respond. "You think maybe you're different from when you went in?" Gideon continued. "You'd have to be. Everybody is."

Thane finally looked up at him. "I thought maybe I wouldn't have changed much because I was innocent."

"Hell, that'd be worse. Besides, nobody leaves Forsman innocent. I don't give a fuck who it is."

CHAPTER

FIFTEEN

THANE SAT AT HIS KITCHEN table, jotting sporadic notes on his legal pad. The clock on the wall read six, and the morning sun was just starting to awaken. Thane was already on his third cup of coffee, which was mixing badly with the adrenaline already surging through his veins.

The past five months had been tough, although it wasn't anything new for Thane. The newspapers had savaged him for taking the case, but the furor had subsided after a couple months. But now that the start of the trial was upon them, the hostility was ramping back up.

Times had also been challenging for Thane and Hannah as a couple, not just emotionally, but also financially. In a way Thane was fortunate because Stone was just as anxious as he was to get this case over with and off the front page. Joseph had been gracious enough to pay him for the rest of the month, even though he had left on the fifth, which had helped. Plus, the salary that Thane had earned during his four months working for Joseph was more than Hannah usually cleared in a year at her bookstore, which gave them at least a little cushion.

But there were new expenses that ate up some of the small savings they had built up. Thane had brought Gideon on as part of his legal team. He felt confident the big man could be helpful at some point along the way, and he also hoped it might increase the odds of Gideon staying out of prison: he was a little surprised Gideon hadn't already killed anybody at Bernie's Burgers. Thane wasn't able to pay him much—not that Gideon was being well-paid for mopping up the fast food restaurant—but it was still an additional expense.

There was another source of money that Thane wasn't ready to tell Hannah about just yet: Angelique Arvand, a reporter for a gossip site with a questionable reputation and deep pockets, had given Thane her card one day when he was coming out of his new office and offered at least a modicum of financial support to tide him over in exchange for a full exclusive interview. The deal was that Thane would not only discuss this trial as soon as it was over, but also address questions about his own conviction and release. It wasn't something Thane wanted to do, but he also didn't want to bankrupt himself and Hannah by taking on this case, so he agreed.

Hannah stood behind him, looking out the window at the trash-covered alley while sipping her tea and nibbling a piece of toast and jelly. She remained resolute that he shouldn't have taken this case, but was no longer trying to talk him out of it. She had expressed her feelings as directly as possible, but once he said he had to do this, she hadn't brought it up again. Thane knew she was struggling, searching for the elusive balance between articulating her anger and not letting anything come between them again.

She put her teacup in the sink, then walked over and stood behind him, putting her hand on his shoulder. He appreciated her willingness to offer a physical connection, rather than tossing out empty platitudes of encouragement he knew she didn't feel. He didn't want to share his fears with her, because he knew he had no right to expect any sympathy for what he was facing. But he had always turned to her when confronted with adversity, and with her hand on his shoulder, he was overwhelmed by his need to talk.

"I'm not blind to what I'm doing here," he said. "Being responsible for somebody's life. Nobody should have that right. Whether somebody lives or dies, having it be up to you. That's not something I would have ever considered doing."

"These are unique circumstances," she said after a moment.

"They are. But I understand that doesn't justify it. I know it's wrong: it's not even a question. And yet, that's what I've done." He reached up and put his hand over hers, turning to look at her. "I'm sorry I'm putting you through this. I really am."

"I know you're sorry," Hannah said, "and I want to understand, but you don't exactly open up to me like you used to." She squeezed his hand, which he took as reassurance that she wasn't totally giving up on him yet.

"You said in the bookstore a few months ago that you used to know who I am," Thane said. "Well, I'm not sure who I am anymore either."

He rose from his chair and stepped around behind her, putting his arms around her waist and holding her close so she couldn't see the anguish in his eyes.

"I'm doing things I never would have done before," he continued. "Is it all just for revenge? And if so, do I have the right? A large part of me feels I do, but I'm scared maybe that just means there isn't much of the old me left."

"I wish you hadn't taken this case."

"I feel it's my last chance to get our life back on track. I'm hoping it will bring me full circle."

"By beating Stone? How does that get anything back on track? All it's doing is dragging you backward." She worked her way around so that she was facing him. "I don't understand how—" She stopped when she saw the moisture forming in his eyes, then pulled him forward and embraced him.

"Here's their case, far as I can tell," Thane said. He stood next to a four-by-five chalkboard he had nailed onto one of his office walls, figuring it covered more holes than it created. "A bus driver says he let Skunk off less than half a mile from Gruber's that night, about an hour or so before the time of the murder."

Kristin sat up straight in one of the side chairs across from his desk, sporting a maroon pantsuit and a silk white top, most likely the best-dressed occupant in the building, if not the entire block. Gideon slumped low on the sofa behind her, his stained T-shirt and frayed blue jeans firmly positioning him on the opposite end of the sartorial scale.

"Can't believe the driver remembers Skunk," Gideon muttered.

Kristin's hand started to shoot up as if still in class. She caught herself, and quickly pulled it back down. "They wouldn't put him on the stand if he wasn't sure."

"Maybe, but I don't want to assume anything," Thane said.

A chalk line was drawn down the middle of the blackboard; one side labeled Prosecution, the other Defense. So far only the prosecution side had a numbered list under it. (1) Bus Driver, (2) MO, (3) Patrol Guards, and (4) Phone Call. Thane looked over the list, then turned to his team.

"Second," Thane continued, "the intruder had the same MO as Skunk's prior break-ins: the way he bypassed the security alarm, the way the locks were picked, what was taken, everything. Third, the rent-a-cops said the suspect had a pronounced limp."

"But they didn't see his face," Kristin added. "They only saw him in the light from a distance for a second, so they can't describe him at all, apart from the limp."

"Which ain't a bad description," Gideon said.

"But they didn't see his face," she repeated curtly.

"And finally," Thane said, "a phone call from Gruber's house to where Skunk worked."

Gideon shook his head in disgust. "Stupid fuck."

"It all seems fairly circumstantial," Kristin said to Thane.

"It's got me convinced," Gideon said as he slid down even lower on the sofa, stretching his legs out in front of him.

Thane picked up the piece of chalk and moved to the Defense side of the board, looking at the blank side for a moment before turning to his team.

"All right, so what do we have?"

The ensuing silence answered his question. Finally, Kristin jotted a note on the fresh legal pad balanced on her leg, talking as she wrote. "No fingerprints at the scene."

Gideon chuckled. "He's a thief. He wore gloves."

Kristin continued ignoring Gideon as Thane thought about it. Deciding it was better than nothing, he started to write it on the board, but Gideon rose from the sofa and lumbered over, taking the chalk from him. He wrote in large letters, 'black con named Skunk says he didn't do it'. He then tossed the piece of chalk to Thane and flopped back onto the sofa.

"Don't mean to rain on your parade, counselor, but that's what you got."

For the first time during the meeting, Kristin turned around and looked back at Gideon. Any demurral she had been showing was now on its way out the cracked window.

"That's the spirit," she said. "Let's gas him ourselves."

"Lookit, I can rah-rah all you want, Barbie, but that don't change shit."

"I don't even know why you're here."

"Cause if you got a criminal trial, who better to help than a criminal?"

"Maybe somebody who knows what they're talking about." Kristin glared at him a moment longer before starting to turn, but whipped back around and pointed a finger at the big man. "And you call me Barbie again, I'll show you what a two-inch spiked heel can do."

Thane walked between them and held a hand up toward each. "Cool it, guys. Kristin, I need Gideon to give me a different perspective on this case—and to be my bullshit detector where the crime is concerned. He'll see things you and I would miss." He then turned toward Gideon. "And Kristin's right. I'm the last guy who's going to take anything Stone says at face value. He had strong evidence against me, too."

"He needed it," Gideon said, "cause you're white and you're a lawyer. Skunk's black. Once you charge a black man, you're nine-tenths the way home. And putting a black man with four burglary convictions under his belt in front of a jury, well, there's your other nine-tenths. Stone can phone this one in." Gideon leaned back, then looked at Kristin. "And yeah, I was making a joke about the other nine-tenths. I'm not that stupid."

Kristin looked at the blackboard again. "So Mr. Burns doesn't have any sort of alibi for that night?"

Thane shook his head. "He claims some guy called saying he had a job for him at Armor Park, which is where he got off the bus."

"At 8:30 p.m.?"

"Yeah. He says the guy told him to not give up on him, because he might be late. So Skunk says he waited until almost midnight."

"What kind of work do you interview for like that?" she asked.

Gideon guffawed. "Not 'work.' A *job*. You know, something illegal?"

Kristin ignored him and scribbled on her notepad as Thane set the piece of chalk on his desk. He looked over the board again, then picked up the eraser and removed Gideon's pessimistic summation.

"I'm not ready to write off Skunk yet. Look, I've got to go meet with the judge before we start jury selection. Kristin, I want you to review Gruber's phone records for the few months before he was killed. See if anything jumps out at you. Not sure what it'd be, but just keep your eye open for anything unusual. Gideon, I want you to look through the police reports that describe the crime scene."

Gideon sighed and slowly lifted his slumping frame off the sofa. Kristin shot up quickly, again in sharp contrast to her colleague. "Why can't he look through the phone records and I read about the crime scene?" Kristin asked.

"Like I said before," Gideon said. "I'm the criminal. I'm pretty sure I've been at a lot more crime scenes than you. Besides, you're the junior associate around here."

"How do you figure?" Kristin said.

"'Cause I'm betting I've also spent a hell of a lot more time in a courtroom than you."

CHAPTER SIXTEEN

UDGE CHARLES REYNOLDS'S OFFICE WAS immaculate, a direct reflection of the precision and order he demanded in his courtroom. Thane sat in a navy blue leather wingback chair across the desk from the fifty-five-year-old judge, watching as he read through a motion submitted by the prosecution. Reynolds looked like a Marine drill sergeant, with his gray hair cut military-style and his long-sleeved white dress shirt looking starched enough to crack nuts against, his pursed lips twitching while he read Stone's motion.

"I'm afraid I don't understand your point, Mr. Stone," Judge Reynolds said.

"Your Honor," Stone replied, "the media will turn this trial into a circus, given Mr. Banning's presence. The past few months have already seen too much publicity about a case that hasn't even started. Now that it's about to actually begin, the coverage will only amplify."

Thane looked back over his shoulder at Stone. "And how would that be my fault?"

"Judge Reynolds, there is no doubt in my mind Mr. Banning is only taking this case because of me," Stone said, not taking his eyes off the judge. "That's borderline legal malpractice."

Reynolds rubbed his temples as he considered this, then looked silently across his desk at Thane. Finally, he flipped his reading glasses up so they rested on the top of his head.

"I have to tell you, Mr. Banning, I do not allow bedlam into my courtroom. A courtroom should be solemn, like a place of worship—not a World Federation Wrestling exhibition. This case, unfortunately, has all the makings of a center stage grudge match, and that concerns me."

"My client pleaded with me to represent him," Thane said. "I did my best to dissuade him, but he's insisting."

"A capital murder case is not real estate law, Mr. Banning. A man's freedom is at stake. Most likely his very life. That is not a small matter."

"Do you think there's anyone in this room who understands that better than me?" Reynolds's nostrils flared, and Thane quickly added, "Please understand I will not embarrass the court in any way."

The judge leaned forward, his low voice sounding as though it was pushing its way through a throat full of gravel. "And you understand you won't be given a gnat's pecker of leeway in my courtroom. You find yourself in over your sorry little head, do not look to me for pity. And don't you even think about trying to back out once we begin. You take this case, then you're damn sure going to be seeing it through to the end."

"I understand."

Reynolds continued studying Thane for a moment, then cleared his throat a couple of times before turning his attention toward Stone and leaning back in his chair. "Putting aside the obvious fact I have no legal right to remove Mr. Banning from this case, it would also be wrong, given the defendant's wishes, injudicious though they may be."

Stone walked around to the front of his chair and stood at attention in front of the desk. "Your Honor, the TV reporters and cameramen will turn this trial into a farce."

"If the District Attorney is concerned about the presence of the media," Thane said, "I would be open to barring press from the courtroom. I would also obey any gag order not to speak with the press about this case, if Mr. Stone were also to agree."

Thane watched Stone's face out of the corner of his eye, knowing full well that the prosecutor wouldn't take the bait. Stone was a publicity hound on the best of days, and this was an election year. One side of Judge Reynolds's lips turned upward slightly at this, suggesting he was thinking the exact same thing.

"I believe the people have a right to an open trial," Stone said, "especially one involving the death of a former police detective."

"You can't have it both ways, Mr. Stone," the judge said. "Given the defendant's wishes *and* your desire to have an open trial, I have no choice but to once again deny your request for a change in counsel."

"But Your Honor—"

"Mr. Stone, I'm confident you're not thinking of saying anything other than 'Yes, sir'. Am I correct?"

Stone instead said nothing, then reached down and picked up his briefcase.

"Thank you for your time, Your Honor," he said at last.

He then turned and stalked out of the judge's chambers. Thane waited until Stone was down the hall, then rose from his chair as well. As he turned to leave, Reynolds stopped him.

"Mr. Banning, I seriously suggest you look deep in your heart before going any further with this. Do not take this case for the wrong reason. Not this case."

Thane looked back at him and could see the man was trying to offer sincere advice. "I know what I'm doing, Your Honor."

The judge leaned back in his chair and clasped his hands behind his head. "That's not the same as saying you're doing this for the right reason."

It wasn't a question as much as a statement of fact. Thane paused, then turned and exited the office.

The low murmur of small talk was lost in the huge courtroom. Only three rows of seats in the gallery were in use, hosting people from all walks of life, bound only by their legal duty to appear that day as potential jurors. When Judge Reynolds entered the courtroom, most of those summoned looked up in deference, although a couple of people—a businessman in a trendy three-piece suit and a sullen college student—scowled.

Judge Reynolds addressed the potential jurors, expressing his gratitude at their participation in this honored system, as if they had a choice. To get out of being considered for jury duty, he said they either had to have served within the past twenty-four months or have a compelling reason for not serving. A very compelling reason. The disgruntled businessman stood and explained that his company needed him if it was to be successful in today's competitive marketplace. The judge stared him down, then said he was confident the man's business could survive without him, unless he was so managerially inept he didn't have empowered employees to carry the ball, in which case it was probably best the man find a different profession. No one else raised their hand.

At that point, the prosecution team entered the courtroom. Stone entered the room first, followed by his right-hand men Wallace Winston and Simon Keaton. All three men were immaculately dressed, and Stone's presence caused a ripple of murmurs from the potential jurors who recognized him, as if his presence sent a signal that if the District Attorney himself was going to try the case, maybe they weren't wasting their time after all.

The low-key buzzing that Stone elicited, however, shifted into overdrive when Thane and his team appeared. Several in the gallery pointed at him, as if it wasn't already abundantly clear that most everyone had already made the connection. And the few who apparently didn't keep up with the news were quickly brought up-to-speed by the person sitting next to them.

Thane and Kristin were both dressed appropriately for the venue, but Gideon wore dark blue Dockers and a collared shirt, both purchased by Thane. The big man refused to wear a tie, but kept tugging at his collar anyway. As they walked toward their table, Kristin stayed close to Thane, trying to distance herself from being associated with her disinterested-looking colleague. When Thane sat at one end of the table, she quickly staked her claim for the chair next to him, as if music had just stopped. Gideon pulled out the chair at the far end and slumped down, looking as though he was waiting to be sentenced. Kristin looked at him with a stern eye, which Gideon ignored.

Interviewing the first four prospective jurors was uneventful. The first was immediately dismissed upon revealing she had helped canvass her neighborhood in support of the District Attorney during his first campaign. Stone tossed her the smile of a politician and thanked her for her support, but said that that precluded her from serving on the jury.

Jurors two and three were dismissed for other reasons, and juror four was found to be acceptable by Stone. Thane also concurred, although he was awkward while questioning the jurors. Stone had a way of immediately establishing a bond of trust and confidence with each person he questioned. Jury selection was not something Thane had done before as a real estate attorney, and he couldn't afford any of those obscenely priced consultants who turned it into a so-called science. Kristin jotted down some relevant questions for him to ask, which was helpful, but for the most part he simply floundered.

The fifth person questioned was a broad-chested man in his mid-fifties named Frank Ferguson, looking like a staunch conservative who proudly flew the American Flag from his porch, weather permitting. He had a quarter-inch crew cut that resembled gray Astroturf, and his ruddy cheeks accented the polyester red tie he wore, the tip of which landed a couple of inches above his belly button. His sports coat appeared too small, most likely not having made its way out of the closet the past few years.

Ferguson was an auto mechanic and was very respectful addressing Stone's questions, firmly attaching a 'yes sir' or 'no sir' at the end of each response, as if they were brethren in the fight against crime. His body language shifted dramatically, however, when Thane rose and approached the witness box. One side of his mouth curled up and his eyebrows furrowed, as if the attorney for the defense was sporting a swastika. Instead of sitting up straight as he did for Stone, Ferguson leaned forward, as if itching for a confrontation.

After a couple of preliminary questions which were met with terse answers, absent any sign of respect, Thane paused and watched the scowling man awaiting the next question, then offered up the one Ferguson was probably hoping to be asked.

"Mr. Ferguson, can you think of any reason why you might not be impartial in this case?"

"How about because I think the defendant's lawyer got away with murder?"

The other potential jurors appeared charged by this response, several of them nodding immediately in agreement, with one of them even muttering a bit too loud "you got that right." Reynolds lightly tapped his gavel.

"Ladies and gentlemen, this is not a group participation process. I must ask that you keep your comments to yourself." The judge then turned to Ferguson. "And sir, while you may think I am going to admonish you, I actually appreciate your candor. I think it's important that everyone be upfront with any possible reasons why they should not serve on this jury. But don't, however, confuse this latitude with an opportunity to be anything other than responsive to Mr. Banning's questions."

Ferguson nodded. Thane glanced back at the Defense table where Kristin was already crossing a line through Ferguson' name and Gideon just shrugged. Thane also noted Stone sharing a smile with his Associates. He turned back to the man being questioned.

"So you think I got away with murder, and that makes you mad."

"Yeah, it pretty much pisses me the hell off." Ferguson again turned to the judge. "With all due respect."

"So if you were on this jury," Thane continued, "you'd want to make sure we convicted the guilty man, and not just whoever was served up to you?"

"Damn straight. People need to take responsibility for their actions."

"And you believe in justice, regardless of the status or position of the man responsible?"

Ferguson crossed his arms and nodded once for emphasis. "Regardless of the status or position. You do the crime, then you do the time. I don't care who the hell it is."

Thane smiled at the man. "I hope you hold on to that commitment." He then turned to Judge Reynolds. "Defense accepts this juror, Your Honor."

Kristin squeaked out a reaction of disbelief, but managed to refrain from crying out. Gideon chuckled.

"You do?" the judge asked. "Well, OK then, I guess. Mr. Stone?"

Stone's smile had been whisked from his face. He leaned over and whispered something to Winston, who then glanced over at Keaton, as if all three were trying to figure out if they were missing something. Unable to figure out what it was, Stone turned back to the judge. "We most certainly accept."

"Yes, I kind of thought you might. Juror number five has been accepted by both parties."

Ferguson eyed Thane with suspicion as he rose and started back toward the gallery, then looked toward Stone for some sort of reaction, but the District Attorney had already moved on to the next name on the list.

Thane returned to his chair and started reading the short summary of facts for the middle-aged woman being escorted to the witness box, then glanced over at Kristin, whose stare of disbelief had not abated. He gave her a half-smile.

"Safe to say you think we should have dismissed him?"

"Oh, I don't know. Guess it depends on whether or not you want to win this case."

"Look, there probably aren't more than a couple of people here today who aren't thinking the same thing that guy was. At least he's upfront about it, so I know where I stand."

"Yeah, but where you're standing is in a big ole pile of shit."

Thane smiled as he nodded. "Maybe so, but with his rabid need for justice, he could become one of our best friends."

"Or you could just get bit."

CHAPTER SEVENTEEN

GIDEON SPRAWLED OUT ON HIS apartment sofa, as hard and lumpy as anything he'd ever slept on at Forsman, though at least the beds in prison got their sheets bleached. Nothing had been clean inside his decrepit apartment at any point during the past forty years. Dirt had worked its way into everything to the point that it was as much a part of the apartment as the wood of the floor and the bricks in the walls. He hadn't expected anything better. For all practical purposes, it was no different from where he'd landed the other times he'd made parole. But he could walk out of this dump anytime he wanted, and that more than made up for the filth.

He swore under his breath at the fifteen-inch black and white TV sitting on an apple crate across the room. He was trying to watch basketball, but the picture was so poor that there was twice the regulation number of players on the court, and the audio sounded like it was coming through a can on a string.

He got up and took another stab at fixing the picture. He jiggled some knobs, whacked the side of the set a couple of times, then picked the whole thing up and shook it, trying to mix up the ingredients inside, all to no avail. He finally gave up, setting the TV back on the box with a low throaty grumble.

"Next time," he told it. "Next time, I'm gonna lose my temper, and then it's over for you."

He ground his cigarette into the coffee table, then scanned the dim room:

He didn't need much, and not much is what he got.

"Fuck this."

He walked back to his bedroom, which was only big enough for a twin bed. Normally it would be impossible for a man Gideon's size to sleep comfortably on something that small, but it had been years since he'd experienced anything larger, so it wasn't a big deal to him. He also didn't want to get used to anything bigger.

He got down on his knees next to the bed, as if getting ready to pray, then with one hand lifted the mattress as easily as if it were a pillow. The other hand slipped underneath and grabbed a dirty, forest green cloth bag cinched with a string. He rooted around inside the bag, then pulled out something shiny and metallic and stuck it in his pocket. Returning the bag to its hiding place, he rose and walked out of his apartment, not bothering to lock it.

He trudged down the sidewalk; even in this violent part of the city, people veered a step or two to the side when approaching him. White people especially gave him plenty of room, if not the entire sidewalk. It didn't bother him anymore. Of course they saw an angry black man: he *was* an angry black man. Everybody was smart to cross the street when he was in that kind of space.

The night air always smelled like freedom. Forsman inmates never got to go outside after four in the afternoon, which was one reason he loved walking the streets after dark. Anything could happen once the sun set, and even though a lot of times what happened was trouble, that was okay: it beat the hell out of boredom.

He thought back to the first time he felt the peculiar magic of night air. He'd been young, just out of his first stint in prison: three years for stealing cars. He was out on the street, strutting, listening while Mick Jagger hollered "Sympathy for the Devil" out of a boom box the size of a microwave, all the smells of a good time wafting along the cool evening breeze. He had a lot of living to catch up on and planned to pack as much as he could into that first night. He ended it in the back of a patrol car after cutting a bartender who refused to sell alcohol to an eighteen-year-old. Given that he had only been on the street for less than twenty-four hours, they packed him off upstate to serve two years for aggravated assault.

Upon his next release, he was determined to stay out for a while. He found work loading boxes into refrigerated semi-trailers, which required a coat and gloves even during the hottest summer days. His boss paid him three dollars an hour less than the minimum wage, telling the parolee that if he thought he could get a better deal elsewhere then he was free to take it. Three weeks into the job, he started stealing tools, figuring if his boss was going to be a thief, he would do the same. Unfortunately, his crime was easier to prove and prosecute, and he was sent away for another two-year stint.

The stakes got raised the next time when he killed a man in a street brawl. He had been minding his own business when a drug dealer sitting on a stoop started dogging him, apparently under the impression that everyone in the neighborhood knew and feared him; but Gideon didn't know anybody, and he especially didn't fear anyone. After one insult too many, Gideon flew up the steps and flung the heroin dealer down to the street. When the man unsheathed a knife, that was all it took: Gideon ripped a three-foot long flower box off the building and brought it down over the man's head, bending the metal fixture in half. Two days later, the tough guy died in the hospital, upping the charges against Gideon from assault to manslaughter.

That was his first trip to Forsman.

During his last bout of freedom, he felt like he was going through the motions until they put him away again. He made it three months—a personal best—before an attempted robbery and assault with a deadly weapon did him in. It was the fifth time he'd been arrested, but only the second after the three-strikes rule had gone into effect. That's when the big clock started ticking for convicts everywhere. And every night after he got out again, he wrestled with the notion that it was probably his last chance to go straight. He didn't want to blow it by doing something stupid—but at the same time, he hated the thought of wasting time pretending to be something he wasn't.

On rare occasions, he wondered if working for Thane would change things for him this time, although he knew in his gut it couldn't be true. Thane couldn't afford to pay him for long, and he wasn't looking for handouts, so unless he could figure out how he was helping the case, he'd quit. The best he could do was hope for a longer taste of freedom this time around, and maybe more fun while it lasted, but that would take money.

He stopped in front of a pawn shop and peered through the barred window: there was no one inside except for the rotund clerk sitting behind the front counter, safely ensconced in a Plexiglas fortress. Gideon entered the store, stopping next to a row of TVs, a quarter of which were probably hot but at least offered a clear picture. Several of the sets were showing the basketball game he had been trying to watch earlier.

He walked up to the counter and thrust his hand into his pants pocket, a move not lost on the clerk, and brought out a silver pocket watch. He dangled it at the clerk's eye level, then placed it in the small pass-through burrowed under the Plexiglas. The clerk used his Metallica T-shirt to wipe the chicken grease from his fingers before retrieving the watch and examining it, looking unfazed. "It's sterling," Gideon said.

"Actually, it's not. I've been doing this for a while." The clerk managed to open the casing with his pudgy fingers and held it up to his ear. "Keep good time?"

"Within a minute a year."

The clerk sighed, as though every item that ever crossed his counter was in mint condition. He closed the watch casing and examined the back of it. "I'm going to need I.D."

Gideon glared at the man for a moment, then pulled out his wallet and slipped his driver's license under the glass where it was scrutinized by the clerk.

"It's an old license," Gideon said, "but it's still me."

"Gideon Spence," the clerk read aloud. He then checked the back of the watch again. "The monogram is T.G. Let me guess: it's your great uncle's."

"Nope. Grandfather's."

"But of course. So what's the 'G' stand for?"

"Stands for gimme some damn money," Gideon said. "It ain't stolen, if that's what you're fretting about."

"Perish the thought."

The clerk pried open the back casing and surveyed the inside mechanisms, then put the cover back on. He stared at the counter for a moment without moving, the wheels turning inside his head. He finally gave a professional shrug of indifference.

"Forty dollars—and before you start acting all outraged, let me tell you the monogram really cuts down the value. Plus, who do you think carries pocket watches anymore? My only chance to sell it is going to be some old geezer who can't see shit."

Gideon scowled at the clerk but knew the figure wouldn't change. The man likely wasn't the owner of the shop and would be just as happy for Gideon to storm out so he could go back to watching the basketball game.

"Forty dollars. That's fucked up. Can't hardly buy nothing for forty dollars."

"You can get a good buzz on."

"Yeah, cause I'm a black man and that's all I'm looking for. Fuck you, you greasy fat piece of shit. Just give me the forty."

The clerk pulled out a journal from under the counter and copied down the information from Gideon's license. "City requirement," he explained.

Gideon snatched his license back along with two twenty-dollar bills and shoved them in his pocket. He stopped and checked the score of the game one more time before leaving, since he wouldn't be able to afford a new TV that night.

His team, of course, was losing.

Thane sat on the window seat of his and Hannah's apartment at 3:00 a.m., a legal pad resting on his lap and his eyes watching the street below. The neighborhood had called it a night; even the gang of teenagers who rose like vampires when the sun went down had packed it in.

The trial opened in seven hours. He had spent the last five working on his opening statement, but his mind was blank now. Previous drafts lay crumpled on the floor around him, numbering in the dozens. Kristin had offered to write his opening remarks for him— he knew she would have worked the entire case for free if she'd been allowed to present it in court—but Thane said the words needed to be his. Now he just had to find them.

On the sidewalk below he caught the movement of a strolling prostitute, constantly tugging the hem of her dress as she ambled down the street. Thane had noticed her in the area before: she lived a couple of blocks away, but didn't work the neighborhood streets. He wondered what she had been like before turning to prostitution. Even now she carried herself with spirit, shoulders back, chin high, announcing that she was who she was, no apologies needed. Thane wondered whether or not he would get to that point himself.

CHAPTER EIGHTEEN

O NCE AGAIN, THE RUBBERNECKERS WERE forming a line outside the courtroom long before the morning newspapers were delivered. Murder trials always attracted groupies like this, but today was different. Today, nobody cared about Skunk or the dead Ted Gruber. They wanted to watch Los Angeles's rock star District Attorney do battle with Thane Banning again.

Thane and his team huddled in a small meeting room across the hall from the courtroom. Sitting at a wooden table, his forehead propped up on one hand, Thane crossed something out on his legal pad and jotted down something else in its place. Words and sentences throughout the page had lines drawn through them, making the document resemble a cobweb. The muffled rumblings of a crowd outside the door and down the hall rolled into the room; nothing discernible, but the energy was building.

Kristin paced along one side of the room, occasionally looking outside at the mob of people. She had arrived at the courthouse an hour ago, wearing a brand-new black pantsuit and carrying a leather Prada briefcase. Thane wasn't sure there was anything inside, but she looked formidable carrying it.

Gideon leaned against the opposite wall, looking at nothing in particular—just passing the time like everyone did at Forsman. He had grumbled about there not being a TV in the room, but other than that he was keeping out of the way. He started digging around in his denim shirt's front pocket until he found a cigarette. Kristin immediately stopped her marching and vigorously shook her head, pointing toward a No Smoking sign on the door.

Gideon looked at Thane, but he just shook his head, so the cigarette was stuffed back into the pocket. "Can't smoke in the room," he said, "can't smoke in the building, can't smoke on the steps. What the hell happened while I was in Forsman? Give me a fucking break." He pushed away from the wall and sulked toward the door. "Anybody needs me, I'm driving to Arizona for a smoke." The door slammed hard behind him.

Kristin watched Thane as he stared at his notes, then took a seat across the table from him. She continued looking at him, but he refused to look up, so she finally broke the unbearable silence. "You nervous?"

He stopped writing, leaned back in his chair, and considered the question for a moment. "Once in Forsman, I was working by myself in the laundry. Usually I worked with two other guys, but one was in the hole for jumping a guard, and the other had been taken to the ward for some reason, so it was just me. I started getting a bad feeling, and I looked up to see this nut job convict named Wally—three hundred eighty on a trim day—just grinning at me, holding a butcher knife." Thane looked at Kristin and shrugged. "Then, I was nervous. This is nothing. How about you? You doing OK?"

"I don't get nervous."

"You never met Wally."

He returned his attention to his notes.

"Are you kidding me?" she said. "So what happened in the laundry room?"

Thane crossed through one more sentence, then placed the legal pad in his briefcase and stood. "Nothing. He was just having some fun with me, to see what I would do. Wally was kind of odd like that."

He picked up his briefcase and turned toward the door. "What do you think?" he asked. "Ready to fight for justice?"

The courtroom was so crammed that it was hard to breathe. The overhead fans worked nonstop, spinning in vain. Most of the spectators were observing Thane at one end of the defense table, with Kristin on the other end, leafing through piles of notes. Tucked safely between them in an orange jumpsuit was Skunk, slouched over, staring down at his shoes like his spine was missing.

Gideon sat in the front row of the gallery directly behind Thane, the smell of cigarettes still emanating from his shirt, causing the woman next to him to sniff in disgust. Gideon had said earlier that he'd sat at the defense table enough times in his life, and that he'd feel more comfortable watching the proceedings from the cheap seats.

On the other side of the aisle, Stone conferred with Winston and Keaton, turning as far away from Thane as possible. After Judge Reynolds entered and called the court in session, Stone pushed away from the table and rose, every movement polished and assured. He wanted to make it clear that this was *his* house.

"Ladies and gentlemen of the jury," he began. "I have good news. You have an easy job today. I have phone logs. I have eyewitnesses. I have *modus operandi*. I have so much evidence, in fact, that I don't want to waste a second more of your time talking about it when I could simply show you. I'm just that proud. Usually an opening statement describes each piece of evidence in turn to ensure that you understand what I'm about to present, but everything in this case will speak just fine for itself."

Stone paused for a moment to look across the room at Skunk, then returned his focus to the jury.

"As you all know, this is a capital case. A man's life is on the line. The question of whether or not there is sufficient evidence to take another human being's life is usually a difficult question. This time the answer is easy—and I look forward to showing you why."

He walked back towards his seat, his associates nodding in assent at their boss's performance. Several reporters scribbled in their notebooks, surprise written across each of their faces at the brevity of his opening statement.

Stone sat down, but Thane didn't rise from his seat immediately, instead staring at his written statement without moving. Judge Reynolds waited a moment, then finally called out:

"Mr. Banning?"

Thane remained frozen, then finally rose. He started to turn toward the jury box, then stopped and placed his legal pad face down on the table. He looked up, aware that he wasn't displaying the confidence offered by Stone. He walked toward the jury, haltingly at first, feeling like a nervous kid walking up to ask out a girl for the first time. He started speaking slowly as he neared them.

"District Attorney Stone says this is a simple one. Says this case, your verdict, the final judgment you'll be called upon to make—that they're all going to be easy." He paused, still working out this concept in his mind. "I say that's true—but only if you aren't willing to look deeper."

He walked up to the jury box, placing his hands on the front railing. A petite young woman wearing a pearl necklace leaned back slightly, doing everything but letting out a small 'yip', Thane's proximity obviously making her nervous.

"Imagine you're sitting at a café counter," Thane continued, quickly taking a step back, "and you ask the man sitting next to you to please pass the salt. He ignores you. Doesn't even look your way. You ask again and finally he mutters something and reluctantly slides the shaker your way. You make the easy judgement: that man is a jerk."

Thane turned away from the jury, approaching the witness stand, where he leaned against the cool wood.

"The man then tells you his wife just died. Ah . . . suddenly your opinion changes. He wasn't being rude: he's in shock. Grieving. You're filled with compassion for the man. That, too, was easy." Thane paused, looking down at the floor for a moment, then looked back at the jury. "The man then turns toward you and says he had just killed his wife. My God, what should you do? You are afraid. You want to run and call the police. Again: easy."

Thane again approached the jury box, staying a few feet back from the railing this time.

"Then the man tells you his wife was sick. She suffered horribly for months—terminal cancer. The pain was too much, she begged to be released from her agony, but it was hard for him because he loved her so very, very much. Finally her anguish was more than he could stand, so he turned up the morphine in her IV, just like she asked. Within an hour she was dead. You feel sorry for the man. Your heart breaks for him. That, too, was easy."

Thane quietly stepped forward until he was once again leaning on the front railing of the jury box. This time the nervous woman didn't lean back.

"Ladies and gentlemen, the truth is not always easy. What is right, or fair, or real, is not always easy. I'm not here to tell you I have all the answers or that everything I say is going to be perfectly obvious to you. I simply ask that you not blindly accept the first scenario offered to you. That you not accept what someone else tells you is easy. I ask that you dig for the truth. If you truly want justice—if you *demand* justice—then you're going to have to question what you're being told. Because believe me, this case is anything but easy."

CHAPTER NINETEEN

THE FIRST WITNESS FOR THE prosecution was Vince Struthers, a highly decorated police detective only five years from retirement. Thane could see why Stone had picked him for a first witness: Struthers sat comfortably in the witness chair, looking for all the world as if he were merely sitting on his back porch, sharing a few drinks with friends.

Stone walked the detective through the murder scene, starting from the time Struthers and his partner arrived at the scene until the coroner's confirmation of the cause of death, although a bullet to the head made that simply a formality. Struthers rattled off the necessary details requested by the District Attorney so that no piece of the story was left out: the location of the body, the estimated time of death, the list of items suspected to have been stolen.

"So, Detective Struthers," Stone said, "you're saying you identified Mr. Burns as a suspect within a couple of hours?"

"Yes, sir. The intruder bypassed the security alarm with a couple of twisties—like you find in the produce section. Mr. Burns had the same MO from previous break-ins. As far as I was concerned, he might as well have signed his name at the door."

"So you had a suspect. What did you do then?"

"We got lucky. We checked phone logs from Detective Gruber's home and found the number to a factory where Mr. Burns worked.

We estimate the call was made about ten minutes before Mr. Gruber was killed."

Stone nodded. "Good work, Detective."

Struthers turned his head and looked directly at Thane. "It's not always that easy. But sometimes it is."

The corners of Stone's mouth kinked up. "Yes, Detective, I have to agree with you on that," he said. "No further questions."

Thane stood without speaking for a moment, simply looking at his notes. He had never cross-examined a witness before. "Detective," he began, "the twist-ties you mentioned: were they stripped completely clean?"

Struthers looked bored.

"No, just the ends were stripped."

"You have detailed knowledge of my client's MO, Detective. You've read his file. Isn't it true that Mr. Burns stripped all of the plastic coating off during his previous string of burglaries?"

Struthers shrugged nonchalantly. "Maybe. I think you might be right, but Burns is the only one we know who used them at all, stripped or not. I don't really see what difference it makes."

"It could make a big difference, Detective. A few minutes ago, you mentioned some of the stolen items: a DVD player, a coin collection, a wallet—but isn't it believed that a computer disk may have also been stolen?"

"A number of disks were scattered on the floor, but I can't say whether or not any were taken."

Thane stepped away from his table and toward the witness for the first time during his cross-examination. "The disks were numbered. You put them back in order, didn't you? And found one was missing?"

"There was a gap in the numbers, yes, but that's not to say the disk was ever there. For all I know, the victim tossed it. Or lost it. I didn't even know anyone still used disks anymore. Who knows how old they were?"

Thane looked down at the floor and shook his head, as if he were trying to make sense of this but it just wouldn't take.

"That may be, but Detective Gruber kept them right next to the computer, so we can assume he used them. And the way the disks were scattered on the floor, we can assume the perpetrator deliberately went through them—trying to find something, perhaps. I mean, why else would a burglar waste his time with something that obviously wasn't worth anything? He would have simply left them in the case. Plus, although you mentioned a few things that were stolen, there were still a number of valuable objects in plain sight, untouched. Some of them were worth more than all of what was stolen put together. That seems a little strange, doesn't it? Why rifle through all those disks when there was a fortune sitting on the mantelpiece in the next room?"

Struthers shrugged again. "I don't know," he said. "You'd have to ask the burglar."

"Detective Struthers, you testified that my client's name came up within a couple of hours. Were you the one to make that connection?"

For the first time, Struthers hesitated slightly. "No, District Attorney Stone read the police report and remembered this guy's MO," he replied at last. "It was real impressive. He had all the facts from the previous case up in his head already. When he suggested we look into him, we made the connection to the phone log."

Thane glanced back toward Stone. "So it was Mr. Stone who suggested you investigate the defendant."

"Yes, but we would have come up with it ourselves in time. Mr. Burns's dealings were well-known amongst our team."

"That was nice of Mr. Stone to give you all the credit today for putting my client on your radar. So it's safe to assume Mr. Stone knows a lot about my client's criminal history, since his office prosecuted him on a couple of occasions before . . ."

Stone tossed his pen on the table and stood. "Objection, Your Honor. Relevance?"

"Sustained." Judge Reynolds looked down at Thane. "Let's move this along."

"Detective Struthers, you said you reviewed the victim's phone records, but you didn't mention that those records also showed three calls to District Attorney Stone's office earlier that week. Why is that?"

The sound of the reporters' pens started scratching fast.

"Yes, we did see that. But I didn't feel that that's relevant."

"I'm sure you don't, Detective," Thane cut him off with a wave of his hand as he walked over to the jury box, facing them but still addressing Struthers. "So the DA calls and tells you who you should consider in your investigation, and when you look into it you find that this professional thief, a man who in all likelihood has only been caught a small fraction of the times he's broken the law, *called his work* from the home he was allegedly robbing? I'm not here to claim that my client is an honest man. His track record has shown otherwise. But I think history will also show he's not a *stupid* man."

Thane turned back around so that he was once again facing Struthers. "Detective, I can see why you say it was easy. In fact, in my opinion, it was suspiciously easy."

Stone once again stood. "Your Honor, is there a question in any of this?"

Before the judge could answer, Thane started walking back to his chair. "I think a lot of people here have a question, but it's not one the witness can answer. Nothing further, Your Honor."

As Thane retook his seat, Kristin leaned over. "What was all that about?"

"A start. But if it's going to work, I'm going to need you to focus your energy on figuring out what's on that missing disk. Or at the very least, find out what's on the other ones."

The next witness called was Roy Vale, a thirty-something factory supervisor who looked pissed he had to waste a weekend in court.

"Mr. Vale, you're the night supervisor at the B&D Factory, correct?" Stone asked.

"Yeah, that's right. Which means I should be asleep right now."

"Well, I appreciate your losing a little bit of sleep to assist in a murder trial. And the defendant, Scotty Burns, works for you?"

"He did. We had him cleaning up the floor during the night shift. Sweeping, cleaning up spills, that sort of shit. Ah, stuff."

Stone handed the witness a piece of paper. "This is a copy of a telephone log listing calls made from the victim's home the night of the murder. Do you recognize the highlighted number?"

Vale held the paper out in front of him, and after squinting like someone caught under a spotlight, he nodded and handed the page back to Stone.

"Yeah, that's my work number."

"And did you get a call from Mr. Burns that evening?"

"Yeah, he said he was sick or something and wasn't coming to work."

Stone turned away, looking satisfied. "No further questions, your Honor."

Thane rose, but remained standing behind his table. "Mr. Vale, how well do you know the defendant? Have you spent much time with him?"

"It's a factory, not a social club. I got work to do." Vale offered up a slight sneer, but Thane stared him down until he finally shifted his weight in the witness box and shook his head. "No, I don't spend time with him. I don't know nothing about him, except he's another of those parole losers we get sometimes."

"So if you don't know Mr. Burns very well, how did you recognize his voice?" Vale considered this but did not answer, so Thane continued. "If I were to play you a recording of five or six different people saying they were Scotty Burns, do you think you would be able to pick out my client's voice?"

"Lookit, the guy called and said he was Burns. You asking me did I recognize his voice? No. I'm just telling you what the guy said."

"Well, District Attorney Stone also said this was a slam-dunk case. Obviously, you can't always believe what someone says."

Stone sprung from his chair, but before he could sputter out any words, Thane raised his hand toward the judge. "I apologize, Your Honor. No further questions."

The last witness for the day on the side of the prosecution was a heavyset man in his early sixties named Willy Woolf. A bus driver for thirty years, the clothes on his back looked like things he'd owned for at least that long. The tip of his unfashionably thick green tie was frayed, but he was in court and obviously wanted to show the proper respect.

Woolf fidgeted in the witness box, trying to settle his bulk in the tiny chair. Stone asked him a few basic questions—his name, his age, his occupation—obviously trying to set the man at ease. But it only took a couple of minutes before the underarms of his shirt had soaked through to his sports coat. The DA's tone was unusually soothing, but Woolf looked as though he would rather be stuck in rush hour traffic with a bus full of screaming children.

Stone walked Woolf through his story, up until the point where Skunk was on the man's bus. "And it's your testimony, Mr. Woolf, that the defendant got off your bus at 17th and A Street around 8:30 the night of the murder?"

"Yes, sir," the witness said, then turned and leaned toward the microphone. "Yes, sir, that is correct."

"A stop only half a mile from the victim's home, only an hour from the time of the murder. No further questions."

Woolf emitted a booming sigh of relief, relaxing for the first time since reaching the stand. He started pulling himself up from the witness chair, but Judge Reynolds raised his hand.

"Not quite yet, Mr. Woolf. I tend to prefer giving both sides a chance to ask questions. I'm funny like that."

Woolf looked at the judge, flushed from embarrassment. Nodding, he sheepishly settled back down into his seat, taking out a handkerchief and dabbing his forehead before round two began.

Thane looked at his notepad for a moment, then turned his attention to the witness. "Mr. Woolf, how many people do you carry each evening on your bus?"

Woolf shifted in his seat, but managed to maintain eye contact with Thane. "Depends on the day, I suppose."

"How about on a Friday. Just give me an estimate. Would you say it's rare to have fewer than five hundred riders on a Friday?"

As the court waited for an answer, Thane saw Stone lightly nudge Winston, who smiled and nodded.

"Oh yeah," Woolf said, "definitely more than that. I got people coming on and off my bus all day long. Oh yeah, sure, more than that."

"And yet you can say with certainty that my client was on your bus the night in question. I must say I'm impressed."

Woolf beamed, relaxing under the compliment. "Thank you."

Judge Reynolds rapped his gavel to quiet the chuckling that rippled around the gallery, although he himself couldn't suppress a smile on his face. Thane pursued his point again.

"Can you please tell the court how you are able to say with certainty that Mr. Burns was on your bus on the night in question, given the number of riders you see each day?"

Woolf nodded, his smile dropping away, replaced with a look of concentration. "There weren't many people on the bus at the time. He was a talkative little feller—kind of twitchy, but seemed nice enough—so I asked him if he lived in the area and he said yeah, he lived around there, then he said he was going home but first he said he was going to a bar near there before walking on home. That's what he said."

"And you remember that?"

"Yeah, because there ain't no bars around there. I've lived in that neighborhood most my adult life, so I should know. So that sort of made me wonder what he was up to, not like it was a big deal or nothing, but that's how I remember him."

More than a few heads in the jury box whipped down, writing rapturously in their notebooks. Ferguson looked over at Thane and grinned, but the smile didn't reach his eyes. Hushed murmuring came from the spectators.

Thane froze for a moment. He glanced back over at Kristin, but all she could do was return his look. Finally he turned back toward Woolf. "And you're sure that was the twenty-eighth of July? Almost five months ago?"

"Yes, sir, because the next day I read about the murder and Mr. Gruber's address. I thought wouldn't it be something if that guy on my bus had done it, because he'd lied about the bar, and he had a limp. Paper said the guy who done it was limping. Course I didn't really believe he'd done it, otherwise I'd have called the police. After I saw his picture in the paper, though, I felt real stupid I hadn't told anybody about it, but you gotta believe me that at the time I didn't figure I was right. I sure remember thinking it, though."

Thane tried to speak, knowing the jury would pick up on his discomfort. He twice started to ask a follow-up question, but stopped himself before getting past the first syllable of the first word. He looked one more time at his notepad and finally faced the fact he had nowhere to go except back to his chair.

"Mr. Banning, are you through?" the judge asked.

Thane nodded and sat down. Kristin tried to meet his eyes, but Thane didn't return her look, frustrated enough with himself as he was. So Kristin waited a respectable thirty seconds before leaning over and whispering:

"Let me know if you want to bounce questions off me for the upcoming witnesses. Before you do anything else that stupid."

CHAPTER
TWENTY

Hours after the last witness stepped down from the stand, Gideon lumbered into a run-down Korean grocery store right before closing time. He had spent the last hour canvassing the stores that faced the park where Skunk claimed to have sat for hours the night of the murder. The neighborhood saw more than its share of violence on a regular basis, and store owners took note when Gideon walked through their door: he didn't just look like someone with a potential for violence; he looked like a man who carried it with him wherever he went.

After the trial's first day had wrapped, everyone working for the defense knew they had to come up with something to clear Skunk, which was why Gideon was stomping from store to store, having so far been met with indifference at best. But he was willing to see it through, because given Thane's disastrous performance in the courtroom, Gideon knew it would take a hell of a lot of luck to get someone like Skunk kicked free. It's not as though he felt some sort of obligation to help out Skunk—caring what happened to other people wasn't exactly his strong suit—he just didn't enjoy feeling like Thane's charity case.

This store was the ninth he had visited. He walked toward the front counter of the five-aisle grocery store where Mr. Song, the Korean storeowner who looked old enough to have nine or ten grandkids, was bent over slightly, feeling for something on the lower shelf.

Gideon shook his head. "You don't need your gun," he said. "I just want to ask you something."

Gideon held up a picture of Skunk, but it took a moment before Song was willing to take his coke-bottle glasses off the intimidating visitor to look at the photo. When he finally did, it wasn't long before he snapped his attention back to Gideon.

"Don't know him," Song said.

"Well, at least *pretend* to look carefully. Lookit, I'm not here to rob you. Just look at the damn picture."

Song huffed but did not reply.

"I'm trying to help somebody," Gideon said. "He says he was across the street in the park the night that detective got murdered. I just want to know if you remember seeing him. I know people around here don't like to get involved in nothing, but I'm trying to find someone who believes in doing the right thing. Don't need to say it was that night, 'cause it was a while ago, but does he look familiar?"

Song grudgingly took the picture from Gideon and studied it some more, scrunching his nose up as he handed it back.

"He stopped in my store one time, tried to steal a bottle of beer. Not just little bottle; one of a thirty-two ouncers. Told him get the hell out of my store. He then go sit in the park rest of night."

Gideon's eyebrows shot up. "You sure? When was that?"

"You said I didn't need to say what night," Song complained, but Gideon glared at him. "I don't remember. Many months ago maybe. I don't know."

Gideon held out his hand in appreciation, but the storeowner just stared at it. Gideon pulled it back and shoved it in his pocket. "Thank you. Somebody a whole lot nicer than me will probably be by to talk to you more about this."

He looked around and grabbed a couple of packs of gum off a shelf next to the cash register, pulling three bucks out of his front pocket and slapping them down. "You're a good man, even if you ain't very friendly."

Gideon walked out of the store and pumped his fist. He dug deep in his front pocket for some change, then looked up and down the street. He ended up walking fifteen blocks before finally coming across a payphone. He stuffed two quarters into the slot, then dialed and got the answering machine at Thane's office.

"Where the fuck all the payphones go while I was away?" Gideon asked. "Christ. Maybe you oughta get me one of them little phones. Anyway, I found somebody who remembers seeing Skunk. Korean dude works in a grocery store right across the park from where Skunk said he hung out. You need to talk to him. Name of the store is uh, Song Yi Convenience Goods." Gideon started hanging up, then brought the phone back up. "And I want a raise."

He hung up, chuckling to himself. This called for a beer. Maybe two. Thane never mentioned an expense account, but he figured he'd earned it.

Stone returned to his desk following a seven o'clock meeting with his staff that morning. He had been at the office since five, about an hour earlier than normal. Working twelve-hour days was not unusual for him, and that was only the time spent in his office. As DA, even going out to dinner with his wife was always work-related: a city event, a government function, a banquet honoring the latest name on the latest plaque. But he knew what he'd signed up for, and he wouldn't be running for re-election if he couldn't handle the life. And while the thought of running for higher office had crossed his mind more than once, he never wanted to be one of those Hollywood DAs that used the office as a ladder-rung to bigger, better things. This was where he could do the most good for the most people.

This was where he was meant to be.

He stood behind his desk looking through the list of calls taken by his secretary when Winston knocked on the open office door.

"You ready to review the security guard's testimony?" Winston asked.

Stone waved him in. "How's Sheri doing?" he asked, not looking up from the list of phone numbers.

"There are good days and bad days. I'll tell you what, you wouldn't believe how much her medical care runs. Without insurance, we'd be out on the street. Seriously. It's staggering, the cost of . . ." Winston trailed off, realizing his boss wasn't listening.

Stone looked closer at one of the telephone messages he was holding, making sure he had read it correctly. He thought for a moment, then jabbed at the intercom button. "Jeannie, have my car brought around. Now."

Winston walked over to Stone's desk. "What's up?"

Stone handed him the slip of paper. "This came in during this morning's meeting."

Winston read the note then looked up, concerned. "Want me to talk to him?"

"No, I'll do it. Something like this, I want him to understand we're not fucking around. He better make damn sure what he's saying." Stone grabbed his jacket and headed toward the door.

"Think there's any way it's true?"

"No. It's just a nuisance, but if I don't do it now, it'll turn into a headache later." Stone put on his suit coat and headed out his office. Chances were fifty-fifty this storeowner was either looking for publicity or didn't know what the hell he was talking about. As Stone walked down the hall, he couldn't remember if his secretary had written the name of the person calling in the tip.

Thane watched Gideon strut into his office without a scowl for the first time since working this case. He didn't look excited—not exactly—but he met both his and Kristin's eyes as he strode in, which was a first. Even his black T-shirt was tucked in, albeit only in the front.

Thane leaned back in his desk chair but didn't say anything, his hands knit behind his head. Kristin sat mute on the sofa, slouched against one of the cushions, looking exhausted. Gideon nodded at her, then sat down across from Thane.

"You get my message?" Gideon asked.

"Yeah, I did."

Gideon waited for a moment, but when Thane didn't say more, his smile started to fade. "I kind of thought you'd be happy. Like a 'thank you' or somethin'. Like maybe I was actually earning my keep around here. Ain't you ever heard of positive reinforcements?"

Thane sat up in his chair, looking beaten down. "I appreciate the effort, really I do. But Mr. Song says now he's not sure he saw Skunk at all."

Gideon slammed his hands on the desk. "I'll get him to remember." His eyes were wild, like a boxer who'd just weathered a body blow and wanted to return the favor.

Thane waved him off. "Forget it. He won't testify. You did a great job, but it's not going to happen."

"What the hell happened?"

"I have my suspicions."

Kristin pulled herself off the sofa. "Stone?"

Thane nodded.

"But how?" she asked. "Gideon just called last night."

Thane leaned back and stared up at the ceiling. "Now that's something I *don't* understand."

"Damn, this day's starting to suck," Gideon said.

"If you think it's bad now," Thane said, "wait until you hear who's been added to this morning's witness list, after the neighborhood security guard testifies."

"Another fucking bus driver?" Gideon asked.

"Yoder," Thane said. "And knowing that asshole guard, he'll do anything he can to finish us off."

CHAPTER
TWENTY-ONE

OURT GOT OFF TO A slow start that morning. One of the jurors had tried to beg off duty to get back to work, resulting in a long conversation in the judge's chambers. By the time the actual testimony began—with the complaining juror once again firmly ensconced in his seat—it was well after eleven.

The first witness of the day, Wes Omernik, was already up and striding toward the witness box before the bailiff could finish pronouncing his name. The security guard who had chased the suspect the night of the murder marched toward the stand like a champion boxer climbing into the ring. Thane noticed a laundry tag safety-pinned to the back of the man's jacket.

Stone was brief with his questions. He quickly led Wes through his credentials, including his years at the company that patrolled Detective Gruber's neighborhood, and asked about the events leading up to seeing the intruder. After spending considerable time on the suspect's limp, Stone had Skunk limp across the floor in front of Wes, despite Thane's objections. After walking back and forth in front of the witness stand a couple of times, Stone once again turned back to his eager witness.

"Having now seen the defendant walk, you are testifying that his limp is consistent with the man you chased on July twenty-eighth?" Stone asked.

"Objection," Thane said. "The phrase 'consistent with' is inappropriately vague."

Stone shook his head and rolled his eyes for the jury's behalf. "What I'm asking is, is that how the man you saw moved?"

Judge Reynolds angled his head at Thane, directing the lawyer to retake his seat. "Overruled. The jury understands what the prosecution meant."

Wes turned towards the jury. "I've been in law enforcement for over six years, and it is my professional opinion that the defendant's limp is, indeed, consistent with the man I chased on July twenty-eighth. I would stake my career as a lawman on it."

Stone cleared his throat. "Thank you, Mr. Omernik. No further questions."

Thane rose before Stone took his seat. "I'd like a more exact comparison, if you don't mind," Thane said. "Please tell me when you think my limp is identical, not consistent with, but *identical* to that of the defendant."

It was Stone's turn to shout out an objection. Thane faced the judge.

"Your Honor," he said, "I want to make sure the witness can identify the same limp on somebody else, not simply when the defendant walks for him. That's like having a one-person line up. I don't believe that's asking too much."

Judge Reynolds nodded in agreement. "Overruled. Proceed, Mr. Banning, but let's not make a production out of this."

"Mr. Omernik, I'm going to start limping in front of you. I want you to tell me when my limp is the exact same as the individual you saw the night of the murder."

Thane started walking back and forth between the defense table and the jury box, starting with a slow, subtle limp, gradually making it more pronounced until the security guard called out.

"That's about right."

Thane continued limping slowly back and forth across the floor. "So this is what the defendant looked like as he ran away?"

"Yes, sir."

"You're positive?"

"Yes, I'm positive."

Thane slowed down his pace even further, but continued limping.

"That's interesting, because I'm limping on the opposite leg from the defendant." He walked for a few seconds more, giving everybody time to take note, then stopped in front of the witness box.

"Well, I . . . that's not what I was . . ."

"Objection," Stone shouted. "Counsel was stressing the pace of the limp, not the accuracy of the leg."

Thane turned toward the judge, not to Stone. "I never said anything about the pace. I said for him to let me know when the limp was identical to that of the person he saw the night of the murder. Surely the leg of the limp matters."

Reynolds paused for just a moment, then shook his head. "Sustained. Counsel, you were a bit misleading in your presentation."

Thane shrugged slightly, then turned back to the witness. "Then let me ask you this, Mr. Omernik: I limped in such a way as to look like the defendant. Doesn't it stand to reason, therefore, that somebody else could have done the same thing the night of the murder?"

Wes eyed Thane suspiciously. "Maybe," he finally said. "But I don't know why anybody would do that."

Thane stepped up next to the witness stand and looked Wes over, sizing him up. "I understand you've been trying to join the police force, so I'm sure you work to keep fit."

"I spend my time in the gym, if that's what you mean."

"So you're saying you're just in average shape?"

"No, I'm in excellent shape. I was quarterback in high school, made first team conference two years in a row."

"Objection, Your Honor," Stone said wearily. "What in the world does this have to do with anything?"

Before the judge could respond, Thane looked at the jury and said, "I was just wondering how a man with such a pronounced limp managed to outrun the witness?"

Reynolds nodded. "Objection overruled. Proceed."

"Well?" Thane asked. "Weren't you surprised to find the man had disappeared when you reached the backyard?"

Wes gave Thane a hostile look. "Well, it was dark. And he did have a head start."

"Yes, I understand that, but you're obviously in great shape, and you said you weren't all that far behind him when he went around the side of the house. So honestly, weren't you at least a *little* bit surprised that somebody running with a limp that bad was able to cross the backyard and get through the bushes before you even got there?"

Wes paused, then hesitantly admitted, "Yeah, I guess I was kind of surprised."

Thane turned and walked back toward the defense table. "Don't feel bad, Mr. Omernik. Maybe the man didn't really have a limp after all. No further questions."

The Court's lunch recess was almost over, after which Yoder would be called to the witness box. Thane had no appetite. He stood in the small meeting room assigned to the defense team, gazing out the window. He loosened his tie and opened the top button of his shirt, but he still felt winded.

Kristin sat at a table reading through her notes from that morning, occasionally glancing up at Thane. Gideon leaned against a wall nearby, watching Thane closely. He looked up at the clock over the door, then walked over and joined Thane in looking outside at nothing in particular. Without taking his eye off the street below, Gideon asked, "You ready?"

Thane didn't respond. A four-car pile-up could have taken place outside and he probably wouldn't have noticed. He was someplace in the past.

Kristin put down her pen. "So who's this guy again?" she finally asked.

Gideon glanced at Thane. When he didn't answer, Gideon spoke for him.

"Name's Yoder. Prison guard at Forsman. He's just a stupid redneck who probably got kicked around as a pup, and now he likes doing the same to others. If he was married he'd probably take it out on his wife, too, but I can't imagine there's a woman dumb enough to go on a second date with him."

"There's not much we can do to refute his testimony, is there?" Kristin asked. "It's going to be his word against our client's, since nobody else was around. Not even sure it makes sense to cross-examine him. Probably best to let him say what he's got to say and get him off the stand."

"I don't want to make it that easy for him," Thane said as he finally turned around, leaning against the windowsill. His voice sounded hollow.

Gideon walked over and took a chair across from Kristin, turning it so that he faced Thane. "You know there's nothing I'd like more than to see that asshole taste his own blood in front of everybody in that courtroom, but what the fuck can you do? Vengeance is mine, sayeth the lawyer, but just probably not today."

Kristin looked at her notes. "At the deposition, Mr. Yoder—"

Thane brusquely cut her off. "It's just Yoder. Don't dignify him."

She paused a moment, looking surprised at the harshness of his tone. "Yoder said Mr. Burns made a veiled threat to him while being escorted to his cell, saying now that he'd murdered a cop, there was nothing stopping him from taking a shot at anybody else in the prison."

"Bullshit," Gideon responded, spitting the word onto the floor. "If Yoder thought Skunk was saying anything to him other than 'yes sir' or 'no sir', ol' Skunk would be nothing but a bag of bones by now."

"I'm not saying I believe it," Kristin said, "I'm just saying there's no way to disprove it. And given the choice between believing a prison guard or a thief, who do you think they're going to believe? The jury doesn't know Mr.—doesn't know Yoder—like you guys do."

"Then maybe we need to introduce him," Thane said. "Gideon and I know more about him than he realizes. Plus, he's an arrogant prick."

"And dumb as plywood," Gideon added.

Thane walked over and picked up his papers, sliding them into his briefcase. Kristin's observation was dead on target, but he was hoping his knowledge of the guard's history would be their ace in the hole. He didn't know if Yoder had ever testified in court before, but if he thought of Thane as a lawyer rather than an ex-con, there might be an opportunity.

Kristin turned to Gideon. "Why's this guy going to all this trouble to screw over Skunk?"

"He's not after Skunk," Thane said. "He's after me."

He picked up his briefcase and started toward the door. Every previous encounter with Yoder had been inside Forsman, but today the guard was on his turf. He knew the law, he knew his prey: now it was time for Yoder to see what could happen when force wasn't an option.

"Let's go," Thane said. "It's time for Yoder to suffer for his sins."

Kristin paused a moment, then hopped up and raced over to walk with him. Gideon rose slowly. "Maybe vengeance is ours after all," he said, grinning.

Whereas Detective Struthers was every prosecutor's dream witness, Yoder was a ball of lightning on the witness stand. Even Stone had to have picked up on the sadistic streak running through this man. It was obvious to all that Yoder wasn't a bad ass just when the situation called for it: he was wired that way. But Thane knew Yoder's testimony was too important for the DA to ignore. The guard had reported Skunk's alleged comments to the Warden, who then contacted the DA's office. Stone most likely talked with the Warden to make sure there weren't any possible ulterior motives that would have caused Yoder to concoct this story; perhaps Yoder didn't like Skunk. Thane could imagine the Warden laughing, telling Stone that Yoder didn't like anybody.

So far, though, Yoder was getting a passing grade on the witness stand. He actually cleaned up pretty well, and he answered each of Stone's questions clearly and concisely, even tossing in an occasional 'yes sir', a sign of professionalism Thane never would have guessed resided within the coarse man. That's not to say the words sounded comfortable on Yoder's lips, but he appeared to be coming across to the jury as a credible enough witness.

Thane looked at his notes until Judge Reynolds asked if he was ready to cross-examine. He slowly lifted his head until he was facing Yoder directly for the first time since the guard had taken the stand. Thane stared at him, expressionless, then moved to a point about eight feet in front of the witness box.

"You say the defendant just . . . freely offered to you that he had killed an ex-detective. Even while claiming innocence to everybody else in the prison. Doesn't that seem a bit odd to you?"

"To be honest, I always thought ol' Skunk was a little odd to begin with." Yoder chuckled.

"Your Honor, please direct the witness to refer to the defendant as Mr. Burns. I don't have the patience for this sort of insolence."

"It's the court's patience that I'm concerned about, Mr. Banning," Reynolds said. The judge then turned toward Yoder. "Witness shall refer to the defendant as either 'the defendant,' or 'Mr. Burns.'"

"Sorry, Your Honor."

Thane offered Yoder a subtle smile. "Apology accepted." He could see the guard's teeth clench as his face flushed with anger.

"You've been a guard at Forsman Prison," Thane continued, "for almost twenty years, as the District Attorney mentioned. And you've held that same rank all those years. There have been a few difficult points in your time at Forsman, haven't there?"

Stone raised his hand toward the judge. "Objection, Your Honor. The witness deserves better than to be submitted to character assassination by the defense."

Thane turned toward Stone, holding up his hands, palms out. "I haven't even said anything yet. What makes you think I'm planning on attacking this man's reputation?"

Reynolds rapped his gavel, redirecting Thane's attention toward the bench. "Mr. Banning, I'm going out on a limb and guessing that what you're about to offer is not exactly warm and fuzzy. If that is true, what is the relevance?"

"Credibility, Your Honor. District Attorney Stone mentioned some of the witness's accomplishments during his time at Forsman. I feel I deserve a bit of leeway to establish the other side. Besides, Your Honor, what I'm about to review with the witness is documented and on the record. It simply shows a day in the life of a prison guard. And to be honest, I don't think even the witness will consider this hostile questioning."

The judge studied Thane carefully. "Proceed, Mr. Banning, but I can assure you this won't take long."

"Yes, sir." Thane walked back to his table and picked up his notepad. As he glanced up, he noticed Hannah in the back of the room. He froze: seeing her in the courtroom brought back memories of her sitting behind him during his trial five years ago. He wanted to walk her out, to shepherd her away from this place, but at the same time he found her presence reassuring, reminding him why he was there, why he was doing what he was doing. He paused, then turned back towards the witness box.

"Eight years ago, you killed an inmate, Joey Sanchez, who you said came at you with a knife, is that correct?"

"Yeah, that's right. Sanchez pulled a knife he had somehow gotten hold of, and started toward me. I drew my handgun, directed him twice to stop, but he didn't, so I put him down."

"You shot him."

"That's right."

"You killed him."

"That's what we're trained to do," Yoder said. "Anybody who thinks I should have tried to shoot the knife from his hand watches too many movies. There were scores of witnesses, and the review showed I did everything by the book."

"I didn't mean to imply you had done anything wrong. You're correct: the record is quite clear and confirms what you just told us. In fact, I believe you received a commendation for your actions. I simply want to review some of these incidents, then I will ask my question."

Thane returned his attention to his notes. He felt strong, finally having this man in his arena, being forced to answer his questions. He would have liked to ask Yoder a whole host of questions under oath, few of which pertained to this trial, but he knew the answers would be lies.

"Over the next four years, you had to 'put down' Pauly Giradello in the laundry room, Howard Jameson in his cell, and Corey Carlson in the courtyard. Each time you claimed the inmate in question was coming at you with malicious intent."

"Yeah, inmates in a maximum-security prison sometimes tend to have 'malicious intent'. But in each instance I was cleared."

"Yes. Again, the record shows that."

Stone half-lifted his hand in the air. "Your Honor, any possibility of moving to something actually relevant to the matter at hand?"

"Your Honor," Thane said, "I have just one more incident. I feel these are important for the jury to get a sense of the responsibilities of a prison guard."

"I'm not sure they're important at all, but you may offer one more—and then I'd appreciate it if you could question the witness regarding something related to this case."

Thane looked at a blank page and pretended to be reading something; the prison grapevine, which had always been surprisingly accurate, was about to be introduced into a court of law.

"And a year and a half ago, you killed Ricky Hernandez while he was working in the prison kitchen. You claimed self-defense on this one as well. Said he came at you with a frying pan and you had to beat him back with your metal baton, resulting in his death."

Gideon looked up at the name Ricky Hernandez, then immediately returned his focus to the floor.

Yoder paused for a moment, then nodded. "That's correct. I didn't have time to pull out my gun, he was that fast. A frying pan may not sound like much of a threat to most people, but if it had hit my head, I wouldn't be here today."

"You remember the incident that clearly?"

"Hernandez was a hard man. He came at me, I figured I wasn't gonna live to see retirement. I got lucky."

Thane nodded. "I'm sure you were quite scared."

Yoder gave a piercing glare at Thane's choice of words. "I wasn't scared. But it was him or me. I still remember that look in his eyes."

Thane turned and positioned himself in front of the jury box. "Then why, in your official report, did you state that Tony Hernandez had been beaten by a fellow inmate in the kitchen?"

Stone glanced quickly at Winston then started to rise, but Judge Reynolds caught his movement and with his palm turned downward directed Stone to return to his seat. Gideon put his hand over his mouth to hold back from laughing out loud.

"I don't know about—I'm not sure that's correct," Yoder stammered.

Thane pulled out a report and handed it to the judge. "I'd like to submit the official prison report related to this event. The witness's statement was that he came across inmate Hernandez lying against the wall, bleeding to death, his head caved in by a small rolling pin used by prison cafeteria workers. A rolling pin, by the way, the same dimension as a guard's metal baton. He claimed the incident took place before he got there, and there was nothing he could do to save the prisoner. He said the reason the man's blood was all over his uniform was because he tried to resuscitate him."

Yoder started squirming. He glanced at Stone, then over at the judge. "I remember that now. I got the names mixed up with another time, is all."

Thane walked quickly toward the witness box until he was standing immediately in front of Yoder. "It was only a little more than a year ago."

"Like I said, I just got the names mixed up."

"But there are no other reports where you beat a man to death with your baton for coming at you with a frying pan, so it's not as though you just got the names mixed up. Tell me: why the sudden change in stories? Why did you tell the prison inquiry board that you came across Mr. Hernandez after he had been beaten, but today you said you killed him in self-defense? No, I remember now: *the look in his eyes*. Very scary."

"You said I killed him with the baton. That's what you said," Yoder yelped.

"But you were certainly quick to agree with it. Almost looked as though you were reliving that frightful day all over again. Except, of course, for the fact it never happened."

Yoder glared at him, probably one breath away from launching himself over the top of the witness box and onto Thane. He then turned and gave a death glare toward Gideon, who scratched the side of his nose with his middle finger.

"Is it possible you simply couldn't remember which lie you told regarding this inmate's death?" Thane asked.

Yoder leaned forward, grabbing the front of the jury box. "I'm telling you that Skunk told me—"

Thane wheeled back toward Yoder. "I told you not to call him—"

"Fuck what you want! That piece of shit told me he beat that cop down and that he'd do the same to me."

Reynolds banged his gavel and turned toward Yoder, but Thane didn't slow down.

"But the detective was *shot*, not beaten," Thane said. "You're the one who beats people to death. Sure you don't want to retry your story yet again?"

Stone rose. "Your Honor, there's obviously been some misunderstanding on the part of the witness. I suggest the counsel for the defense ask any more questions he might have regarding Mr. Yoder's earlier testimony . . ."

Thane waved Stone off. "Why should I waste a second more of my time talking to this witness?"

"Your Honor!" Stone shouted.

The judge nodded his agreement. "Mr. Banning, if you have no other questions, I shall dismiss this witness."

"No further questions, Your Honor. However, I hope the District Attorney's office will look further into the events described during today's testimony. It's clear the witness should be dismissed from more than just this witness stand."

CHAPTER TWENTY-TWO

OURT ADJOURNED IMMEDIATELY AFTER THANE finished with Yoder, but many of the spectators were slow to leave, talking amongst themselves. When the bailiff started directing the crowd to leave the courtroom, Thane stood to see if Hannah was still at the back. Yes, there she was—but unlike the other gawkers, there was no curiosity in her eyes. Just shining admiration.

Thane picked his way through the crowd towards her, pulling her to the side to let the mob skirt by them, most of them not hiding their stares. "I didn't know you were coming today."

"I didn't either. It was just the spur of the moment. I hope you don't mind." She reached over and took his hand. "I was afraid I would make you nervous."

"I'll be nervous all the time until this is finished. I appreciate the support."

"Is that guard someone you knew at Forsman?" she asked hesitantly.

"He was there. Nothing special." If and when he ever felt comfortable talking about Forsman, he wouldn't give Yoder a significant role in that story. He put his arm around his wife's waist and turned toward the door.

"Buy you a drink?" he asked.

"I have to close the store this afternoon. Why don't you come by around six and we can get a drink then? My treat."

"Deal. I'll see you there."

As he turned to rejoin his colleagues, Hannah put her hand on his shoulder. "Thane? You were really impressive today." She leaned over and kissed his cheek, then exited the courtroom.

He walked back to the defense table where Kristin was reading a document, pretending not to have been watching them. Gideon, on the other hand, simply chuckled as Thane approached.

"You had a good day there, Counselor."

Kristin sprang up, her eyes looking as though they could start emitting sparks of electricity. "Oh my God, that was so amazing. You rocked up there. When you started reading from the official record and Yoder's face just froze up and he started sweating . . . I swear to God I thought smoke was going to start pouring out his ears like in the cartoons. Jesus—that was better than sex."

Thane and Gideon looked at each other, then started laughing.

"Damn, girl," Gideon said. "I know crackheads mellower than you."

Thane looked at the now-empty witness chair. During all his time at Forsman, he never imagined he would get to do something like that. He just hoped his stunt had worked—that Yoder would get arrested, or at least thrown out of Forsman for good.

The three of them exited the courtroom and started down the long marble corridor leading to the elevators. Immediately they were mobbed by reporters like hornets streaming out of the trees.

"What was your experience with Mr. Yoder while at Forsman?" a bleach-blonde reporter hollered out to him, her deep voice rising above the maelstrom. "Did he ever mistreat you?"

Thane held his hand up, futilely attempting to quiet the pack of journalists. "What you heard today was just one example of Yoder's abuses. I'd love to comment more, but my guess is that this will become a legal matter soon, so I'd rather leave it up to the police. But if it doesn't get looked into further, I hope you'll be asking why."

Thane and his team walked on down the hall, ignoring the second volley of questions. Thane was trying to find a quicker way out of the building when he saw Hannah being hassled by a TV reporter and cameraman. She looked like she was trying to move past them, but the reporter kept blocking her way forward, and his cameraman was keeping her from retreating.

Thane turned and moved quickly down the hall toward her with long, determined strides, leaving Gideon and Kristin behind. As he neared, he heard Hannah trying to politely get away from Jag Colter, the court reporter for Channel 4. His jet-black hair was slicked back—Thane could almost smell the styling mousse caked in it.

"I just want to know if you support your husband taking on this case," Colter asked. "How's he been since his release? What do you say to accusations that he's risking a man's life because of his dislike for the District Attorney?" He jabbed a microphone in front of Hannah, who flinched backward.

"Please stop," Hannah pleaded. "Just leave me alone. I'm trying to ask you nicely."

Hannah put her arms out in the hope that she could gently move Colter to the side, but he was too sturdy for her to budge. The obese cameraman behind her kept crowding closer, his lights coming dangerously close to burning her.

"A lot of people feel Mr. Burns is going to get the death penalty because your husband's desire for revenge is keeping him from accepting a plea deal."

Suddenly Thane's voice boomed off the marble walls.

"Leave her alone."

Thane pushed past the cameraman, causing the large man to stumble a couple of steps to the side, though he didn't stop filming.

Hannah turned and took hold of Thane's arm. "It's okay. I'm all right."

He shook his arm free with one strong movement. Colter's eyes lit up.

"Jag Colter, KXLA News. I wanted to know how your wife feels about you putting a man's life at risk?"

"She has nothing to say to you. If you want to be an asshole, come at me, but leave her alone, understand?" He tried steering Hannah around the microphone, but Colter leaned around Thane.

"Mrs. Banning, has it been difficult having your husband back after so many years?" As he thrust his arm past Thane, the microphone got too close and struck Hannah in the forehead.

In an instant, Thane had grabbed the reporter by the lapels of his jacket, picking him up off his feet. Colter's eyes grew round as the distance between him and the floor kept increasing. Thane carried him across the corridor and slammed him against the cold marble wall. The cameraman never pulled his eyes away from the viewfinder, though he did take a few steps back.

Colter looked shaken, but his voice never wavered. "You learn that move in Forsman?" he asked.

Thane shoved the smirking reporter to the ground. "Keep the hell away from her! Didn't you do enough damage the first time?"

Colter tried holding his microphone up toward Hannah. "Mrs. Banning, has your husband been violent with you as well?"

Thane knocked the microphone out of Colter's hand; it spun down the hall like a game of spin the bottle. "I said, leave her alone!" he roared.

By now, the other reporters were making a mad dash toward this breaking story. Thane saw them coming and turned to Hannah, who looked lost, her eyes glazed over.

"Get out of here," he said.

"Thane, what are you doing? Come with me."

She started toward him, but froze as he wheeled on her.

"Leave, damn it!"

She looked at Thane, who only minutes ago had been holding her hand. Her expression grew hard, as did her voice. "I may have to."

Thane stopped cold. He watched her turn and walk down the corridor away from the approaching reporters, slowly at first, then breaking into a run as if chased by ghosts. She reached the stairwell at the end of the hall, shoving the bar on the door open and disappearing down the dimly lit stairs.

The reporters caught up with Thane, who positioned himself firmly between them and the door through which Hannah had just vanished. They began peppering him with questions, not one of them checking to see if their fellow journalist, who was gingerly lifting himself up off the floor, was injured.

From the rear of the pack, Gideon forced his way through toward Thane. Kristin followed close behind him, like a running back following her All-Pro blocker. When they reached him, Gideon said to Kristin:

"Get him out of here."

She walked over and lightly placed her hand on Thane's shoulder. He looked at her with a face full of fury. She pulled back slightly, then once again rested her hand on him, turning him toward where Hannah had just escaped.

"Come on. Let's go outside. She's safe now."

As Thane and Kristin turned and started toward the stairwell, he glanced back and saw Jag Colter brushing himself off and looking over at his cameraman with a gleam in his eye, his hair somehow still perfectly coiffed.

"Tell me you got that," Thane heard him say.

The heavyset man held up his camera like a trophy and grinned, as though he'd just won a free dinner.

"Hell yeah."

CHAPTER TWENTY-THREE

THANE SAT AT THE BAR at Tucker's, a musty hole-in-the-wall joint he always passed on his way to Hannah's bookstore. At three thirty in the afternoon, the only patrons were himself and a couple of derelicts. He had been in the bar for less than five minutes, just long enough to throw down a shot of whiskey and rebuke himself for sitting in a bar, rather than finding Hannah.

He looked at the other two men sitting three stools down from him, draped over their drinks as if afraid someone was going to run by and snatch them. He caught his own reflection in the mirror, lurched over as well. He shook himself, grabbed a mint from the ashtray, threw a ten-dollar bill on the counter, and slid off his bar stool.

He walked down the sidewalk, still wired from court and his encounter with Jag Colter. He'd never wanted to feel like this, but he could sense a kind of bitterness worming its way down inside of him, like termites in an old house. Bitterness toward Bradford Stone, who let him go to prison for a crime he didn't commit; toward the bastard that had killed Lauren; and toward the whole blasted system that had torn his life apart, fractured his marriage, and poisoned his soul. Perhaps a better man would know how to move on, how to put it all behind him—but he was not that man. At least this time, when he saw Hannah getting hassled, he'd been able to stand by her side and protect her.

But he hadn't stood by her side: he'd yelled at her.

The look in her eye made him wince whenever the image bullied its way back into his consciousness. The fear in the face of the woman he loved, confusion as she tried to understand why the man she loved was acting like an ugly drunk.

He entered the bookstore, this time not caring whether there were customers inside or not; but the only person he saw was Caitlin, curled up in her usual chair. She glanced up at him, her eyes springing wide. Her mouth dropped open a couple of inches, but nothing came out.

"I need to talk to Hannah," he told her.

She stumbled up out of her chair, clutching the book to her chest like a shield. She glanced toward Hannah's office, then back at Thane, throwing her shoulders back and trying not to sound so much like a kid.

"She's not here. She's not working today."

"She told me she was closing up this afternoon. She in the back?"

Caitlin shifted back and forth on her feet and pushed back a lock of hair that kept falling over her left eye. "You shouldn't be here."

"That's not for you to decide," Thane said.

He started toward the back of the store. Caitlin looked as though she was going to step between him and the hall, but she quickly backed out of the way, her hand going up to her mouth and then back to her side.

"I'm serious, you really shouldn't be here. Right now . . . it's not a good time. Please believe me." She nervously glanced at her watch.

Thane didn't break his stride. As he neared the door, Caitlin was still calling out to him. "I'll call the police. I mean it. Please, you need to leave."

Thane paused in front of the office door, but only to catch his breath. He lightly tapped on the door, then slowly opened it after he hadn't gotten a response. Hannah sat, staring at the top of her desk, her fingers steepled in front of her mouth.

"Hi," he offered, keeping his voice soft. Hannah didn't look up.

He walked into the office, shutting the door behind him. "I was worried about you. I'm sorry about this afternoon. I don't know what to say. It's just . . . when I saw that reporter harassing you, it brought back memories of the first trial, when I wasn't around to protect you."

She spoke without taking her eyes off the clean desktop. "I didn't feel protected. I felt threatened."

Her voice was quiet and flat, betraying no emotion whatsoever. "I'm sorry. That wasn't what I meant to do."

She finally looked up at him. Her eyes were red and she looked exhausted, beaten down. "Thane, I just want you back."

"You have me."

She leaned back in her chair. "No. I don't. I felt like I was starting to, but then you took this case. Now you're slipping away, just like I was afraid you would."

He walked over and stood in front of her desk, glancing at the chair next to him, but afraid that if he sat down he wouldn't have the strength to stand again. "I have to do this."

Hannah jumped up from her chair. "*No you don't.*" She stopped and took a deep breath. "No, you *don't* have to do this. You're *choosing* to do this."

Thane looked into his wife's face—and for a moment, he could have done it. He could have walked away from the trial, from Skunk, from Bradford Stone . . . But the moment passed as quickly as it had come. He wished he could explain what he was trying to do, but he couldn't conjure the words. Of everyone he knew Gideon, and probably Joseph, would understand. But not Hannah. Never Hannah.

"I'm hoping this will allow me to move on."

She looked at him as if he were a puzzle. A curiosity. She closed her eyes, her jaw working as she thought. Finally, she shook her head.

"I don't understand how."

"I know you don't. I wish you could trust me."

She opened her eyes again. "Trust you? Who is it I'm trusting?"

She stared at him, waiting for an answer. Then her voice grew quieter, but strong like a wire. "You need to decide. Are we going to move forward—together—or are you going to keep waging war with the past? With Stone. With Forsman. I waited five years for you, Thane. I'm not going to wait any longer."

He knew she was serious. Although she had obviously been thinking about everything since the incident at the courthouse, he felt she had just come to this conclusion. He had spent five years wishing he could get back to Hannah, and she was finally back in his life. Things could go back to the way they used to be.

And yet . . .

"I have to do this," Thane said at last.

"Then do it alone."

She looked up at him, her eyes glassy. Thane couldn't move, struck with the sudden fear that if he left her office, he might never see her again.

"Stone knew I was innocent, but he convicted me anyway. I will not let him do that to another innocent man. I won't."

"This isn't about him," she said plaintively. "Baby, this is about you and me. Right now, there's just you and me. It wasn't easy for me either, you know. I waited years for you—"

"I never asked you to."

She slammed her hand on the desk, jolting it from the force of the blow. "Goddamn you—that wasn't your decision to make. It almost killed me when you cut me off. But now you're home and I will not lose you a second time because of another one of your stubborn choices."

Now the tears started to flow.

"Thane," she almost screamed, "why are you doing this to us?"

Her sobbing filled the room. Thane started to move toward her when the office door flung open. In the doorway stood a man Thane had never seen before.

"Get the fuck away from her, you son of a bitch."

Thane's body tensed. The familiar alarm of violence again flooded his body. He wanted to look over at Hannah, but he wasn't about to take his eyes off this man. "Who the hell are you?"

"Paul, don't," Hannah said. "What are you doing here?"

Paul stared at Thane for a moment longer. "Caitlin called me when you got back. Said you had returned from the courthouse all upset, she thought you might need someone to talk to. I just wanted to see if you were okay."

"She doesn't need help," Thane said. "I don't know who you are, but this is between my wife and me. You need to leave. Now."

"I don't give a damn what you want." Paul locked his hand into a fist, then started to move around Thane to get to Hannah, but Thane stepped in his way.

"This is between Hannah and me. She's fine. Just go."

Paul tried to brush by him, but the moment the other man touched him, Thane felt an electric jolt surge through him. When Paul grabbed hold of Thane's wrist, he maneuvered his hand up and over his attacker's wrist, instinctively twisting the arm and forcing the other man to the floor—the same maneuver that had saved his life so many times at Forsman. He kept the pressure on Paul's wrist, pushing it backward, subduing him with minimal effort.

"Thane," Hannah said. "Please don't . . ."

"I don't want to fight you," Thane said to Paul, trying desperately to keep the jagged edge out of his voice. "I'm just trying to talk to my wife. I don't know who the hell you are, but I understand you're trying to help her. But she doesn't need it. You don't want to push this any further."

"Or what? Are you going to kill me too?"

"No, but you'll get hurt," Thane said.

"Paul, it's okay. Really."

Paul struggled a moment longer, then finally stopped. Thane waited a moment before letting go, but he knew what would happen. There was a pause, then as Paul rose from the floor, he sprang at Thane, his right arm swinging through the air like a club; but Thane leaned back, just as the fist slashed by his head. He brought his left fist up into Paul's stomach, forcing whatever air was left in the lungs to burst out. Hannah started to scream, but Thane could barely hear her. Two more rapid blows to the stomach, solid hits like he was working a punching bag, then a cracking left uppercut under the chin. This last strike sent Paul wheeling into the edge of a file cabinet. He crumbled to the floor, sitting dazed against the bottom drawer.

"Stop it!" Hannah screamed as she scrambled around her desk, shoving her way past Thane and dropping to the floor beside Paul.

Thane's teeth ground against each other, red tinting his vision at the corners. His focus disappeared, however, when he saw his wife kneeling down and putting her hand on the man's head, stroking it. She looked up at Thane, and this time, there was no fear in her face—only rage.

"*Get out,*" she said.

Thane just stood there looking at the two of them, stunned.

"I said get out!" Hannah shouted again.

Thane turned and staggered out of the room, his breath gone, feeling as though he had taken every punch he'd just thrown.

CHAPTER
TWENTY-FOUR

THANE STOOD IN THE AISLE of a dingy drugstore, staring blankly at a row of toothbrushes. The store was only a few blocks from his office, but he'd never come inside before today: the shelves were bent and all half-empty, the chipped linoleum floor was littered with gum wrappers and magazine inserts, and even the safety-sealed packaging was yellowing. A strong aroma filled the store, almost a medicinal smell, or like the scent of men's deodorant.

He still couldn't get his bearings. He'd returned to the apartment from the bookstore to collect some things, but as he threw handfuls of clothes into a gym bag, his head was spinning, as if he'd just stepped off the Tilt-a-Whirl at the fair. He hadn't thought to get anything from the bathroom, which is why he now found himself here, staring at toothbrushes for the last five minutes.

He shook himself and grabbed a toothbrush at random, then dragged himself over to the aspirin. The expiration date on the box had passed two months ago, which almost made him laugh—who'd ever seen expired aspirin before? Glancing at some of the other boxes on the shelf, he saw that more than a quarter of them were expired. Five years ago, he would have been outraged: tonight he simply tossed the aspirin into his basket.

As he searched for shaving cream, he felt eyes on him. It wasn't the store cashier, who was focused on a bum pretending to check prices on mouthwash. Thane didn't turn around right away. Instead, he tossed a pack of razor blades into his basket, then discreetly scanned the store as he turned around. He saw no one. It was probably nothing, but five years in Forsman had taught him to trust his instincts.

He walked toward the cashier as the front door was closing. He sat his basket on the counter, and as his items were being rung up, he walked over and peered out the door, but didn't see anything. He was used to being watched everywhere he went, but this felt different. The cashier took his money and made change without taking his eye off the guy studying the mouthwash.

Thane walked out of the store carrying the thin paper bag with his items. He surveyed the street stealthily, but the few people he saw walking at that late hour looked like they belonged to the neighborhood. Making his way down the sidewalk, he stopped to look in a liquor store window, using the reflection to try and spot anybody following.

There—he picked up the shadow of a person across the street, moving close to the side of a decrepit brick building.

He turned, ready for the confrontation, but the shadowy figure slipped down the alley that ran parallel to his office building. The streetlight on the corner had burned out, so the street was dark. Thane reached into his bag and tore open the pack of razor blades, then stomped on the plastic casing and picked up one of the blades, placing it between his first and second knuckle as he formed a fist. He crossed the street.

He kept close to the building until he reached the alleyway, paused, then stepped forward quickly, his fist holding the razor at chest-level. But there was no one there. He couldn't see very far into the alley and didn't hear any movement. The fire escape on the building opposite his was pulled down, but the one attached to his building was a good eight feet off the ground, impossible to reach from the outside.

He took a couple of steps into the alley, then stopped and listened again. The alley was nothing but shadows and smells, barely distinguishable from the brick buildings. A memory struck him like a blast of wind, of an alley very much like this one:

The alley where he'd found Lauren's body all those years ago.

He retrieved his bag, entered his building, and walked up the three flights of stairs and down the hall toward his office. It was probably just a bum—and anyway, there was no force on earth that would make him walk down an alley like that ever again. Especially not tonight. Inside, the office building was dark; most everyone renting there had no interest hanging around after the sun went down. That was one advantage of having been in prison: every other place seemed as safe as Disneyland in comparison.

Once more, the image of Hannah kneeling next to the unknown man as she screamed at Thane wrenched its way back into his mind. He knew on an intellectual level that Hannah must have dated other men while he was inside. Emotionally, however, he could only imagine Hannah with him.

At least until a couple of hours ago.

He unlocked his office door and slipped inside, locking it behind him. He placed his ear against the door, but didn't hear any noises in the hall. He turned on the light in the front room, then walked into his office. He reached down to turn on his desk lamp when he suddenly stopped. He then walked over and stood to the side of his office window, peering through the Venetian blinds at the building across the alley, the roof of which was directly across from his office window. He didn't detect any movement, but that didn't mean anything. The darkness could hide anything.

He leaned back against the wall, trying to steady his nerves. He wasn't the type to jump at shadows, but he also knew from experience how dangerous shadows could be. He leaned down and unplugged his desk lamp from the outlet on the wall, then walked over and flipped the switch to the lamp. Going back to the outlet, he crouched low against the wall and plugged the lamp cord back into the electrical socket, bathing the room in light once more.

Three blasts from a shotgun rang out.

The window exploded inward, showering Thane with shards of glass that fell like sleet. The room plunged into shadow—one of the blasts tore apart the lamp. Thane raised his hands to cover his face, and they came back bloody. He swept his gaze around the room: the wall to either side of the window had busted clean through, and the shelves behind the desk had absorbed a lot of buckshot, as did the back of his desk chair.

He pressed up against the wall. After a couple of minutes, he heard an engine turning over down the block, and he peered hesitantly out the corner of the window, feeling secure now that the office was dark once more. He studied the rooftop across the alley, but whoever had been there was long gone. He then looked down toward the street, where the only movement was an old pick-up truck driving away from his building.

Thane slid back down to the floor, leaning against the wall and ignoring his bleeding hand. The assassin was gone for the night, but they'd be back once Thane reappeared in court, alive. He knew he wouldn't be reporting this to the police, not only to avoid even more publicity, but because he was going to handle it his way—and his way didn't include the police. He figured the odds were against anyone else in this neighborhood reporting the incident as well; it wasn't the sort of area that sought police involvement.

The wheezing AC unit had never done much to help cool his office, so there was no way it would be able to cough up any sort of air flow to offset the heat now flooding in through the shattered window. He also knew that sleeping on his office sofa was going to be like sleeping on a pile of gravel, but all things considered, his comfort was the least of his concerns right now. Just the same, he hoped the expired bottle of aspirin still had at least a little of its medicinal power left.

Thane managed to claim a couple hours of sleep despite the lumps in the sofa. The sound of the entryway door opening woke him, but he didn't move until he heard careful footsteps outside his door, at which point he grabbed the baseball bat next to him. He rose and silently maneuvered over to the side of the door, bat raised and ready.

His office door opened far more deliberately than normal, as if someone were trying to sneak up on him, but he lowered his weapon when he saw the bright pink nail polish on the hands that carried two cups of coffee.

Kristin froze when she spotted the bat.

"Whoa, Trigger. Maybe I should have brought you decaf." She extended one of the cups to him. "No need to be so jumpy." Then she noticed the remains of the window and the debris strewn across the office floor. "On the other hand, maybe there is. What the hell happened here?"

Thane stirred his coffee with a plastic spoon. "Somebody took a shot at me."

"Oh my God! Are you kidding me? Who was it?"

"I don't know. I seem to have an enemy."

Kristin conducted another quick visual survey of the damage. "Ya think?" She turned back toward Thane. "Are you hurt? Oh my God—you have blood on your neck."

"I'm fine. Just some pieces of glass. It's from my hands."

"Let me look." She stood in front of him, lifting his chin with one hand then licking her napkin and running it lightly across the small streak of dried blood to wipe it off.

"I always hated when my mom did that," he said.

"You used to get shot at as a child, too?" Once the blood was off, she ran her index finger along the side of his neck, feeling for shards of glass. "This was not how I was expecting to start my morning."

"Look, I'm fine." Thane replaced the back-sofa cushions where they belonged, then sat down. He took a long drink of coffee, the aroma counterbalancing the gas fumes and garbage smells wafting in from the alley below.

Kristin approached his desk, eyeing his gym bag. "You spend the night here?"

"That's a whole 'nother story."

She ran her hand along the back of his desk chair, moving her fingers across the pellet holes as if she were reading Braille. His desk and the books on the shelf looked as though they had been attacked by burrowing insects.

"Your life certainly has no shortage of drama," she said. He ignored the comment, continuing to focus on the coffee, so she walked around to the front of the desk, brushed away the remains of the demolished lamp with a book that was also filled with buckshot, and hopped up on the edge of it.

"You want to hear something interesting?" she asked. "I mean, good interesting, not someone-shot-my-office-all-to-hell interesting?" Thane looked up at her and simply stared, tired, so she continued. "You know I've been trying to get a copy of Gruber's computer disks, right? I was getting to the point where I was thinking I was going to have to sue their asses for withholding evidence, but then I started dealing with this young officer who I think kind of has the hots for me, so I implied—only implied—that if he gave me the information, I might—only might—consider going out with him. Once he heard that, suddenly he was—"

"Kristin, I didn't have the best of nights. Any chance we can just jump to the point where it gets interesting?"

She tilted her head down and lifted her eyes as if she were looking over a pair of invisible reading glasses. "I think I like you better when you haven't been shot at. But OK, I got a copy of the disks, and most of them contain notes about cases he's worked on."

"Like police reports?"

"Sort of. More like a journal—more informal than a police report, although nothing especially revealing. Just general notes from over the years. Reads sort of like something you could get out of a newspaper, for the most part. It's like he was making notes on crimes he had worked, maybe in case he got called to testify on any of them, or maybe for his memoirs."

"I'm not sure that rises to the level of interesting."

"Then how about the fact that the missing disk covered the time period August through September, 2014?" Thane looked up at her as if she'd just slapped him. "Ah," Kristin said, "I seem to have your attention."

Thane rose slowly. "Lauren McCoy was killed in August of 2014." Kristin did, indeed, have his attention. All roads that he now traveled emanated from that night in the alley. "I want you to go through Gruber's phone records again for calls he made. Start four weeks before he was killed, although we might have to go back further than that. I want a list of names and businesses he called during that time. That something you can do?"

"Sure, no problem. You looking for anything in particular?"

Thane shook his head. "I'm hoping we'll know it when we see it."

The phone rang, despite sporting several holes in one side of it. Thane walked over to answer it just as Gideon entered, stopping in the doorway as he took in all the destruction.

"You two been scuffling?"

"Somebody took a shot at him," Kristin said.

"Took more than one, from the look of things."

Gideon looked out the glassless window at the building across the alley. As Gideon surveyed the office, Thane grabbed a pen and started writing on the back of a manila folder. "When?" Thane said into the phone. He jotted down a time. "What'd they find?" He started writing then stopped, dropping his head toward his chest for a moment, then regaining his composure. "Please email the report over to me."

He hung up the phone and looked over at his colleagues, both of whom were expecting the next piece of bad news: he didn't disappoint them.

"That was Detective Struthers. They recovered the stolen goods from Skunk's apartment building. Hidden in the drop ceiling in the hallway right outside his front door."

CHAPTER TWENTY-FIVE

IDEON SHOOK HIS HEAD AND spit out of the broken window. "Skunk always was a dumb shit."

Kristin kicked the leg of the desk and flopped down onto the sofa. "Son of a bitch. I never even got interviewed on TV."

Gideon smirked from behind her. "Yeah, now you're just another law grad newbie."

Kristin whirled. "Hey, I'm not *just* another anything."

"I know it doesn't look good," Thane said.

"*Doesn't look good?*" Kristin parroted. "What planet are you from?"

"This just confirms my suspicions: somebody's framing Skunk. This is all too convenient."

Gideon sat on the end of the sofa, tilting his head at Thane. "You have any idea how much that shit was worth? Somebody'd have to hate Skunk a hell of a lot to give up all that just to frame him. What do you think he done to make somebody that mad? Skunk can get on a guy's nerves, but not enough to do all this. Don't make no sense."

"I know," Thane said. "But do you honestly believe he would hide all that outside his apartment, where somebody else could come across it? Maybe he's the patsy. Being set up to take the fall for the real murderer. So help me out here: who would know enough about Skunk's habits to set this up?"

Gideon just shook his head again. "Yeah, right, okay. Framed. Sure." He stroked his chin, gazing up at the ceiling. "As far as who would know how he operated, that narrows it down to . . . the basketful of cops who arrested him, the prosecutors who locked him up, any judge who ever met him, and every convict at Forsman who spent more than three minutes listening to him brag about shit. But as for people who'd want to frame him—I've got nothin'."

"Look, we can talk about this later. We're due in court in two hours," Thane said. "And I don't want you guys looking like we've already lost. Kristin, follow up on those phone records. We're not beaten yet."

She didn't move, but instead slid lower into the sofa, sulking. She stared at her shoes until Thane added:

"You find something, you can talk to the press."

She thought about it for a minute, then shrugged and made a beeline for Thane's file cabinet. "Where are those phone records we subpoenaed?"

"Officer Novak," Thane began, addressing the fresh-faced young cop in the witness box. "I thought the police searched the defendant's apartment after he was arrested."

Novak slouched nonchalantly in the hot seat. His blond hair was almost translucent, and a pronounced case of acne speckled both cheeks.

"That's right," Novak said, "we did search the apartment. But then we went back later and searched the hallway ceiling *outside* his apartment."

"The hallway ceiling? Did you search anyplace else?"

"Didn't have to. We found the stolen items. Nothing else to look for."

"Lucky you," Thane said. "How'd you know to look there?"

"District Attorney Stone received a call telling him where to look, and he passed it along to us."

Thane looked back at Stone, then glanced at the jury before returning his attention to the Officer. "And who was it that called him?"

"I believe it was an anonymous tip."

Thane nodded his head. "But of course."

"Objection, Your Honor," Stone said.

"Sustained. Please curb the sarcasm, Mr. Banning."

Novak leaned forward, puffing out his chest. "A lot of cases get solved through anonymous tips. People have info, but they don't want to get involved. Maybe a neighbor saw him put it up there. In any case, it turned out to be good intel, so I got no complaints."

"Well then—that's good enough for me. Was everything accounted for?"

"Yes, as far as we can tell."

"The DVD player, the wallet, everything else?"

"Yes, it was all there."

"Including the missing computer disk?"

Novak started to answer, then glanced over toward Stone, as if the DA could offer direction. Not receiving any, he shrugged nonchalantly. "There wasn't any computer disk found. We don't even know if one was taken. You're the only one saying that."

Thane raised his eyebrows to convey surprise, then looked over at the jury. He then turned back to Novak. "So hardly anything else around the desk was disturbed except for a box of disks, the contents of which were scattered across the room. The disks were numbered and all still there except for one, and you're saying I'm the only one who says *maybe* it was taken? Now, I'm not saying it's a fact, but are you trying to tell me that L.A.'s finest aren't even making note of it? Really?"

Novak squirmed a little. "I'm sure the detectives investigating the case are taking the missing disk into account, but as far as I'm concerned, it's not relevant."

"How long have you been on the force, son?" Thane asked.

"It'll be a year next month."

"Then with all due respect, I don't think whether or not you believe the disk is relevant matters much at all."

"Your Honor!" Stone yelled.

Thane looked at the judge and smiled sheepishly. "I did say 'with all due respect', Your Honor." Before Judge Reynolds could admonish him, Thane was already back in his seat. "No further questions."

Novak started to respond when Stone stood and glared him back into silence. Then he turned to the judge. "The Prosecution rests, Your Honor."

"In that case, court will resume tomorrow at 9:00 a.m. at which point the Defense will present its case. Until that time, this court is dismissed."

Thane and his colleagues stepped out of the courthouse and into an L.A. sun that overwhelmed even the lights rigged up behind the TV cameras. Staking out the foot of the steps, as always, a swarm of reporters buzzed amongst themselves.

Thane leaned over to Kristin and nodded toward the pack. "You interested in saying a few words on behalf of our firm?"

"Are you serious? Because if you're just messing with me . . ."

"Keep it brief—but when they ask what we have planned for tomorrow, just say we still believe the absence of the lone computer disk is more relevant than the prosecution is willing to admit, and we intend to pursue that as we continue to present our case."

"Got it."

She started off down the steps, but Thane grabbed hold of her arm. "And I'm serious: keep it brief. Don't get into specifics."

"Do we even *have* specifics?" she said as she started down the steps.

A chuckle slipped from Gideon's lips. "Go get 'em, counselor," he called out.

Thane looked over at him. "I'm going back to the office. Stick close to her, all right? If it looks like she's turning this into a reality show, reel her in."

"Gotcha."

As Gideon started down toward Kristin, Thane called out to him. "Give her a little time in the sun, though. I want her to get something out of this."

Gideon nodded and plodded down the steps, ignoring the reporters, who edged around him warily, no doubt remembering their last encounter.

While the press's attention was focused on Kristin, Thane slipped by them unnoticed. He reached the bottom of the steps and looked back: he could already hear her going to work on the press mob, working them like an old pro. She was going to be a top-notch lawyer one day, if her ambition didn't yank her off the rails.

He turned to head down the sidewalk when a fist drove into his gut, dropping him to his knees. He tried to stand, but a dead-eyed Russell McCoy clamped a huge paw onto the back of his neck. For a moment, Thane wished that Hannah was by his side, stroking his head and yelling at McCoy to stop.

"My daughter was everything, you son of a bitch, and you took her from me. It's time you started feeling some of that pain."

McCoy cocked his leg like a field goal kicker preparing for a fifty-yarder, but before he could strike, Gideon appeared out of nowhere. He slammed his shoulder into the man's chest, the two of them crashing against the side of a parked news van, leaving an impressive dent in the metal.

Before either man could get their bearings, two nearby cops sprung into action. One wrestled McCoy into a full-nelson, while the other stood hand-on-revolver in front of Gideon, who looked electrified by his first taste of blood in quite some time. Thane managed to get to his feet and staggered over to grab hold of his friend's flexed arm, but Gideon didn't acknowledge him, instead snarling at McCoy like an angry Rottweiler.

"Come on, Gideon, let's get out of here," Thane said, but the big man didn't move. "Let's go. You don't need to be breaking parole over something like this."

Gideon continued to eye McCoy, who was also refusing to back down. Kristin joined them, cautiously putting her hand on Gideon's other arm as though it were a live wire. Her touch seemed to at least bring him back to earth, but he didn't immediately lower his fists. Finally, he grunted and turned to leave with them, but not before glaring down a couple of reporters who had been lurking on the sidelines and trying to follow Thane.

"She was only thirty-three," McCoy shouted. "You're going to hell for this, Banning. You're going to burn in *hell*."

Thane didn't look back, but nodded slightly and muttered to himself, "You're probably right."

After assuring Gideon and Kristin that he was all right, Thane broke away towards the City Coroner's office, one hand pressed to his ribcage as he walked up the steps. The building's bright yellow façade, with the ornately landscaped flowerbeds outside the front entrance, stood in stark contrast to the grisly work done inside its four walls—like putting a smiley face sticker on the lid of a casket.

He was directed to the rear of the building on the first floor, where medical records dating back seventy-five years were kept in immaculate order by Earnest Privey, a small man in his sixties who probably stood no more than five feet when he wore dress shoes, and maybe a second pair of socks. Privey did a double take as Thane approached the front desk, then skitted over to the counter as Thane handed him a request slip.

"Figured I would have seen you before now," he sniffed as Thane walked up.

"Why's that?"

"I know you're not a criminal lawyer, mister, but in a murder, pretty much everybody wants to see the coroner's report. Just one of those things you do first off." Privey's voice was bored, yet strangely condescending at the same time, like a stern teacher delivering orientation to a group of boisterous youngsters. "You got the form?"

Thane handed the triplicate paperwork over. Privey ripped the back page off and handed it back to him, rolling his eyes.

"This is your copy," he sighed, then turned and skittered over toward the medical files, glancing at the form while he walked. He was partway down one aisle of records when he stopped abruptly, holding the form at arm's length in order to re-read it more carefully before turning back toward Thane and eyeing him quizzically.

"Just bring me the record," Thane said.

Privey looked at the form again, then changed directions toward another aisle, looking rather stunned. His haughty demeanor suddenly appeared diluted by this unexpected curve ball.

"Huh," he said to himself, as if it were unusual to catch him by surprise.

CHAPTER TWENTY-SIX

THE USUAL BUZZ IN THE gallery ramped up as a bruised and bandaged Skunk hobbled into the courtroom, his limp even more pronounced than usual. Gideon let out a low whistle, and Thane and Kristin leapt up to help Skunk into his seat. "What the hell happened?"

"Ah, you know the drill," Skunk said. "Yoder and a couple of the other screws played a pretty mean game of Kick the Skunk."

Thane eased him into his chair. Kristin put her arm around his shoulders in a quick half-hug, but even this touch made him wince in pain.

"I'll get you some water," she said, her voice cracking with emotion.

"Skunk, I am so sorry," Thane said. "I really am."

"Damn, Banning—you don't got to apologize to me. You kidding? Any other public defender woulda bolted by now, and I'd be sitting on death row."

"You didn't deserve any of this, no matter which way this falls."

"Yoder's a thug. We always knew that. You just showed the rest of the world. 'Sides, yesterday was his last day at Forsman. He's finished."

"I'm going to make things right. I promise."

"The bruises'll heal. They always do. Just don't let them send the juice through me. That's all I'm asking. I ain't ready for that."

Everyone stood as Judge Reynolds entered the courtroom. As he sat down, his eyebrows shot up when he spotted Skunk's bandages, and he looked over his reading glasses at Thane, who simply stared back at him. Reynolds shook his head knowingly, looking disgusted.

"Is Defense ready, Counselor?"

"Yes, Your Honor. Defense calls Drew Chamberlain."

A tall, fit man in his early thirties rose and strutted to the witness box, wearing a dark suit tailor-fit to his toned body and a teal tie that was probably that month's "power color." His blond, tussled hair was full of product and looked as though it could house a family of birds without anyone knowing, yet he still managed to look professional.

"Please state your name and occupation to the court," Thane said.

"Drew Chamberlain. I'm a literary agent for Henkler Publishing."

Several members of the gallery exchanged glances.

"As an agent," Thane said, "people come to you with books they've written, or ideas for books, and you decide if you want to publish them, is that correct?"

"That's the simplified version, but yes."

"And was one of those people who contacted you Detective Ted Gruber?"

"He called me a couple of times, the first call being two or three months before his death."

Thane handed a piece of paper to the Bailiff. "Defense offers Exhibit One, the phone records of Ted Gruber. Mr. Chamberlain's phone number has been highlighted on the page." Thane turned back to his witness. "Did Detective Gruber have an idea for a book?"

Chamberlain looked at the jury. "He said he wanted to write about the dirty side of the court system, station politics, that kind of thing. Said it was 'dynamite stuff,' if memory serves." Chamberlain spoke with a bemused expression. "This is so strange, you know, I feel like I'm in the plot of a book myself. A true-crime courtroom drama."

"And did you follow up with him on the book idea?" Thane pressed on.

"No. To be honest, it sounded like he had a grudge to settle. I'm interested in publishing great stories, not helping people carry out vendettas. After the second conversation, I asked him to quit calling."

"And we can assume, Mr. Chamberlain, that Detective Gruber would have called other publishing houses once you turned him down?"

"Objection," Stone said. "Calls for speculation."

"Sustained."

"Then let me rephrase. In your professional experience, do most would-be authors submit their ideas to just one publisher, or do they make the rounds once they've been rejected?"

"Most authors make the rounds," Chamberlain said. "Any writer who accepts the first rejection isn't going to get very far in this business."

"Thank you, Mr. Chamberlain. No further questions."

Stone rose, but did not move from his table. He looked at the witness, then looked over toward the jury, finally offering up a slight shrug of his shoulders.

"Mr. Chamberlain, did you ever actually meet with Detective Gruber?"

"No, sir."

"And perhaps a more relevant question is, do you have any idea what in the world any of this has to do with a murder trial?"

Chamberlain let the first hint of a grin slip out. "No, sir, I can't say I do."

"Yeah, me neither," Stone said as he retook his seat. "No further questions."

Thane's next witness was Lee Song. The Korean storeowner scooted his way to the witness stand, hopping up into the seat and wringing his hands. He looked guiltily over toward Stone a couple of times, but the DA ignored him, conferring with Winston. Song also glanced once at Gideon, but just long enough to see the big man glaring hard at him.

Thane leaned against the far corner of the jury box. "Mr. Song, you own a store across the street from Armor Park, is that correct?"

"Yes, but I didn't see nothing. Nothing." Song spurted the words quickly, as if they had been perched in his throat for hours.

"I understand. And I appreciate your desire to make sure we know that. But Mr. Song, is it true you told my associate you thought you recognized the defendant as someone sitting in the park near your store the night of the murder?"

Song's eyes flicked to Gideon and back. He blanched, lowering his eyes before he answered.

"Yeah, but I realized I was wrong."

"That's fine. Did District Attorney Bradford Stone visit you just a few hours after you spoke with my associate?"

"Objection," Stone said with an edge to his tone.

"Your Honor," Thane said, "I'm simply trying to establish a timeline. There was a contradiction in what the witness told my associate and what he's saying now. I want to know precisely when he changed his mind."

"Objection overruled. But proceed carefully, Mr. Banning. *Very* carefully."

"As always, Your Honor," Thane said. "Mr. Song? Did Mr. Stone visit you early the morning after you spoke with my associate?"

Song fidgeted. "Yes, Mr. Stone visited my store."

"Did you call Mr. Stone? Did you call anyone after talking with my colleague?"

Song shook his head sadly, then sighed. "No, sir."

"Mr. Song, I'm not trying to get you into trouble. But just so I make sure I understand this correctly, you told my associate you recognized the picture of the defendant, then Mr. Stone came to visit immediately after, and now you're certain you didn't see anything. Do I have that correct?"

Stone leapt to his feet so forcefully it made Song jump. "Your Honor, this is outrageous!"

Reynolds rapped his gavel four times, his face growing red. "Counsel to my chambers. Right now!"

"You were given the benefit of the doubt when you took this case, Mr. Banning," Judge Reynold growled. "I'm now beginning to think Mr. Stone was right when he said you were taking this case solely to try to embarrass him."

"I did not, Your Honor."

"It sure as hell looks that way to me, and that sort of bullshit will not go on in my courtroom." Reynolds threw his shoulders back, daring Thane to take him on.

"I was just trying to—"

Stone interrupted Thane, his face so flushed Thane was surprised he couldn't hear the DA's heartbeat from across the room. "We both know damn well what you were trying to do," Stone said. "You've continually implied impropriety on my part, and I will not stand for it."

"More importantly," Reynolds added, "neither will I."

"Your Honor, if this was a cheap trick, then the jury will see through it and penalize me for it. But you tell me: a witness tells my colleague he saw my client in a park, then the District Attorney pays him a visit—and god knows how he even learned about it—and suddenly the witness saw nothing. You saw him up on that stand: he wanted to make damn sure we all knew he didn't see anything, afraid what might happen if he said otherwise."

"Mr. Banning, with all due respect, anyone could take one look at that 'colleague' of yours and easily see where a person would affirm whatever he was being asked. I have little doubt Mr. Song would have been willing to say he had seen Santa Claus that night."

Stone, who had been standing on one side of the room looking concerned he wouldn't be able to constrain himself, strode over and joined the two men at the judge's desk.

"I demand a formal apology from this man in front of the jury," Stone said.

"Well, that isn't going to happen," the judge answered. "But I'll tell you what is, Mr. Banning. You go down this path again of implying illegal behavior on the part of Mr. Stone without any evidence to back it up and I will cite you for contempt of court. You might even experience the pleasure of a jail cell once again, even if just for the night. Do you understand?"

Thane's stomach seized at this threat, especially after what he had done to Yoder in court. Whatever jail he was sent to, retribution would be swift, certain, and quite possibly fatal. The thought of once again being behind bars, being subjugated to the sadistic whims of anyone with authority and attitude, made him want to bolt from the room. He had vowed never to be locked up again, but he was now seeing where that could be a distinct possibility, especially if things played out as he expected.

"Do you understand?" Reynolds asked again.

CHAPTER TWENTY-SEVEN

THANE STOOD BETWEEN GIDEON AND Kristin in front of the elevators, but his mind was far away. Neither had asked what happened in the judge's chambers yet, although he knew Kristin would only be able to contain herself for so long. When the elevator reached their floor, Stone appeared from the side, stepping in front of the opening door, blocking them from entering. Stone motioned for Thane to get on, then turned toward Gideon and Kristin.

"Take the stairs," Stone said.

Gideon didn't budge. "How about I take you with me?"

Stone took a step forward. "You sure you're in a position to threaten a DA, buddy boy?"

"You sure you want to call me 'boy'?"

Thane shook his head. "I'll meet you downstairs," he said. He ushered the DA inside the elevator, as much for his well-being as Gideon's. "Go on," he said. "Take the next car and we'll meet downstairs."

The elevator doors had to shut before Gideon's glare was broken. As soon as they were alone, Stone immediately shifted his threats toward Thane, taking advantage of the privacy offered by the elevator.

"If I thought you had any respect for the law, I wouldn't worry about you ignoring the judge's order."

"Respect for the law? That's a joke, coming from you."

"Your antics are getting old, and they're going to stop now if you want to keep that Neanderthal from going back to Forsman."

"Say what you have to say."

"Several nights ago your pal out there pawned a silver watch belonging to Ted Gruber. Care to tell me how he got it?"

Thane stopped breathing.

"You're lying."

"No reason for the pawn shop owner to lie, and the video camera damn sure doesn't lie. Ask the tough guy, see what he says."

"What do you want?"

"His ass in jail, for one thing. I'm assuming he stole it when you visited Gruber's home, and since pawning stolen goods will be his third strike, that means he's out of the game for the rest of his life."

"Yet here we are, talking. So again, I'm asking you, what do you want?"

"First, you quit insinuating I've broken conduct. Second, this case is over. No more witnesses, no more testimony, no more cross-examinations. Nothing. Third, you will not speak my name to the press again, ever, or your big friend goes away for good."

Thane turned away. "There's the Bradford Stone we know and love."

"I'm not here to be loved. I asked you to step away from this case before all this started, but you didn't listen. I don't care what beef you have with me—but you're after my office now, and that's when I fight back. I'm not trying to be the bad guy here, but you fuck with me one more time, I will rain justice down all over your miserable head. That's a promise."

Thane turned back slowly toward Stone, black thoughts rising inside him. And even though Stone had been more than comfortable standing up to Gideon, whatever he saw in Thane's eyes made him step back. As soon as the doors opened, he quickly slipped past Thane and out onto the main floor, glancing back at Thane as he exited the elevator.

"We're done here," he said over his shoulder. "You understand? We're done."

Stone breezed past Gideon and Kristin, who were winded from hustling down the steps to meet the elevator.

Kristin was the first to ask, "So, what'd Prince Charming have to say?"

Thane ignored her, grabbing Gideon by the forearm and pulling him toward an empty meeting room off the main corridor. If his friend had been a smaller man, Thane's grip would have pulled him off his feet. As it was, Gideon went along willingly.

They entered the small room, Thane slamming the door behind him. His rage was building, but he tried as best he could to mollify his tone. "When we were at Gruber's, did you steal something?"

"What do you think?"

"I think you're not answering my question."

"Then there's your answer," Gideon said matter-of-factly.

"Goddamn it, why?"

"'Cause that's what I do."

Thane kicked a chair, sending it clattering across the floor. He wanted to pick it up and smash it over his friend's head. "Don't give me that bullshit. You're out of Forsman. You're free. Why do you want to screw that up?"

Gideon put his hands on the table, acting as if he were ready to flip it over. "Because I'm tired of living in a dump. Tired of not having money to get a decent meal or even buy a fucking beer. Yeah, I'm free, but sitting in a shithole with nothing to eat isn't any better than jail."

"Oh that's right, I forgot: we had to ask permission to piss in Forsman, but at least they gave you a good meal. Look, I'm trying to help you, but—"

"Then stop trying. I don't need your help, and I sure as hell didn't ask for it. You don't owe me nothin', so maybe you should quit acting like you're my white knight come to raise me from the ghetto. And maybe we should just stop pretending we have anything in common 'sides doing time together. We're from two different worlds, amigo, and those worlds are getting ready to collide. You shoulda seen it coming, so get off my back."

Gideon scowled and headed for the door. Thane reached out and once again grabbed hold of his arm as he passed.

"Don't you walk out on me—"

Gideon wheeled around and clamped hold of Thane's shoulders with a grip that could have crushed his bones and pushed him toward the wall.

"Don't you *ever* grab me—" Gideon roared, but Thane managed to twist and reverse the hold, using their momentum to slam Gideon's chest against the wall, his cheek flattened against the paneling.

"Listen, you stubborn son of a bitch," Thane said breathlessly.

"Stone's playing hardball now—and you're the ball. *He knows.*"

Gideon stopped struggling.

"He threatening me to get you to back off?"

Thane nodded, easing up on his grip, letting the big man peel off the wall to face him. "He's Bradford Stone. That's what he does."

"Fuck him. You can't quit."

Thane hoped he'd never understand the thought process of a career felon. Total disregard for consequences or risk-versus-reward, where spending the rest of your life in prison was just the price you paid for showing someone they couldn't push you around.

"Does the phrase 'three strikes' mean anything to you?" Thane asked.

"Yeah, that's the number of times I'm going to take this chair upside your head if you roll over for him."

Gideon grabbed the chair that Thane had kicked across the room and sat down, slumping about as low as he could without sliding out of it.

"What do you want me to do?" Thane asked.

"I think you need to keep doing whatever you can to help Skunk—whatever it takes, whether it's legal or not."

And there it was. Thane was surprised it had taken this long for Gideon to say it. "Jesus, Gideon, I can't just—"

Gideon flew back out of his chair. "Didn't you learn nothing I taught you at Forsman? If somebody hits you in the leg with a stick, you bash them over the head with a pipe. You don't do no eye for an eye. You take the entire head."

"I'm not in prison anymore."

Gideon stood over Thane. "But you still got the instincts. I can tell by watching you. You can't tell me you didn't learn a thing or two in prison. I watched you develop that edge. Hell, I helped you *get* that edge. You're just scared to use it now that you're out, 'fraid of what it means if you can do those things. Take what you learned inside Forsman and start *using* it. Quit playing by their fucking rules."

"That's not how the legal system works."

"*The legal system,*" Gideon muttered. "Ain't that the same system that put you away? The same system that ripped you and your wife apart? How's it working out for you now? You know Stone bullied that storeowner to change what he said. He playing by the rules? Time you start doing whatever you need to beat that son of a bitch. You're due one. Take it."

Thane had no answer for this.

"Skunk is counting on you, man," Gideon continued. "If you roll over and let Stone step on you a second time, I'll turn myself in over that watch. I'll send myself back to Forsman just to spite you."

"You're not that stubborn. Or that stupid."

"I'm both. Daddy didn't raise no Honors student."

Gideon slapped Thane on the back and headed for the door. Just like that, the conversation was over.

"Come on," he said as he walked off. "We got work to do."

Gideon returned to the office, ostensibly to look through police reports and the various depositions the team had collected so far. He was supposed to be reading through the documents with a criminal's eye. He had to laugh at that: everything he picked up he read with a criminal's eye. But that didn't mean he didn't get bored with the reading part.

The front office door creaked open, and Gideon glanced up to see Thane's wife leaning into the office. She looked emotionally beaten down, like a first-time convict after his first week in Forsman: a dazed look in her eyes, and hesitant with every step.

"Oh, I'm sorry," she said quietly. "I'm looking for Thane."

"He's out."

He lifted himself off the sofa and extended his hand. "Gideon."

"Hannah. Hannah Banning. I'm glad to finally meet you. Thane's talked a lot about you."

Gideon grinned. "I'm honored."

"You should be. You're the only part of his time there he ever talks about."

Silence took over the room. Gideon had never been comfortable talking to women. He wanted to say something else, but was afraid that whatever he'd think up would be taken the wrong way—crass, profane, or just plain dumb. So he stood there, watching Thane's wife until she spoke again.

"Do me a favor," she whispered. "Don't tell Thane I stopped by. Maybe I'll try calling him later."

After a moment more of standing in a daze, she turned slowly to leave. When she reached the door she paused, standing like that for several seconds. "Have I lost him?" she asked without turning around.

"What do you mean?"

She turned back around, the water in her eyes reflecting the light in the room. "I know who went into prison. But I'm not sure who came out."

"You expected the same fella you married?"

"Don't get me wrong. I understand what he went through, but—"

"Whoa," Gideon said, holding up his hand as if stopping traffic. "Let's get that straight right now: you don't. No damn way. Not trying to be rude or nothing, but however bad you think it is, the picture of it in your head is still a walk through Candyland next to the real thing."

She walked over and looked out the window. "After his second year at Forsman, he didn't let me visit anymore. Didn't respond to my letters. He said he wanted me to get on with my life."

"Sometimes it's hard for those on the inside to hear about life outside. Kind of a cruel reminder. Besides, he loved you. Probably figured you was wasting your time waiting for him."

She continued staring out the window. "I just want him back." Her voice cracked with emotion. "But I'm scared."

"You wanna know why I took your husband under my wing?" Gideon asked. "He was the only man I'd ever met in there who I really thought was innocent. A good man. I'd never met a guy like that before—not in Forsman, not anywhere."

Hannah finally turned back around to look at Gideon. "But five years is a long time."

"Hell of a lot longer than you know, sister. It's like dog years. A long time to get bitter. Long time to have anger eatin' away at you. Question now is, will he be able to get past that anger, or will it be a part of him forever?"

Hannah nodded. "That's what I want to know."

"Tell you the truth, I think he does too. Listen, I did everything I could to help him survive on the inside, but between you and me, I'm kinda out of my element on this side of the fence. It's up to you now to help him survive."

"How?"

"Just be there for him, even if you don't understand what he's going through. He needs you; it's just he's been conditioned not to ask for anything. Prison will do that to you. But one thing you got to keep in mind, no matter what happens, is he's doing all of this for the two of you. For whatever reason, he thinks this is going to bring him through to the other side of that bitterness, crazy as it sounds. Hell, it don't make no sense to me neither, but I don't question nothing. Even though I ain't got no college degree, I know one thing for sure, and that's that he doesn't give a damn about anything 'cept getting on with your lives. He just thinks he's gotta do this first. So have a little faith in him, huh? He needs you. He's still a good man—despite what he thinks."

CHAPTER
TWENTY-EIGHT

RMOR PARK DIDN'T LOOK LIKE a park to Thane. Four busted-up benches were scattered across thirty yards of dirt, with an occasional tuft of grass bullying its way through the rock-hard soil. The only other hint of color came from some tall, mostly dead shrubs, which divided the park in half.

Thane and Kristin stood at one end of the lot, surveying the stores surrounding it. A couple of sullen teenagers in the middle of some sort of transaction claimed the opposite side. One of the guys was exchanging packages with a shiny-faced youth in a shiny car, who looked like he was probably between classes at a nearby university. The other teen involved glanced over at Kristin and Thane, but paid them no mind—he was probably the lookout. He could probably tell they weren't cops, but just the same, the well-dressed white couple didn't exactly fit the picture.

"What were you hoping to find here?" Kristin asked.

"I don't know," Thane said. "I'm just grasping."

Kristin glanced from side to side. Despite her earlier attempts at bravado, she clearly didn't like being in a place like this, even during daylight hours.

Of the four benches in the park, they walked over to the only one that had wooden slats in the seat, and Thane saw that even those could be lifted up without much effort. A wall of hedges ran directly behind the bench, providing some shade and cover from the rear. They sat down.

"This must be the bench where Skunk sat awaiting the mysterious caller," Thane said.

"I can see why Gideon had trouble finding anyone who would place Skunk here," she said. "I'm betting there's not a lot of civic-minded people around here. Not that I blame them."

Kristin paused, then glanced at Thane. "A lot of people are saying you took this case just to get back at Stone. Is it . . . is it true?"

He didn't answer right away, but also didn't look away from her. Finally:

"Yes."

She cocked her head in surprise, then nodded and turned back to the street. "Then I hope you kick his ass."

A black BMW SUV crawled down the street, the darkened passenger-side window rolling down a quarter of the way, then silently sliding back up as the car drove past. Kristin again glanced around the park, shifting on the bench. It wasn't dark enough for the feeble streetlight next to the bench to illuminate them, but if they didn't leave soon, the light would make them just that much more conspicuous.

Thane knew it was time to head back, but not because of the growing darkness. Hannah had left him a voicemail an hour ago, asking him to come home. He'd almost canceled the trip to the park just for the wobble in her voice. He wanted to be back with his wife, but he had to see this through. He didn't, however, have to take long doing so.

As soon as he stood, Kristin was quick to follow suit. They walked around the hedges and headed across the park where they had left his car.

"What time is it?"

Thane held up his watch-less wrist, then nodded toward a flashing neon time-and-temp display on the wall of the bank on their left. Seven o'clock: definitely time to get back to Hannah.

When they reached the other side of the park, Thane saw that the small grocery store across the street to their left was once again manned by Mr. Song, who was wheeling in a cart of fruit from the sidewalk. Thane stopped and watched Mr. Song go back into his store. He then looked at the bench next to him, the one with no slats on the seat.

"What's up?" Kristin asked.

"Song originally told Gideon he saw Skunk sitting on a bench in the park most of the night."

"Yeah?"

"But he wouldn't have been able to see him sitting on the other bench. The hedges would have blocked his view."

"But he obviously didn't sit here," Kristin said.

"Then how could he have seen him?"

Kristin shrugged. "But later he said he didn't see him at all, so who knows what really happened?" She glanced around again. "Maybe we should be getting back," she said. "This doesn't feel like the safest place to hang around after dark."

"Where is nowadays?" Thane said. "Everywhere you look, there are bars on the windows, padlocks on the doors, security systems . . . I can't imagine working at a convenience store or liquor store around here."

When they reached the car, Thane pulled out his keys, then stopped. Kristin tugged the locked door handle, then looked up to see him staring straight ahead at the bank.

"You okay?"

He looked back over at the park bench, then turned his gaze to survey the neighborhood. Finally, he turned back toward Kristin, closely scrutinizing her for a moment to size her up.

"In school you learned the book version of the legal practice," he said. "But if you're really as ambitious as I think you are, I'm wondering if you're up to seeing how the game's really played."

Thane sat in the worn reading chair in the living room with a folder of papers balanced on one leg, but that was all he was doing with it. He had instinctively picked up the folder filled with police reports and other testimonies pertaining to their case, but he couldn't motivate himself to review it. He knew that what was to come wouldn't have any corroborating report in his files. From here on, pieces of paper were irrelevant.

The sound of Hannah putting away dishes spilled out from the kitchen. He had offered to help once they were through with dinner, but she told him to go into the living room to relax.

She made some pasta with shrimp and vegetables, and opened the last bottle of wine she had bought when Thane was released. Over dinner, she told him about life on her own, and about her relationship with Paul. She said that she always knew in her heart of hearts that she wasn't ever going to marry Paul, but he did so much to help her rebuild some semblance of a normal life. She was grateful to him and fond of him, but she was not in love with him—not the sort of love she had always felt for Thane. She also spoke of the fear she had felt, first in the courthouse when Thane yelled at her, then again in the bookstore when he was fighting Paul. She simply wanted all of this to go away and for life to get back to the way it used to be, but she realized it was naïve of her to think there wouldn't be challenging times. She said she also realized she was ready to take on those times and see them through, as long as it meant coming through to the other side with Thane.

He sat in the living room, listening as she rinsed out the sink, the dishes now washed and put away. She walked into the living room, drying her hands on a bright red dishtowel, then seated herself on one end of the sofa.

"How's it coming?" she asked.

"Little by little."

He tossed the folder of papers onto the coffee table and leaned forward in the chair, exhausted. Hannah stood, walked behind him, and started massaging his shoulders. His body immersed itself with the feel of her touch. He couldn't imagine being away from her again, and he would do whatever it took to make sure that never happened.

"Tell me what you're feeling," she said. "You don't have to keep things locked up anymore."

He didn't speak at first, unsure if he could trust himself to stop if he opened up. There was so much he wanted to talk to her about, to share with her as he always had prior to his arrest, but he had spent the past five years creating crevices within himself to hide feelings and thoughts. It was necessary in order to keep the magnitude of their situation from overwhelming him. He finally said what he could, even though it was only stating the obvious.

"I feel bad for Skunk, being back in prison. He doesn't deserve this. But I'll make it right by him."

"I'm committed to seeing this through with you, but I have to ask: What will this do to you if you lose? What will it do to us?"

"I'm not going to lose. I know that sounds delusional, but please trust me. I have a plan."

Hannah massaged his tense muscles a few moments longer, then stopped, resting her hands on his shoulders. Thane knew she was trying to be as supportive as she could, but that the enormity of all this still weighed heavily on her.

"But if it does go the other way?" she asked.

"I won't be doing this again. Capital murder. Going up against Stone. It's a one-time shot, I swear to you. And then I'll move on."

"I think it's time."

"Just about," he said. "Just about."

He reached up and took hold of one of her hands, clutching it tight as if afraid some unseen force was going to come and try to pull her away. He then closed his eyes, but didn't release her hand.

"Thank you," he whispered.

Thane went back to work around ten, following the first real night's sleep he'd gotten in what seemed like weeks. Being back with Hannah was like leaving a great wilderness—but as safe as he felt, the bond still seemed fragile, as though there was one more piece that needed to fall into place.

And he knew what that was. He had always known.

He entered his office and saw Gideon stretched out on the sofa, an open bottle of beer on the floor within easy reach. "You sure spend a lot of time here," Thane said.

"Hard as it might be for you to imagine, this dump is nicer than my place, even after it got shot up."

Thane was embarrassed to admit he hadn't really imagined Gideon's life on the outside, although he also knew there wasn't anything he could do about that just yet.

"Where's Valley Girl?" Gideon asked.

"It's Sunday."

Gideon grabbed his beer and sat up, scratching his head with his free hand. "Guess that explains why I was the first one here. Keeping track of what day it is isn't something I've gotten used to yet." He took a deep swig, wiping his mouth with the back of his shirt sleeve. "She's got spunk, I'll give her that. But at the risk of sounding all negative, you sure we can trust her? I'm just saying—you know somebody told Stone about me talking to that Korean fuckhead. Maybe the mighty DA is tailing us, but I doubt he could do that without me knowing it. So I'm thinking maybe somebody must have fed him that info."

"And you think it was Kristin?"

"I'm just saying she wants to get ahead, is all. And I can't imagine Stone would turn down her help, especially if she had information he wanted."

"Well, we'll find out soon whether or not we can trust her. She and I went to the park yesterday where I got an idea. If she goes and tells Stone about it, then we're screwed."

"I was born screwed," Gideon said, "so that don't bother me much. You got some things to live for." Gideon tipped the bottle up to his mouth until he had drained the last drops. "I met Hannah," he continued. "She stopped by yesterday. Asked me not to tell you, but I never could keep a secret."

"Did you talk to her?"

"A little. I like her, but she seems kind of confused."

"Being with me will do that to you."

"I'm impressed she waited five years for a loser like you."

"She shouldn't have."

"But she did. Damn, if I had a woman like that in my corner, well, I'd spend more time in my corner."

"We used to be perfect together," Thane said. "Now I don't know. Things have changed. I've changed."

"So change back."

"It's not that easy."

"You love her. Who gives a damn if it's easy?"

Thane sat up straight. "After this case, I'm going to try and change back. I just have to see this through first."

Gideon chuckled. "You sound like a criminal. *Just one last job.*"

Stone leaned against the edge of his desk and motioned for the young woman standing in his office to have a seat. It wasn't unusual for him to be working on a Sunday afternoon; in fact, he considered it a regular part of his work week.

It was, however, far from routine to be meeting with a junior member of the Defense team.

But the young graduate had been insistent when she called him at home the previous evening. He didn't know how she had gotten his phone number, but if there was one thing he could tell about her, it was that she was resourceful. That, and she had a strong desire to succeed at any cost. It was this more than anything else that made him agree to meet her.

Kristin stood behind one of the chairs positioned in front of Stone's desk, holding onto the back of it. "I appreciate your willingness to meet with me on a Sunday, Mr. Stone," she said.

"To be honest, it's not entirely appropriate that we're meeting at all."

"I understand. Just out of curiosity, why did you agree to do it?"

"I've been watching you in court. I think you have a bright future in law, even if you've had the poor judgement to involve yourself with Thane Banning."

"He's not as bad as you think he is."

"I know. But we all have our parts we have to play. And while I think I understand *why* you went to work with him, I'm still not sure it was your best move. As for why I'm meeting with you, you sounded troubled when you called. I thought I could help you."

Kristin bit her bottom lip. "I have a lot of big plans, and I don't want to mess them up before I even finish my first case." She hesitated. "Thane found something that might prove our client's innocence."

Stone's stomach tightened, but he stayed alert, studying this young woman's face, wondering if he was being conned. But on the other hand, he had dealt with liars for his entire prosecutorial career—if she wasn't on the level, he'd know. He was sure of that.

"So why come to me?"

"Because if the evidence doesn't prove Mr. Burns's innocence, it will prove his guilt, in which case Thane plans to destroy the evidence."

"Which is illegal."

She nodded, dejected. "He told me that it was time for me to learn how the game was really played. I know I'm young, and maybe I'm naïve, but I've never considered this a game. But more than anything, I can't risk being disbarred before I'm twenty-five. Christ, my parents would kill me."

He studied her for a long moment, his mind working. Her left foot tapped the floor relentlessly, keeping beat to a tune no one else could hear.

"So where do I fit in?" he asked.

She fidgeted, then drew in a deep breath. "I figured if I told you, off the record, you could check it for yourself. If it helps convict our client, so be it. But if it proves his innocence, you can't hide the evidence, since I already know about it."

Stone shot her one of his trademark glares, immediately sending her verbally scrambling. "Not that you would! I didn't mean that. I'm sorry. It's just . . . this is the best solution I could come up with. If both sides know about the evidence, then we'll let the truth speak for itself. That's all I want. Thane won't call until tomorrow to try to get it, so you can get there first if you decide to. Obviously it's your call, but at least I can feel like I've done the right thing."

Stone considered her story. Every prosecutorial cell in his body screamed out in alarm, but the more he thought about it, the more he realized it couldn't be a trick: if both sides knew about a piece of evidence, it couldn't be much more straightforward than that. It was what the legal system was built on.

He reached over his desk and grabbed a legal pad and a pen.

"What kind of evidence are we talking about here?"

CHAPTER
TWENTY-NINE

ONALD DAVIS, CHIEF OF SECURITY of the Union Bank of Los Angeles, pulled up to the gray stone bank where Bradford Stone and Simon Keaton had been waiting outside for over half an hour. A trim man in his early fifties wearing a bright red and blue plaid shirt, he had both men show him their badges before unlocking the door to the bank. Stone figured Davis had to have recognized him from TV, but was probably just trying to make things a little harder for them in retaliation for being called into work on a Sunday afternoon. After they entered the bank, Davis locked the door behind him.

"I appreciate your coming down here on such short notice," Stone said.

"You pulled me away from my daughter's birthday party," Davis grumbled. "If we can make this quick, that would be good."

"Soon as I get the security footage, you can be on your way."

Davis led the two men to a small office off the main lobby of the bank, which served as his work area. The desk looked as if it belonged to a hoarder: stacks of files, documents, and folders teetered on every inch of its surface. A small bookshelf on one side of the room, however, was immaculately organized with video boxes and DVD jewel cases. Davis walked over to the shelf, scanned the labeled cases with his index finger, then pulled one of the DVD's off the shelf, handing it to Stone.

"Here."

Stone looked at the shiny DVD inside the clear plastic case. "This is July twenty-eighth?"

"It covers all of July. That's the period of time you said you wanted."

"And it covers twenty-four hours a day?" Stone asked.

"Each and every one of them. Can I go home now?"

"Go and tell your daughter you gave her a safer city for her birthday."

"She'd rather have an iPhone."

Half an hour later, Stone sat at the end of a mahogany conference table, the centerpiece of his personal conference room. Winston, looking out of place in a pair of khaki shorts and a L.A. Laker's T-shirt, entered the room hurriedly, huffing and puffing from hustling down the hall.

"I got here fast as I could," he said. "What's up?" He dropped into a chair immediately to Stone's right and looked over at Keaton, who was setting up a portable DVD player in the middle of the table. A flat screen monitor on the wall flickered on, glowing bright blue, ready for showtime. Stone stared intently into the glow, ignoring his colleague, so Winston turned to Keaton.

"What's that?" Winston asked.

"There's an ATM across the street from Armor Park. We got the machine's security video."

"Play the damn thing, would you?" Stone barked.

"It's almost ready. Let me punch in the date and time."

Keaton thumbed a few buttons on the remote control. An image appeared on the monitor, a surprisingly clear shot of the area around the ATM. While the main focus was the space in front of the machine, part of the background was also in frame, enough for the three men to identify the individual sitting on a park bench across the street: Scotty "Skunk" Burns.

Stone shot up out of his chair, sending it clattering away.

"Goddamn it! Fast forward that thing."

Keaton obliged. Stone simply stood at attention, watching the images flash by. Skunk kept sitting on the bench, barely moving. Finally, Stone signaled Keaton to turn off the projector.

Keaton took out the disk, looking as if he wanted to snap it in two. "How the hell did the cops not think to check the ATM security camera?" he asked. "It's right across the street!"

"Because when they checked the park, there was only one bench with a place to sit down, and it was out of view of the ATM machine," Stone said. "The cops assumed that's where Burns sat, but Banning must have figured maybe somebody moved the slats off the bench where Burns was that night—the damn boards just lift up—and the police report didn't mention checking the security tapes. He must have noticed that, too."

Keaton put the disk back into the machine and punched some numbers into the remote. The date read July twenty-ninth at 8:00 a.m., the morning after the murder, then he hit the fast forward button. At around 9:30 a.m., footage showed a homeless man picking up the slats from the seat in the bench across from the ATM machine and carrying them around the other side of the shrubs and out of sight of the camera.

"A drunk wanting to sleep in the sun," Winston said.

"I don't fucking believe it." Stone got up and walked out of the conference room. Winston and Keaton looked at each other, then reluctantly followed.

Back in Stone's office, Keaton paced in front of his boss's desk while Winston wilted in his chair. Stone, however, sat ramrod straight behind his desk, his mind racing.

Keaton leaned over Stone's desk. "Could we just lose the disk?" he asked.

Winston looked at Keaton in disbelief and spoke before Stone could respond. "What if this is just a copy?"

"It's not," Keaton responded. "We called the bank's security chief at his home and got to the bank before he did. He didn't make a copy. And I'm not recommending we lose it; I'm just throwing out possibilities."

"I can't believe the son of a bitch is innocent," Winston muttered.

Stone slammed his palm down onto his desk so hard it sounded like a gunshot. "He is *not* innocent. He's a thief, and he'll be back in jail regardless if he's found guilty here. And for whatever reason he ends up going back, it will be his third strike, which means life for him— even if it's just shoplifting."

"I know, I know," Winston said, more to himself than to the others. "I just mean he didn't murder Gruber. How can we be talking about letting him take the rap anyway?"

"I understand what you're saying," Stone said, "and ninety-nine times out of a hundred that's the right instinct, but let's talk it through. Is this the one time we have to do something extremely distasteful for the greater good? I don't know. Maybe. Sometimes we have to make tough decisions that we could never have imagined making because it will keep scores of others from being hurt. We've gone out of our way to state unequivocally that Burns is guilty, and just coming back and saying 'whoops, our bad' won't cut it this time. There will be repercussions. We do damn important work here. Violent crime is down eighteen percent since we took office. Eighteen percent. People are safer than ever. You know how many murders we've prevented during our time in office? How many lives we've saved? But we can't do it from the unemployment line, and that's likely where we'll end up."

Stone stood slowly and walked around to the other side of his desk, sitting on the edge of it right in front of Winston. "That's the only thing I hate to see end: the impact we've had making this city safer. That's all. We've made a difference. We've made a real difference." Stone looked at Winston until he made eye contact. "I know you've transitioned smoothly from one administration to another in this office, but if we end up looking like a joke because of this case, I'll be voted out of your office and the next DA sure as hell won't want you or Keaton as a reminder of this fiasco."

Keaton rejoined the discussion. "Even if we could lose the evidence, we wouldn't have to go after the death penalty."

"Of course not. We're not barbarians. We're realists. But tell me honestly, Wallace, do you have any doubt at all that Scotty Burns will be back in jail for life in the near future, regardless of this case? Any doubt at all? If you do, then I swear to you, I'll let it go right now. I'm not looking to send an innocent man away. But this is not an innocent man."

"I know," Winston said. "The recidivism rate for guys like him is something like ninety percent. And like you said, it would be his third strike."

"Christ, even Burns admits he was in that park to set up another job," Keaton added.

"But I know where you're coming from, Wallace. Besides, there are other jobs out there for us. It's not as though we can't have an impact in other ways. Things work out. We'll still find a paycheck. Still have health insurance."

Stone didn't have to look at Winston to know he'd scored on that note. Winston wasn't at an age where a new job would come easily, and health insurance was the only thing keeping him and his sick wife in their home.

Winston's jaw tightened. "You're right: that piece of trash is going to end up back in prison anyway," Winston said. "And of course we wouldn't actually follow through on the death penalty. We could deliberately make some sort of procedural error that would keep it from being enforced when the time came."

Stone nodded. "But we can't just lose the disk. Little Miss Teen Lawyer knew we were going to see it, and the bank's security chief will say he gave it to us if Banning asks. She knew what she was doing."

Winston rose, looking as if he were making a point of order in a courtroom. "We bring the tape forward ourselves. That'll at least limit the damage."

"Not much," Stone said, "especially with Banning trying to convince the jury I orchestrated the arrest. And you can be damn sure he'll let the press know how we came to learn about the tape, claiming that's the only reason we cut Burns loose." He paused to think again, finally heaving a resigned sigh. "But I don't see any other options."

Keaton looked at the DVD player. "I do," he said.

Thane leaned back in his desk chair as Kristin stared out the window, shifting her weight from foot to foot. Gideon, as usual, was stretched out on the sofa, the sports page covering his chest like a homeless man's blanket. The office felt like the waiting room outside a surgical theater, thick with silent tension.

Gideon, however, wasn't one to wait quietly for long.

"So ol' Stone-head didn't tell you what this new evidence is?"

Thane shook his head. "He just said Judge Reynolds gave him permission to introduce something big, but I've got a sneaking suspicion I know what it is." He shot a glance Kristin's way, but her attention didn't stray from the window. "Let me ask you both a question," Thane said. "If you were trying to get under Stone's skin, what would you say to him?"

"That I was screwing his wife," Gideon replied.

Kristin turned around to participate. "I'd challenge his reputation as a tough guy. Call him a coward. Tell him he isn't as tough on crime as he likes to think."

"That's what I was thinking." Thane looked over at Gideon. "Not that yours wouldn't work, too."

They heard the door off the hallway open and Stone appeared in the doorway.

"Sorry to intrude on your Monday morning, Counselor. I wanted to give you an opportunity to review this before tomorrow." Stone set a notebook PC on the desk and looked around the shabby office.

"I figured you didn't have DVD capability in this office. I'm assuming you at least have electricity."

"What the hell is DVD?" Gideon grumbled.

Stone ignored him and pulled out a jewel case from his jacket pocket. "This is bank surveillance footage showing Armor Park from the ATM across the street. I made you your own copy. If it's all the same with you, I'm keeping the original."

Thane shot Kristin a harsh look, but she looked away, flushing red. "You're a member of the twenty-first century," Stone said, turning towards Thane's young associate. "I assume you know how to operate this?"

"I can operate it," she said.

"All right then. Enjoy the show." He turned to leave, pausing in the doorway. "Oh, and bring the computer to court with you tomorrow. It's city property." As he made his exit, his footsteps sounded like the DA had some spring in his step.

Thane stared at the jewel case for a long moment. "Okay," he said at last, "let's see what we have."

Kristin booted up the laptop and loaded the DVD. Thane walked around to the other side of his desk and stood behind the sofa as Gideon sat up and leaned forward for better viewing. When everything was ready, Kristin pushed "play" and took a seat on the sofa next to Gideon.

The image in front of the ATM from the 17th Street bank appeared on the screen. Across the street in the background, they could easily see a side angle of the park, as well as a number of the neighboring buildings. Along the bottom of the image was the date: 7/28/19, as well as the time, which advanced with the images. While the picture wasn't crystal clear, the empty park bench in the background was evident, illuminated enough by the streetlight to at least make it visible. Kristin looked back at Thane, who gave her a nod; she pushed a button, and the footage juddered by at fast-forward.

Various customers zipped up to the ATM and dashed away like characters in a silent comedy, but apart from one young couple, no one appeared on the bench. In just a few minutes, two hours' worth of surveillance tape played, with no sign of Skunk. Thane walked around and stopped the machine, then retook his position behind his desk.

Gideon waited a couple of moments before speaking. "I say we at least hock the machine."

"Damn," Kristin said. "Damn, damn, damn, DAMN!"

Thane shook his head slowly. "Something's not right. I still can't see Skunk killing somebody, under any circumstances."

"That sounds naive to me." Gideon said.

Thane took out the DVD and looked at it, then held it up to Kristin. "Is there any way he could have altered this?"

"I don't think there's any way they could have digitally removed his image from the bench, if that's what you mean."

"Maybe Skunk actually did it," Gideon said. "At what point are you going to face the facts?"

"If this came from anybody but Bradford Stone, I would accept it, but he brought it here himself—as far as I'm concerned, this means nothing. But if we can't prove that he tampered with it, this trial is over."

"Like it's not already," Gideon muttered.

Thane looked at him, then put the DVD back in the jewel case, pocketed it, and left the office without a word.

Kristin and Gideon stayed seated on the sofa for a couple of moments without moving or speaking, until he finally glanced her way.

"I wish I knew what he isn't telling us."

Thane sat on his apartment floor, his back up against the reading chair, watching the security footage on the TV over and over. Rewind, play, rewind, play. The pad of paper on the floor next to him was still blank. Hannah entered and sat sideways on the chair so that her legs dangled over one of its arms. She put her hand on Thane's shoulder and watched the images with him.

"How long are you going to keep watching this?"

"Until I'm satisfied."

"And when will that be?"

"When I figure out how he did it. I know Skunk didn't kill Gruber. I know it just like you knew I was innocent. But the jury isn't going to give a damn what I think. So that leaves me with trying to figure out how Stone changed it."

Hannah said nothing, which he thanked her silently for: he knew what she had to be thinking. The tea kettle shrieked from the other room, and Thane sighed as he stood.

"I'll get it," he said. "Maybe a break will help."

He handed Hannah the remote control and walked out of the room, leaving her to study the TV screen. He poured himself a cup of tea, trying to figure out if there was a way around this latest piece of evidence. He knew there had to be. Skunk wasn't a killer.

He stood in the kitchen doorway as he sipped his tea, watching Hannah watch the DVD images that she now had on fast forward. It looked like she was reaching for the remote to stop it when something on the screen appeared to catch her eye. She leaned forward and stared even more intently at the images.

"What are you looking at?" Thane asked.

Hannah slid off the chair and down onto her knees, moving closer to the TV as she put the DVD back on regular speed, backed it up, then sped it up again. She then hit the pause button.

"Come here," she said, motioning for him to kneel down next to her. She started the DVD again, hit reverse for a couple of seconds until she reached a certain number on the time stamp, then hit the pause button. She pointed at something on the screen.

"Just focus on this right here. When I speed this up, tell me that it doesn't look a little shaky for just a second."

She hit the fast forward button. Thane watched for a moment, not seeing anything different, then suddenly looked over at her: she was watching for his reaction. He stared at her for a moment, then looked back at the TV. He leaned forward so that he was about a foot in front of the screen.

"Run it again."

CHAPTER
THIRTY

THANE BANNING ENTERED THE COURTROOM Tuesday morning knowing the case was over, even if he had no idea how it would end. While the final witness was being sworn in, Stone stood at attention with his shoulders thrown back and his chin thrust forward—clearly, he also knew the case was over, and smelled victory in the air.

A seventy-two inch flat-screen monitor was wheeled into the courtroom, set up to play the evidence Stone had brought Thane's team the day prior. While the jury had the best view of the monitor, it was positioned such that everyone in the gallery could see it clearly as well.

Kristin leaned over to Skunk while the large monitor was being plugged in and spoke in a whisper. "You're going to see and hear some things that might confuse you, but it's vitally important you not react to anything because we don't want the jury to be focusing on your response. We want them to listen to what is being said."

"OK," Skunk said, already looking puzzled.

"I'm serious. Whatever Stone shows on that monitor, it's imperative you don't display any emotions. Understand?"

Skunk nodded solemnly, then whispered back. "What's 'imperative' mean?"

Donald Davis swore to tell the whole truth, so help him God. He was dressed in his usual workday uniform, sans handgun, which wasn't permitted in the courtroom. The uniform itself looked freshly pressed.

Stone rose and approached the witness. He moved slowly, almost ponderously, as if to lend portent to his every motion. "Mr. Davis," he asked, "what is your occupation?"

"I'm the Chief of Security for the 17th Street branch of the Union Bank of Los Angeles."

"Your bank is located across the street from Armor Park, where Mr. Burns claimed to have been sitting the night of the murder."

"That's correct."

Stone walked back to his table and picked up a jewel case that held a DVD. He held it up for effect, examined it, then walked over to the DVD player.

"You have an ATM machine directly across from the park, is that correct?"

"Yes, sir."

"And your security camera operates twenty-four hours a day?"

"That's correct." Davis nodded with every answer, in case it might not be enough for the jury to simply hear his response.

"This past Sunday afternoon, you gave me a DVD that includes security footage from the month of July of this year," Stone stated.

"Yes, sir."

Stone turned on the monitor, the bright blue light from the screen coating the jury in a warm glow. He reverently inserted the disk into the DVD player, then took the remote control over to Davis and handed it to him.

"Ladies and gentlemen of the jury, this disk can be searched by day and by time of day." He turned back toward the witness. "Mr. Davis, please go to the date in question, July twenty-eighth. And take us to 8:00 p.m."

Davis punched a few buttons on the remote, and the grainy video image from the surveillance camera appeared on the monitor. The date and time stamp appeared at the bottom of the screen in white numbers about an inch tall, along with a smaller, fourteen-digit code.

"Union Bank has a number of ATM machines. How do you know for sure that this is from the machine in question?" Stone asked.

"In the bottom right-hand corner of the screen there's a tag number which identifies it."

Stone pointed to the long identification number appearing under the time and date. "Then you can confirm for us that this is from the 17th Street ATM?"

"Yes, sir. That's the code for that particular bank."

The DVD continued playing. At one point, a teenage girl with an extreme punk-rock hairstyle and a hodge-podge of rings through her nose and eyebrows walked up to the ATM. One of the older women in the jury shook her head slightly, sniffing in disgust. As the girl on the monitor reached for her bank card, she dropped her purse, spilling the contents everywhere.

Stone turned toward the jury and chuckled. "Oops."

Several of the jury members smiled with him. A number of people in the gallery also offered up some laughter. Stone stepped closer to the monitor and pointed to the image of a park bench across the street, where a young couple sat.

"I ask that the jury focus on this particular park bench in the background. This is Armor Park, and the bench you see is where the defendant told police he spent most of the evening of the twenty-eighth. If you'll remember, Detective Struthers testified the other day that only one bench in the park had slats on it." He turned back toward Davis. "Sir, could you magnify that portion of the image for us?"

Using the remote control, Davis drew a box around the park bench in question, then enlarged that portion of the screen. While the image was somewhat fuzzy and out of focus, it was nevertheless clear enough to definitively see a young white couple sitting on the bench talking.

"This couple confirms that the slats were on this bench the night of the murder, meaning it's the only bench where Mr. Burns could have sat that evening. And now, Mr. Davis, please run these images on fast forward." The image of the park bench stayed the same as cars zoomed by at blinding speed, and occasionally the view of the bench was blocked by customers racing up to, and away from, the ATM machine. After a couple of minutes, the couple left the bench.

"Members of the jury, you'll notice that the couple is no longer sitting on this bench. But almost an hour has elapsed, and still no sign of the defendant."

Skunk looked at Kristin in disbelief. After a hard look from her, he shook himself and calmed his features.

Thane decided it was finally time to stop this production.

"Objection, your Honor. How do we know this tape hasn't been altered?"

Before the judge could answer, Stone couldn't help but respond. "By *whom*, Mr. Banning? Mr. Davis has been Chief of Security at this bank for over twelve years. Believe me, sir, this gentleman is beyond reproach."

"I didn't mean by him, your Honor," Thane responded.

Judge Reynolds stared down at Thane from the bench. "Mr. Banning, don't even think of going there."

"Your Honor, is inquiring about the chain of evidence out of line? I'm not accusing any one individual of changing the footage: I simply want some assurance that it went directly from Mr. Davis to the District Attorney's office and didn't, for example, lay unattended on someone's desk."

Stone looked at the judge. "I obtained this security footage myself directly from Mr. Davis—and at no time has it been out of my direct control."

Thane reluctantly retook his seat. The image on the monitor continued to play on fast forward until it reached 12:00 a.m. Stone nodded at Davis, who stopped the DVD.

"We're now far past the time Mr. Burns claimed he sat on that bench, and as you can see, he didn't show. Mr. Burns's alibi simply does not bear out." Stone once again gave a look of appreciation to Davis. "Thank you very much, sir. Your assistance has been invaluable. No further questions, your Honor."

Stone returned to his table, where Keaton gave him a quick pat on the back. Winston's face didn't display the same pride that Keaton's did, but he nodded in agreement as Stone took his seat.

Thane remained sitting, looking first at Davis, then over at Stone. He finally rose and approached the witness. "Mr. Davis, would you please restart the footage from 8:00 p.m.?" Davis once again punched in some numbers, and the image reappeared on the monitor. Thane walked over to the monitor and studied it closely.

"At my signal, I want you to pause the picture. Don't stop it: just put it on pause." He held up his hand for a moment, then dropped it. "Now."

Davis pushed the pause button, freezing the image on the monitor.

"Perfect," Thane said. He pointed to the upper right-hand part of the monitor. "Please do me a favor and enlarge this store window from the other side of the park." An unidentifiable red jumble of lines filled the monitor, like red worms in some alien formation.

"Thank you. Go ahead and start it again."

The red reflection remained on the screen for just a moment, then disappeared, only to reappear in a different configuration of lines, equally unintelligible, which again disappeared after a couple of seconds.

"Can you tell me what that is, Mr. Davis?"

Davis studied the image for a moment: red lines made up of sections, almost like hieroglyphs. He shook his head—then the confusion on his face melted into recognition.

"Ah, that's the reflection of the time-and-temp sign outside the bank. It's reflecting on that store window."

"That makes sense. Okay, I want you to freeze the image again—now!"

Once again, the image froze. Thane turned on an overhead projector that was set up next to the monitor and copied the shape of the red reflection onto an overhead transparency, taking his time to ensure he copied the lines as displayed. The courtroom was dead silent, the gallery seemingly mesmerized by the image shining on the wall of the courtroom.

"I believe your neon display also gives the date. But since we're viewing the reflection in the store window—" Thane turned the transparency over: it now read 7/23/19.

For the first time during Thane's cross-examination, Keaton looked uncomfortable. Winston looked nauseous. But if Stone felt anything, it didn't show on his face, even when Thane looked directly at him.

"The twenty-third?" Thane remarked. "I thought we were viewing the twenty-*eighth* of July."

Davis looked at the remote control. "That's what I entered. I swear."

"Mr. Davis, if someone wanted, could they make a copy of July twenty-third footage and lay it over the July twenty-eighth footage?"

"I suppose so, but the date would still be on it."

"Maybe so," Thane said. "But would it be possible to digitally add a white line, filling in the three to make it look like an eight? Tell you what, do me a favor and enlarge the date for us please, as large as you can. Have it fill the screen to the degree possible, and then start it again."

Davis glared at Stone for a moment, then focused on the request at hand, enlarging the date until it filled the screen.

The left side of the number three occasionally appeared less solid than the rest of the number, a couple of times flickering in an unsteady way. If the line wasn't there, the eight would clearly be a three. Several members of the jury glanced from side to side, and the murmur from the gallery started to grow.

"That doesn't look right to me," Thane said.

"*Objection*, Your Honor," Stone demanded.

Judge Reynolds leaned forward. "And that objection would be?"

Stone stood for a moment, then slowly sat back down without saying a word. Thane walked over and stood next to the witness stand. Davis shifted in his seat, turning toward him.

"Mr. Banning, I swear to you I did not change this tape."

"I believe you, Mr. Davis. As our District Attorney stated, you are beyond reproach. He also said it hasn't left his possession. But just out of curiosity, could you please punch in the date July twenty-third at 8:00 p.m.—just for kicks?"

The monitor once again filled with the image of a park bench with the same couple sitting on it, the new date in question appearing at the bottom of the screen. Within a matter of seconds, the same punk-rock teenager approached the ATM, and once again the young woman spilled the contents of her purse.

Thane turned and looked coldly at Stone. "Oops."

But this time no one in the courtroom smiled. Several members of the jury turned and looked toward Stone, who rose quickly. "Your Honor, I can assure you that this DVD is exactly what Mr. Davis gave me. I had no reason to alter it."

"Unless, of course, Mr. Burns appeared in the original," Thane said. This time there was no reprimand from the bench.

"I have no idea," Stone said, "and we may never know. Your Honor, I ask that you instruct the jury that they should not assume Mr. Burns appeared on the missing tape simply because of a surveillance error. Believe me, I wish we had accurate footage."

As Judge Reynolds considered Stone's request, Davis quietly offered a suggestion. "I brought the original."

Stone stopped cold. He glanced toward Keaton and Winston, but only Keaton would return his stunned look. Winston continued staring at the base of the witness stand, looking dazed.

The judge leaned over and looked at the witness. "This *isn't* the original?"

"No, sir. I would never give out the original. Mr. Banning's assistant," Davis nodded toward Kristin, "came to my office Saturday morning and said Mr. Stone would likely be coming by for a copy of this footage, so I made him one. If I'd known he was going to call on a Sunday, I would have dropped it by his office after I made it. Ms. Peterson asked me to bring the original today."

Stone's eyes burned as he looked over at Kristin, who simply nodded in his direction. "Looks like you get your wish," Thane said.

Davis pulled a second DVD from his jacket pocket and handed it to Thane, who inserted it into the machine. Davis held up the remote control. "I'm assuming . . .?"

"If you would, please. July twenty-eighth."

A new image appeared, eliciting a buzz in the courtroom when Skunk Burns eventually walked into the picture and settled onto the park bench. He glanced around from side to side a couple of times, then slumped down on the bench, looking as though he was preparing for a potentially long evening.

"Fast-forward, if you would," Thane said.

The image and the corresponding time once again raced by, but Skunk never left the park bench—until almost 11:30 p.m., well after the time of the murder.

The judge banged his gavel, but the room did not come to order for almost a full minute. Once the crowd finally quieted down, he turned toward the Prosecution's table and stared at the District Attorney for a moment. He finally spoke, his tone uncharacteristically harsh.

"Mr. Stone... Can you explain this?"

Stone remained seated and silent; he could only manage to shake his head. Judge Reynolds continued studying him, but Stone wouldn't blink first. The judge sent the jurors out of the room, then turned to the DA's colleagues.

"Mr. Winston and Mr. Keaton, if either of you are able to shed any light on what just happened here, now is the time to speak up. I can't prove this was the result of wrongdoing within your department, but

I have strong suspicions already—and rest assured, somebody will be looking into it. If nothing else, I hope you will speak up as a matter of professional pride."

Keaton refused to make eye contact with the judge. Winston stared at the floor. He slowly shook his head, almost imperceptibly, as if in shock. His body language was shouting so loud the judge zeroed in on him immediately.

"Mr. Winston," boomed Judge Reynolds, "I'd like to speak with you in my chambers."

The judge started to rise from his chair, but at first Winston didn't move.

"Mr. Winston. *Now*, if you would."

Winston continued staring blankly at the floor. If he weren't sweating so profusely, he would have appeared catatonic. He remained seated for a moment longer; then, under the unwavering gaze of the judge, he lifted himself up from his chair with great effort. He ignored the stares as he mechanically made his way across the room like a man walking down death row.

Judge Reynolds looked at Winston like a disappointed parent, then turned his attention toward the DA. "Court is in recess until this afternoon at 2:00 p.m." He banged his gavel almost angrily and disappeared into his chambers with a whirl of dark robes.

After the judge and Winston left the courtroom, Thane walked over to the railing that separated him from the gallery and addressed the reporters.

"I'm sure the members of the press have the same questions the judge has, and I can answer them for you. The security footage was changed to cover DA Stone's involvement in the murder. Detective Gruber knew Mr. Stone had been involved in the death of Lauren McCoy. The missing computer disk covered notes the detective had made during the time period when the young woman was killed. Check the dates on the missing disk. Detective Gruber was blackmailing Mr. Stone, threatening to write a book about this case, so our law-and-order District Attorney had him killed."

Stone rose—but he did not respond, only shaking his head in utter disbelief.

Thane didn't take his eyes off the rapt reporters. "I will meet any members of the press who are interested in hearing more outside in ten minutes, at which time I will share some facts I think you'll agree prove my accusation."

Journalists grabbed their gear and scrambled for the door like the building was on fire. A few of them stayed behind and hollered out questions at Stone, but when the DA refused to even look at them, they too left the courtroom.

Thane returned to the defense table where Kristin stood next to Skunk, her arm around his shoulder. While their client still looked a little confused, Kristin sported a megawatt smile.

"Funny," she said. "They never taught me any of *this* in law school."

"Guess you were right," Thane said. "This case is a media magnet."

Gideon walked up to them, grinning and nodding his head like a bobble head doll. "Damn. This lawyering stuff can be kind of fun."

"Is that it?" Skunk asked. "Is it over?"

"Not quite," Thane responded, "but just about. I need to do one more thing right now. Unless I'm mistaken, somebody's going to want to talk to me before I get outside." He pulled a business card from his shirt pocket and his cell phone from his jacket as he walked toward the door to the courtroom.

CHAPTER
THIRTY-ONE

THANE MADE HIS WAY DOWN the courthouse corridor, ignoring the curious stares of the audience filing out of the gallery. One older guy in a flannel shirt even clapped his hands together loudly; Thane was surprised how strange it felt to have a fan.

He turned the corner to head toward the elevator and saw Stone standing next to the small conference room reserved for the prosecution. A policeman stood nearby, and when Stone nodded, the cop ushered away the few people who had been milling around to watch in case anything of interest happened.

As Thane approached, Stone stepped in front of him, blocking his way. "You know I didn't kill Lauren McCoy," Stone said. "Throw all the mud you like, but it won't work. It'll only make you look petty."

"I'll let the reporters decide how it makes me look."

"You've got nothing. Whatever you tell them will just be some bullshit fantasy you made up."

"What about the ether, Stone? Did I make that up?"

Stone's eyebrows rose in confusion. "Ether? What the hell are you talking about?"

Thane stepped closer and lowered his voice. "At my release hearing you said Lauren McCoy had been knocked unconscious with ether before being dragged down the alley and stabbed. But there was no mention of ether in the original trial. The police report never mentioned it, at no time does it appear in the court transcript, and your star witness testified he saw me *walk* with Lauren McCoy into the alley. How did you know something that never came out in court?"

Stone's brow furrowed. "So I got it confused with another case. Big deal."

"No, I read the coroner's report, a copy of which I have with me to give to the press. Lab tests detected a small amount of ether, but not enough to jump out during the investigation unless you were looking for it. So how did you know she was knocked out unless you killed her or know who did?"

Stone drew in a slow breath, then opened the door to the little conference room and waved Thane inside. "Nobody comes in," he called out to the cop standing guard. Thane followed him into the room, and Stone shut the door.

"You are so wrong it's not funny," Stone said. "Gruber wasn't blackmailing me."

"Someone called a publisher from Gruber's home and said he had information on a big scandal," Thane said. "A call was also made to your office not long before he was killed. You're the one who suggested to the police that the MO of the burglar fit my client's. You went to Mr. Song immediately after he said he saw my client and got him to change his story. And you're the one who got the 'anonymous tip' about where the stolen goods were hidden."

"I swear to you, those things happened. I know how it looks, but they just happened that way."

"And now we find out you altered evidence that would clear my client. You killed Gruber because he knew of your involvement in the McCoy murder, and then you took step after step to ensure my client took the fall. You're no better than the criminals you prosecute."

"You're delusional. I didn't kill Gruber."

"You think the reporters are going to buy that?" Thane asked. "Especially after you altered the security footage?" Stone started to protest, but Thane cut him off. "Stop it. You telling me you think Winston is going to hang tough under Judge Reynolds's questioning? Are you kidding me? He looked like he was going to throw up. You know he's already folded. You *know* it."

Stone didn't respond.

"Come on, Stone. It's just you and me now. The reporters are going to look at everything I just told you, including your knowledge of the ether and you changing the security tape. You think I need to lead them there? Who's delusional now?"

Stone continued to glare, but his fury couldn't hold much longer.

"I remember reading about you campaigning for DA while I was in prison," Thane said. "You boasted about being willing to make the tough decisions. Being tough on crime. Turns out you're nothing but a hypocrite and a coward. A weak, self-serving, sniveling *coward*. It's time the public knew the truth."

"Don't talk to those reporters," Stone said. "You don't understand. You'd be doing more harm than you could ever imagine, and not to me. I'm talking about harm to the city."

"Right. Because you only care about your citizens."

"I do care about the people of L.A. They're why I've done . . . everything I did."

"Right." Thane turned and walked toward the door. As his hand grabbed hold of the doorknob, Stone called out to him, almost pleadingly. "I didn't kill Lauren McCoy. Gruber did."

Thane froze as the words soaked in, then looked back over his shoulder and saw Stone leaning on the table for support. "Near the end of your trial," Stone continued, "I discovered evidence implicating Detective Gruber in the girl's death. Gruber killed her. Not me."

For a moment, the honk of a car in traffic outside was the only sound in the room.

"When you learned that Gruber and your star witness knew each other, you figured out they lied about not having met so his testimony would hold water."

"Yes," Stone said reluctantly.

"Which led you to learn about Gruber's involvement in the murder."

"I'm not proud of it, but I had to make a tough decision," Stone said.

"Your political future—or my life."

"That is absolutely untrue. It wasn't about me. I swear to God," Stone said. "That's what you need to understand. I didn't learn about Gruber until the trial was almost over. If I'd exposed him, hundreds of his cases would have been overturned. Hundreds of guilty felons, back on the streets. *Hundreds*. Think about that and tell me it wasn't a tough call."

"Just my bad luck, then," Thane said.

"I was sick about doing what I did," Stone said. "But every asshole politician who runs for this office talks about being *tough on crime*, pledging to *make the community safer*. But they'd never do what I did, make the choice I made. Yes, I let one innocent man go to jail—but I kept hundreds of murderers and rapists locked up. Do you have any idea how many lives I saved by doing that? Nobody else would have had the guts to make that decision, but I did, and I stand by it."

"You had to make a tough call."

"You're *damn right* I did," Stone said, almost indignantly. "That's what being tough on crime means. It's not a slogan. It's an altar you sacrifice to."

"And I was the sacrifice."

Stone looked apologetic for the first time. "You were the sacrifice."

"Did you ever think about what you did to my life? To my *wife's*?"

"Of *course* I thought about that," Stone said. "If your point is that it wasn't fair, you'll get no argument here. It was easily the most shameful thing I've ever done. And I'm not trying to diminish what you went through, but if all of those convictions that Gruber had secured over the years were overturned, then a lot of other innocent people would also be finding out how unfair life is when they or a loved one was robbed or raped or murdered."

"I spent five years on death row because you were worried about all the 'what ifs'," Thane said.

"They weren't 'what ifs'. They were certainties. But I was never going to let them kill you, Thane. I left that loophole open on purpose—the one you used to get free. And if you hadn't found it, I would have fed it to you myself."

"That's a lie," Thane snapped. "You argued against my release."

"I knew the judge would side with you. The precedents you cited were perfect. The law is the law and I knew he had no choice but to release you. So yeah, I had to stomp around a little bit that day, but that was just for show. That's also why I didn't push for a retrial once you got yourself released. I knew we could have put you away again—but we didn't. I wanted to see you free. I'm sorry for what you had to go through. I truly am . . . But *I did not kill Gruber*, although God knows I wanted to. I made damn sure, though, that the son of a bitch resigned from the force immediately after your conviction."

Thane walked over to the window and looked down at the front steps of the courthouse, toward a crowd of reporters waiting for him.

"So think about what you'd be doing if you tried making this known," Stone said. "A lot more people would be the victim of violence. And don't you dare tell me I'm a hypocrite about being tough on crime."

"All right," Thane replied at last. "I won't talk with the reporters. Just answer one question for me: How do you justify changing the security footage? Were more criminals going to be released if Skunk went free?" Stone stared back at Thane but couldn't answer. After a minute of silence, Thane shook his head and started back toward the door.

"Yeah, I didn't think so."

"There's no proof of any of this," Stone called after him. "It'd just be your word against mine. And if you talk, I promise I'll send your friend back to Forsman. Today."

"Now we're back to blackmailing. You really are a man of honor."

"I will not sit back and watch you tear down everything I've accomplished. You won't risk your friend's freedom—hell, his *life*—by talking with a bunch of reporters who you know damn well will believe me over you any day of the week."

"I don't need to talk to the press," Thane said. "You just did." He reached into his front shirt pocket and brought out his cell phone.

"You get all that, Angelique?" Thane asked.

"Oh yeah," came a woman's voice over the speakerphone. "You don't suppose District Attorney Stone is open to a few follow-up questions, is he?"

Thane looked up from the phone. "Angelique Arvand from QMZ wants to know if you're up for some questions." Stone didn't move. Didn't appear to even breathe. "Angelique, it doesn't look like he has any comment right now, but maybe you can catch him later. And I recognize I still owe you an exclusive interview, but hopefully this will keep you busy until we can get together."

"Oh yeah, I think I can do something with this."

Thane hung up the phone and put it back in his pocket. "You'll probably be getting a call from her pretty soon." Thane opened the door, the noise from outside flooding the room.

"*Now* we're done."

CHAPTER
THIRTY-TWO

WHEN COURT RECONVENED AT TWO o'clock—four hours after the last recess had been called—the world had changed. Skunk sat between Thane and Kristin, no longer squirming as though he was already sitting on the electric chair. He and Kristin whispered back and forth before the judge arrived; Skunk even giggled at something Kristin said, but Thane couldn't imagine what it could be.

Across the aisle from Thane at the prosecution table sat only one man: the distinguished-looking State Attorney General, Ian Lord, reading through some papers as though it was just another day at the office. He gave Thane a warm handshake and a pat on the shoulder when he first came into the room, even though Thane knew what he had done would no doubt consume the A.G. office for months to come.

The gallery was packed to capacity, with a throng of spectators standing in the back of the room.

News from the morning's session had been broadcast for the past four hours, with two of those hours being dominated by Angelique's coverage of Bradford Stone's confession, complete with audio. Reporters who had only yesterday trumpeted the travesty of justice that came with Thane representing a cop-killer were now scrambling to turn him into some sort of folk hero. There were no *mea culpas* being served up by any of them; there were too many fast-breaking exclusives to waste time wallowing in hindsight.

Hannah sat near the front of the gallery next to Gideon. She occasionally leaned over and said something to the big man, who just kept smiling and nodding, smiling and nodding.

Everyone rose as Judge Reynolds entered the courtroom. He looked through a couple of pages from a file in front of him as the crowd retook their seats, then looked up at the crowd.

"First of all, I would like to thank the State Attorney General for agreeing to fill in this afternoon. As I'm sure most of you already know, District Attorney Stone and his team have been removed from this case. Mr. Lord, it is my understanding that the State is requesting that all charges against Mr. Burns be dismissed?"

"That is correct, Your Honor," Mr. Lord said as he rose to face the judge. "Given the recent evidence, the State of California requests that all charges be dropped, and I want Mr. Burns to know that the State is truly sorry for what has happened to him this past week." Several people in the gallery broke out in applause. The first rap of Reynold's gavel, however, quieted them immediately.

"Mr. Burns, you are free to go," intoned the judge. "I can't even begin to apologize for what was done to you, although I'm quite sure the city is going to try. Normally I would suggest you find a very good lawyer to help you through that process, but I believe you already have one."

Reynolds then turned his attention toward Thane. "And Mr. Banning . . ." He looked at him for a moment and shook his head. "I have no idea if words can even begin to describe the injustice you've endured for over five years. I am usually extremely proud to be a part of this great country's legal system. Today I am not. Today I feel ashamed. I just wish . . ." Reynolds stopped, and could only once again shake his head. "There are no words." He then grabbed his gavel, brought it down half-heartedly, and said, "This case is dismissed."

He rose and strode from the courtroom.

Half of the journalists began hollering questions at Thane. The other half raced from the courtroom, determined to be first on the air with the afternoon's events.

Everyone at the defense table stood and Gideon stepped up to the front of the gallery next to them. Kristin wrapped her arms around Skunk's neck and gave him a tight hug, the stunned expression on his face making him look as though he had stopped breathing. When she finally released him, Thane reached out and shook Skunk's hand.

"My friend, you should be in a strong position to sue the city for a whole lot of money."

"You really think?" Skunk asked.

"Count on it. So don't be going out on any more 'job' interviews. You're going to be set for life."

Gideon reached out and squeezed Thane's shoulder, the closest he would probably ever come to giving another man a hug. "However much Skunk here's going to get, I'll betcha you'll get fifty times as much."

"I don't want their money," Thane said.

"Man, I do," Skunk said, flashing a true smile for the first time in years.

Thane looked past the journalists calling his name, most of whom had a different tone in their voices, and found Hannah in the crowd. The look on her face hovered between a smile and tears. He worked his way through the mob and when he finally reached her, she wrapped her arms around him, putting her face in his chest. The tears came fast and hard as years of sorrow poured out.

"I couldn't have done this without you," he whispered.

More than an hour after the trial ended, the corridor outside the courtroom remained packed with spectators, including workers from other parts of the building, who scurried up to the fourth floor as soon as word got out that the trial was over. The clamor finally died away when Thane and Hannah made their way out of the courtroom. They had hung back, hoping the crowd would subside, but finally ventured out when they realized the mob wasn't going anywhere.

Thane was used to conversations going silent when he appeared, but this time something seemed different. A respectful hush fell across the huge crowd—and then applause started rippling down the hall, growing louder and louder as it swept through the building. He looked down the corridor, hoping to find someone from security who could clear a path for them. He spotted the press surrounding Skunk, peppering him with questions, each of which Kristin answered with grace and confidence.

Thane looked the other way and saw Joseph leaning against a nearby wall, smiling. Thane and Hannah made their way over to him and were greeted with an extended hand, which Thane quickly accepted.

"Congratulations!" Joseph exclaimed. "That was incredible."

"It ranks right up there, doesn't it."

"When I heard what that son of a bitch had done, I had to get down here to watch." His broad smile started to fade, blanketed by a look of discomfort. "Look, buddy, I'm sorry for what happened. I—"

"You did what was right for the firm, Joseph. I don't blame you. Really."

Hannah took hold of Joseph's hand and squeezed it. "Thane told me he shouldn't have put you in that position. There's nothing to apologize for."

Joseph's smile snapped back into place. He gave Hannah a quick hug, then turned back to Thane. "Any chance of your coming back?"

"As luck would have it, if I clear out my office by midnight, I won't have to pay next month's rent. I'm thinking maybe I'll spend part of this evening doing just that."

"Then give me a call Monday and we can talk more then. With the publicity you'll get after this, I'll have to add another floor to the building. But for now, you two go enjoy yourselves." He shook Thane's hand one more time then walked away, chuckling and shaking his head, still in disbelief. "Absolutely incredible," he said to no one in particular. "That's my boy."

Thane and Hannah ate a quiet dinner at their favorite restaurant, a small Italian place in Santa Monica called Fellini's where they used to go for special occasions before the arrest. The first time they ate there was when he had accepted Joseph's first job offer following law school. Over the years, they found themselves gravitating back there time and time again for birthdays, anniversaries, or simply when they decided life was too short.

They had not been to Fellini's since Thane's release from Forsman, and this time, the reception inside was much different than their experience in the little diner four months ago. Twenty-four-hour cable news meant that big stories like his hit the press at record speed.

He caught several people looking and pointing, but nobody jeered or called him a murderer or threatened him with a broken bottle. He did catch one middle-aged man staring, as though he was about to storm out of the restaurant in protest, but the man's wife whispered something and his reaction quickly changed to one of surprise.

The owner of the restaurant sent over a wonderfully aged bottle of Gaja Barbaresco with a note attached, which simply read 'so very nice to have you back.' They had never enjoyed a meal more, and they savored every drop of the wine. The whole evening brought back vivid memories of their honeymoon in Italy, when they were young and in love and felt they had their whole lives ahead of them. There was an unspoken agreement between them that during dinner they would not discuss the trial.

There would be plenty of time for that later.

Fine food was abundant and conversation was sparse. They often found themselves lost in each other's eyes like school kids, not needing words to communicate their feelings. Quiet smiles often crept across their faces, even when nothing had been said. For the first time in forever, it felt like old times. They had been given a fresh start.

After dinner, Thane dropped Hannah off at their apartment. He said he wanted to pack things up at his office, but that he would be back as soon as he could in order to continue their celebration. He didn't want to be far from her, but there was still one more thing to wrap up.

He went to his office and glanced out the window at the rooftop across the street, an act that had become habit. He then pulled up the blinds and turned on his office lights. Empty boxes from his initial move had been stored in a vacant room across the hall, so he once again started putting them to use. After half an hour of packing books and desk drawer contents, there was a knock on the door: Joseph leaned in, looking as though the grin on his face had yet to fade from earlier that afternoon.

"Hey, come on in," Thane said.

Joseph entered and surveyed the decrepit state of the office, poking his finger in one of the many holes in the ratty sofa. "Good God, have I been that sheltered, or is this office a slum?"

Thane laughed and waved him off. Joseph walked over and pulled up a chair in front of the desk, examining the cushion closely before sitting down, probably concerned it might contain vermin. "You know me," Joseph said, "there's no way I can wait until Monday to see if you've made a decision. I hope finding you cleaning out your office is a good sign for me."

"It very well could be."

Joseph stretched his legs out in front of him. "I have to tell you, when I heard that tape of you on the news accusing Stone of murdering that girl, I really thought the bastard had done it. I'll bet you were blown away when you heard it was Gruber."

Thane shook his head. "No, I knew Stone didn't kill the girl. He's not a murderer. But when he mentioned the ether in my release hearing, a lot of things came together for me. When Gruber put me in the backseat of his car to take me to the station, I noticed a bottle of ether rolling around on the floorboard. Kind of odd what you remember at times like that, but I remember wondering if cops used it to subdue prisoners who got out of hand. Believe me, I didn't really pay much attention to it, not after what had happened, but it stuck in my mind."

"So you knew Gruber was involved."

"That raised my suspicions. After I got out, I learned that Lenny was Gruber's snitch, so it wasn't hard to figure out that he'd been paid to testify against me."

"Unbelievable," Joseph said.

"Gruber also left the force shortly after I was convicted. I knew that had to have been Stone's doing, after he learned what had really happened."

"The McCoy girl must have had something on Gruber, or she did something to really piss him off."

"No. Gruber was just the hired help, but I promise you, I'll find whoever was behind it. In fact, I'm almost there."

Joseph looked at his watch, then stood slowly, as though he needed to head off to his next appointment. But instead he reached inside his jacket.

"I was afraid you wouldn't let it go."

He pointed a .38 snub-nosed pistol at Thane.

"You couldn't carry a shotgun under your jacket, huh?" Thane said, nodding toward some of the holes blasted in the walls and furniture. "If I don't get my security deposit back, I'm holding you responsible."

Joseph looked impressed. "I'm sorry, buddy, but I can't let you keep digging."

Thane leaned back and locked his hands behind his head. "There's no more digging left. Remember when McCoy confronted me outside my apartment and I asked you about the security company you'd used in the past? You said you couldn't remember the name but would go through old invoices and get it for me. I said I'd be happy to do that, but you insisted I let you. No offense, Joseph, but you never hesitate to delegate that sort of thing."

"Am I really that unwilling to do scut work? Say it isn't true," Joseph asked, aping wounded pride.

"That's why I asked if you remembered what Lauren told me. About her suspicions."

"About the possibility of internal malfeasance?"

"Yes," Thane said, "except I never actually told you about that. I promised her I wouldn't tell anybody what she said. Of course, after I was arrested I told the lead detective, but he said it led nowhere. Yet somehow you knew exactly what she said. So I went ahead and looked through past invoices for security companies and it turns out the actual name of the security company you'd used in the past was different than the one you told me. And, surprise, surprise, it was the same company Gruber worked for part time."

Joseph smiled. "I see all those evenings you spent working late at the office weren't just on real estate."

"What was your connection with Lauren? And how'd you know what she told me? She assured me that neither our client nor our firm had done anything to rig the bidding process."

"That's because she helped rig it. She was in on it. She requested a wide range of records from the city, saying she was working on a case, one of which was the Hexagon bid. She forwarded the information on to us, and we were able to use it to tailor our bid and ensure that Wilson-Scott would win."

"Then why did she tell me she had concerns?"

"Because she was a greedy little bitch," Joseph muttered. "Once you started asking questions, she decided she wanted a bigger cut. She said she told you she had suspicions of internal tampering in case I didn't give her a bigger cut. She'd be able to bring the whole thing down on our heads, and if I said she was involved from the beginning, she could have you testify that she talked to you. And who would doubt the word of an Assistant DA? If she'd just taken the money we'd agreed on, none of this would have happened."

"Right. It was her fault," Thane said.

"So Gruber called you and said he was her assistant and set up the meeting. And after she was unconscious, I used her phone and sent you those texts. I thought the 'hope you won't be angry' line was a stroke of genius. We knew the restaurant was closed, and it made sense you'd wait on that bench. Then it was just a matter of waiting until you found the body."

A police siren filled the night air, soft at first, then progressively louder. Joseph slid over to the window, keeping an eye on Thane, and glanced outside. A police car sped down the street, continuing past the office building on its way to something less important. He walked back over and stood behind the chair.

"But why'd you need *me* to take the fall, Joseph?"

"Because if an Assistant DA is murdered, the cops aren't going to rest until they get their guy. They'd have traced it back to me eventually. I needed to keep the police from looking any further, so I gave them a slam-dunk case."

"You offered me my job back to keep an eye on me."

"And to make it up to you. There was absolutely no reason why we couldn't just start over." Joseph glanced at the gun in his hand, then looked at Thane with remorse. "But, of course, you just couldn't let it go. I'm sorry. I wish there was another way. If only McCoy had killed you when he went after you outside the courthouse. That would have been better for everybody."

"No, he wasn't going to hurt me. That whole thing was orchestrated. He needed to keep acting like I killed his daughter."

"Orchestrated? Yeah, right. I'll have to be sure to ask him about that," Joseph said as he raised his pistol and pointed it at Thane's chest.

"Ask him now."

Joseph looked puzzled at first, but his confusion evaporated when the distinct sound of a cartridge being loaded into the chamber of a gun echoed through the room.

"Put the gun down," McCoy instructed.

The only movement in the room was the beads of sweat worming their way down Joseph's face, all the color draining from his skin. For a minute his eyes flicked around the room, his mind racing, considering every option.

Then he laid the gun on the desk.

Thane picked it up and moved it out of Joseph's reach. His former boss looked at him, staring at him as though he were a puzzle with half the pieces gone.

"When Mr. McCoy confronted me in the parking lot that night outside Hannah's apartment, he said I better tell him who to hate," Thane said. "So I did. I told him about Gruber and the ether."

Joseph looked at him in disbelief. "You set this whole thing up."

Thane nodded solemnly. It wasn't something he was proud of, but if anything, a man like Joseph would understand. "Gruber never would have been convicted," Thane said, "especially after Lenny was found dead. Tell me who you think made that happen? Had to be Gruber tying up loose ends. And I knew McCoy here demanded justice. Besides, I got the death penalty for his daughter's murder, so apparently that was a just sentence. So no, I didn't try stopping him, if that's what you mean."

"I mean—you told him to limp. How to break into the house. And to make the call to your client's workplace."

McCoy stepped to the side of Joseph, his gun still trained on his target. "A small price to pay for the name of Lauren's killer," he said. "And he *was* the killer. Or at least, the one who carried it out. We had a talk about it before I sent him to hell."

Joseph glanced at McCoy, but quickly refocused his attention on Thane. "You put Stone in a position where he'd have to clear his own name. *You* called that publisher, not Gruber. And the computer disks, those were yours."

"I made Stone feel absolutely positive he had the right man, whether it was the stolen items outside Skunk's apartment or the phone call to where he worked. I talked enough with Skunk in prison to know his M.O. And yeah, I broke into Gruber's house one afternoon and made those calls. Once Stone started boasting to the press, I put him in a damn tough situation—but when I left a message at his office about Mr. Song, I didn't make Stone pressure him out of testifying. And I sure as hell didn't make him alter the evidence. He had a second chance to do the right thing. If he'd have turned over the real security tape, that would have been that. But I had no doubt that once again he would find a way to justify sending an innocent man to jail. He deserves everything he's going to get."

"But you . . . You set up your own client. You let him be arrested."

Thane's face betrayed a flicker of pain—the first emotion he'd shown the entire conversation. "That was the hardest part for me, but I also gave him the perfect alibi. I knew about the bank security camera; that's why I had him meet me there for a 'job.' I paid a guy a few bucks to handle the bench seats to make sure Skunk sat on the right bench, and then I had the slats moved the next morning so the police would think he sat on the other side of the park, but I always had that chip available to me. I'm sorry he had to go through this, but I'm sure he's more than happy with how things turned out. He would have ended up back in jail before the month was up. Now he's going to have enough money to live life like it's supposed to be lived.

Joseph looked at Thane as though he had just met him for the first time. "Thane, this isn't you."

Thane grabbed his sports coat from the back of his chair and threw it over his shoulder. "Maybe not before. But in Forsman, a friend of mine taught me that if somebody hits you in the leg with a stick, you bash them over the head with a pipe. *You take the whole head.* You and Gruber took five years of my life. You were going to let them kill me, and in fact, I'm convinced that if that couple hadn't walked by the alley that night, Gruber was planning to kill me right there; it wouldn't have been hard for him to say it was self-defense. Now, I might be biased, but as far as I'm concerned, justice is being served a hell of a lot better now than the first time around."

He handed Joseph's pistol to McCoy, who slipped it in the waistband of his pants. Joseph reached his hand out like there was a chance in hell Thane might accept it, but he simply stepped around it.

"So what happens now?" Joseph asked. "You going to call the police?" his voice cracked in a pleading tone that even he had to have known was wasted.

Thane started toward the office door. "This isn't my fight anymore. You destroyed my life, but you took this man's only daughter. It's his call now." He opened the door and walked out of his office. Joseph called out to him.

"Thane, wait. Where are you going?"

"Home."

CHAPTER THIRTY-THREE

THANE SAT IN HIS CAR, looking up at his office window, which was still illuminated. He didn't know exactly what would happen up there—whether McCoy had questions he wanted answered first, or if killing Joseph was all the closure he needed—but Thane was certain he wouldn't be seeing his former friend again. He leaned back in his seat, knowing he should drive away, but he didn't feel he had the strength to even lift his arm and turn the key.

He was surprised to not feel strong emotions one way or the other: neither remorse over what was about to happen to the man who gave him his start, nor satisfaction at having secured some fractured sense of justice. Instead he felt nothing. He simply drew a deep breath as though he had just finished a hard day at the office.

From the moment Thane first broke into Gruber's house one afternoon to call Stone's office and the publisher—the first of three such break-ins conducted to establish a phone record—he thought he would struggle with what he had done.

When he told Hannah a few days earlier that he knew he didn't have the right to be responsible for whether somebody lived or died, she naturally assumed he meant representing Skunk, but he meant it more literally. Because of him, two people were going to die, and others would have their reputations destroyed.

And yet, despite knowing on an intellectual level that he didn't have that right, he only noticed that it felt much more like justice than vengeance. He wondered what that said about him, not detecting even a quiver of moral dilemma over what he was doing. And that was what troubled him the most.

Throughout this entire ordeal, the only concern that dominated his mind was whether or not he could be the husband Hannah deserved. If the part of him she fell in love with had died in Forsman, was it fair to stay with her? He had just orchestrated the death of another human being, playing the part of judge and jury and delegating the role of executioner to McCoy. He allowed an innocent man to be charged with the crime and manipulated the subsequent hearing to take it where he wanted it to go. He pulled all the strings. Yet he, a man who at one time had great respect for the rule of law and an even greater belief in the sanctity of life, felt absolutely no remorse.

But once the trial was over and he was holding Hannah in his arms outside the courtroom, he felt the darkness ascend from his body like a demon being exorcised from a possessed soul. There was hope for redemption, and that's what he wanted most. He believed everything was going to be all right, and while he recognized time might prove him wrong, he was confident he could live with what he had done. It wasn't right, but he knew that sometimes justice took curious turns along the way—if such a thing as justice even existed.

He finally started his car and pulled away from the curb.

The lease to his office wasn't really up for another couple of weeks, but when he saw Joseph at the courthouse, he figured the thought of him being alone in his office would be too tempting of an opportunity for his former boss to pass up. McCoy was more than willing to chance the possibility of a wasted evening sitting in the empty office across the hall.

He really had intended to not renew his office lease for another month, but sitting there waiting for Joseph, he had time to think about what he wanted to do next. He was serious when he told Gideon he had no interest in the city's money, which would most certainly be his for the asking in a civil trial: he hadn't wanted to make money off this for himself. But the more he thought about it, he realized that an enormous settlement with the city would allow him to practice the type of law that otherwise wouldn't be financially feasible.

He would have the luxury of taking on clients who were at risk of being falsely imprisoned by the system, or innocent people who were already on death row. Clients who couldn't afford anyone but a court-appointed attorney who would already be too overworked to help them. He could try to prevent what happened to him from destroying other lives, and he believed his training in law and his experience at Forsman gave him a unique set of skills to fight for those individuals. And as a bonus, he could hire Gideon to stay on and work with him. Not only would he enjoy having his company, but it would also increase his friend's odds of staying out of prison, especially now that Thane would be able to pay him a very respectable wage.

All of this, of course, was contingent on what Hannah had to say. He thought she would understand, given everything that just happened, but if she wanted him to do something else, then that's what he would do. It was now her turn, and everything from here on out would be for her.

Thane called out for Hannah as he entered their apartment, but got no response. She wasn't in the living room, and when he went back to look in the bedroom, it was dark. He was on his way to check the kitchen when he heard her calling to him from the fire escape outside their window. He looked and saw that she had spread a blanket on the black metal platform, a bottle of wine and two glasses awaiting his arrival.

"Been out here long?" he asked.

"Just a few minutes. I figured you'd be home soon. Come join me."

He crawled out the window and sat behind her. Someone had shot out the streetlight at the end of the alley, which helped make the night feel at least a little darker.

"I thought maybe we'd spend the evening looking at the night sky," she said. She handed him a glass of wine and reclined, nestling against him, her back resting upon his chest. They sat like that for several minutes, her warmth filling him with each breath they shared. There was nothing else he needed.

Hannah tilted her head back and pressed it against his shoulder, looking up at him with her warm eyes. "I was so proud of you today."

Thane put the glass of wine down, kissed her forehead, then wrapped his arms around her waist, holding her even closer. He shook his head almost imperceptibly. "Don't be proud," he said as he stroked her hair. "Just be glad it's over."

They continued sitting together in silence, staring up toward the sky. Thane could make out the faint flickering light from a few stars. He noticed the small points of light, but also the infinite darkness surrounding each star. He felt as though he was looking into his own soul. He focused on the stars: the more he stared at them, the further the light seemed to travel into the dark sky. It gave him a sense of hope.

ACKNOWLEDGEMENTS

Thanks to my family for their encouragement. My mother Harlene (who should always be thanked first, for many reasons), Tom, Nanci, and Jim, who all provided me with feedback upon reading an early draft. And to my friends Karen, John, and Stacy for being my supportive tribe for oh so many (many) years.

Thanks to other friends who, for whatever crazy reason, willingly served as early readers and who offered helpful words and constructive observations along the way: Bill Archambault, Tom and Chee Payne, Donna Spearman, Karen Howe, Susan Kristensen, Connie Koslow, Faye Satterly, Mathew Bowen, Don Davis, Megan Holley, Melinda Lee, and Jeff Graup.

A special shout-out to Anne McAneny, who went extraordinarily above and beyond by providing invaluable feedback, insights, editing, guidance, assistance, encouragement, and support in so many ways (and is thus deserving of her own paragraph). She is also a fine author in her own right.

And the gold medal of thanks and appreciation goes to my wife, Kate, for everything she does, and for everything she means to me.

ABOUT THE AUTHOR

Michael Cordell is a novelist, playwright, and produced screenwriter. He has sold three screenplays to Hollywood, including *Beeper*, an action-thriller starring Harvey Keitel and Joey Lauren Adams. Michael currently lives in Charlottesville, Virginia, where he has taught screenwriting for over fifteen years.

CONNECT WITH MICHAEL

Sign up for Michael's newsletter at:
www.michaeljcordell.com/newletter

To find out more information visit his website:
www.michaeljcordell.com

BOOK DISCOUNTS
& SPECIAL DEALS

ONE LAST THING . . .

Thank you for reading! If you enjoyed reading this book, I'd be very grateful if you'd post a short review on Amazon. I read every comment personally and am always learning how to make this book even better. Your support really does make a difference.

Search for *Contempt* by Michael Cordell to leave your review.

Thanks again for your support!

Made in the USA
Columbia, SC
22 October 2022

69853590R00126